Reggie could not see or hear that he was being sought out. Fast asleep, he could not know that animal that he wanted as his spiritual guide was steadily following his scent, and heading directly to the cabin.

At fifty feet away, the lion's acute hearing picked up the rhythmic inhale and exhale of the two-leg's breath. At twenty-five feet, the lion's acute night vision could see the rise and fall of the two-leg's chest.

On the ground below the raised cabin, the lion anchored its hindquarters with its tail and lifted its front quarters in one effortless ascension. It reached up and unsheathed its two-inch claws and locked them on the outside lip of the cabin floor. At two feet from the two-leg's face, but on the other side of the screen, the lion's whiskers felt the warmth of his body. Although the lion could have cut through the screen and then through the throat of the two-leg in a single swipe, he did not. The two-leg stirred and the animal left as silently as he came.

Praise for *Stalking Los Angeles*

"Nothing seems to be going right in Reggie Youngblood's life...Reggie soon finds his escape in studying mountain lions and his Indian heritage... Read *Stalking Los Angeles* by Tom Berquist to discover how Reggie falls in love, discovers himself and learns some of life's most important lessons. Four out of five stars."

~Litpick.com

"...the storyline was a very original idea... Reggie was likable and easy to relate to. (T)he plot moved along at a nice pace, and it always held my interest. I ... would recommend it to others."

~Taylor H. Litpick.com

"Reggie is likeable... the epitome of a teenage boy...Berquist employs the use of dual narratives, paralleling Reggie's journey with the journey of a mountain lion just reaching his maturity. This dual narrative brings (the novel) to the next level. I believe this novel would be something teenage boys ... could really identify with."

~Shannon A. Los Angeles

"I would recommend this book to teens (who) struggle with who they are and struggling to accept their new surroundings. Stalking Los Angeles shows the perspective of various characters undergoing confusions about life, parents, sexuality, and themselves....(T)his book moved me to try and become more observant of nature and what it has to offer, what it can do to relieve my troubles, and to become more protective of it...Life will turn out ok; there are many bumps, trips, and struggles, but as Reggie proved, most struggles have a better reward at the end and have a great outcome."

~Mel R. Los Angeles

"Stalking Los Angeles is a coming of age story for nature lovers... (A) heartwarming story of conservation and coming of age in a world that is careless and unkind both to mountain lions and to teenage boys. ...(I)t is a good story in which heroes get to be heroes. We could use more stories like that."

~Elizabeth K. Lexington, KY

Stalking
Los Angeles

by

Tom Berquist

Stalking Los Angeles

Cover Art by www.angelheartdesign.org

Publishing History
First Edition, 2015
Print ISBN 978-0-9721379-5-9

Published in the United States of America

Dedication

This book is dedicated to my wife Ellen, who continues to put up with my creative needs and cranky ways.

Acknowledgements

I couldn't have written it without the help of my writing teachers, Children's book writing organizations, critique group partners, editors and readers. Thanks.

Author note

Although a work of fiction, this book is based mostly in fact. The Los Angeles mountain lions are still struggling in this ever-depleting habitat. I have tried to be true to their species and speak from inside their skin. The characters are fictional too, but they represent true conservationists who work hard to protect all our plants and animals. As I have dedicated a portion of sales of my book to wildlife preservation, I hope reading this will inspire you to help.

To learn more about other wildlife and my books please visit my author website on:
https://tomberquist-Author.com

Suggested website links:
http://www.samofund.org/santa-monica-mountains-wildlife-preservation/park-connectivity-wildlife-corridor/
www.mountainlion.org
www.urbancarnivores.org
http://www.nwf.org/
http://www.smmc.ca.gov/WCCA.asp
http://www.nps.gov/samo/
http://www.sierraclub.org/

PART ONE

CHAPTER ONE

When the cub was born, he was not given a name, but instead a scent signature by his family. He smelled like the Lupine flower that bloomed in purple profusion where he was born. Lupine-cub was his scent-name.

One evening when he and his brother and sister were sleeping next to their mother after a warm snack, they felt a sudden jolt. As their mother leaped up into action, they immediately saw a stranger shoot out of a thicket with a savage snarl. Lupine-cub could immediately smell his maleness.

The mountain lion intruder roared and charged, and their mother had just enough time to push her cubs back. She yowled for them to run. They darted away and hid deep in their bramble den, shivering as their mother faced off with the stranger. The branches were too thick, and the cubs could not see, but Lupine-cub heard the screams of battle. There were shattering sounds of fangs hitting fangs, claws slashing claws. Then there was silence. A long silence. The cubs huddled and mewed and wanted to help, but stayed hidden as they were taught.

Then there was a shuffling sound, padded feet moving slowly toward them. Then it grew louder, faster. The cubs shivered in panic as they waited for the stranger to pounce on them, but then they picked up a familiar scent. It was their mother. But there was something different to her scent; they smelled her blood. She crashed through the bramble and collapsed in front of her cubs with deep gashes to her head and flanks. The cubs helped to lick her wounds. She nuzzled them and licked their fears.

In time, Lupine-cub also came to fear the two-legged animals. Living in the dense forest high above their cities, the two-legs seldom entered his homeland. Once he came near one of their wide paths and saw them riding inside growling, smoking beasts with four round legs spinning fast. His sister, frightened, ran onto the path and was rammed by the smoking beast. She was thrown high into the air and died before hitting the ground. It was that day Lupine-cub learned to keep the two-legs at a safe distance. His instincts told him they were not fierce, but what they carried with them made them powerful predators. He'd watch as they took down deer from a great distance with one sharp roar of their long firesticks.

1

****

In the valley below the dense forest, a boy named Reggie Youngblood was sitting at the kitchen table with his mother, Carole. Reggie talked into a computer screen.

"Tell you what; when I get back from Iraq," the man said through the jittery Skype connection, "we'll hike our favorite mountain trails."

"Sure, Dad," the boy answered.

"Let's plan a family picnic as soon as you get back," Reggie's mom jumped in, "we can hike up to Ridgeview Rock just like we used to."

While his mom went on planning their picnic and where the best views would be and how they could also visit the Holyfield's, Reggie's mind trailed off to the last time he went hunting with his dad. It was the first and last time he shot a deer. The whole scene flashed by in seconds. He was only twelve then and not too steady with the 30.06 Remington rifle his dad had bought for him.

He hit the ten-point buck in the hindquarters and they watched it fall beyond the Junipers and then struggle to get up. It had been over three years since that day, but what happened next still made Reggie feel like vomiting. As he and his Dad ran to their fallen prey, they saw the hollow-point round had torn a gaping hole past the buck's rib cage and its intestines were hanging out. The buck made gurgling noises and its tongue flapped as it wrenched its head up and down.

Reggie could still hear his dad yelling, 'Quick, put him out of his misery—give him a shot to the head.' But Reggie bent over and threw up. Then his dad, with a disgusted look on his face, proceeded to grab the rifle from him and took care of it.

"SCRRITT!" A noise in the background. The Skype signal began breaking up and Reggie's dad said something like '...only 126 days...go hunting? ...take c ...love....' The audio dies. The video freezes. Blank.

Reggie turned to his mom. "I'm not going hunting. I'm never going hunting again."

Looking concerned, she offered, "I'll try to talk to him about it, but you know how he feels about taking you hunting. He thinks it's what a father is supposed to teach his son."

"I don't care. I don't care what he thinks he's supposed to teach me. He's already taught me what a man *shouldn't* do—you should remember that."

"I know Reggie," she said, ending the conversation, "it's time we both start standing up to him."

****

When Lupine-cub grew older, his mother took him hunting, teaching him where to find prey and when and how to best hide before the ambush. He watched carefully as she slowly crawled and froze, crawled and froze, repeating this over and over --stalking closer and closer to their meal. He mimicked her every move, and when she leaped, he'd jump as far and high as he could, paying attention to how she landed on top and brought down their prey. And then they would eat.

One day, she left Lupine-cub. His hunger and training drove him to find his own food: squirrels, raccoons, and finally deer. And when he was almost full-grown, another instinct arose; Lupine-cub felt the ancestral, pulsating urge to find his own mate.

His nostrils flared and twitched when he picked up the sweet scent of a nearby female one evening, and he followed her scent trail with earnest. But before he could get a look at her, he heard her yelping. He charged ahead, no longer worrying about crawling and freezing, but when he finally saw her, he was crushed to see her wrestling with an older, much bigger male.

His instincts told him the older mountain lion could, and would, kill him. But Lupine-cub remained transfixed as he watched the older lion mount her and then lay down to rest. Lupine-cub was unaware that the bigger lion had picked up his scent, until he saw him look in his direction and growl. The old lion made a huge leap at the intruder, just missing catching his rear legs with his huge claws.

The young lion bolted through the grass and bramble and then leaped across a wide ravine. The older lion gave chase, growling and coming at him with murder glowing in his yellow eyes, his fierce screams echoing through the canyon. But Lupine-cub was too fast; the old lion grew tired and stopped the chase; his instincts to mate were stronger and he soon returned to his female.

When Lupine-cub became Lupine-boy, he felt a change in his body and a change in the wind. He didn't know it, but on one fateful day, he was given a new name by the two-legged animals. It was night when he caught a seductive but foreign scent near the edge of a meadow. Curious, he slowly crouched toward it, but as soon as his whiskers touched the pungent pile, 'Snap! Whoosh!' Something bit his rear leg and held tight.

Lupine-boy roared and reared to face his enemy, but nothing was there but a sharp pain and an invisible tight grip. He struggled to escape, rolling on the ground, dragging his sides in the dirt, but the pain only strengthened. It would not let go. His sharp teeth and strong jaws could not bite through it. He was trapped.

Exhausted, he dropped to his belly and slept until dawn. In the morning, he felt another sharp pain, this time in his hindquarters.

3

Rising to fight on three legs, he saw no enemy; he only saw a feathered thorn sticking out where the pain was. Suddenly, he heard movement all around him, and then he saw the two-legs coming with firesticks. As they grew nearer, they moved slower and slower until they blurred in Lupine-boy's eyes. His body felt weak and he fell to the ground like a lifeless lump.

When he woke up later, the two-legs were gone. The young lion felt a weight and an itch around his neck. It smelled both of leather and the two-legs, and he couldn't get it off. Still groggy, he hobbled away as far as he could from the smell of the where the two-legs had handled him.

****

In the valley below, school buses returned to their parking lots and cars crammed and choked up the roads on their evening commute. Reggie Youngblood heard his mom come home, but didn't leave his room to greet her.

"You in there, Reggie?" his Mom called.

"I'm here," he grunted, "But I'm busy." *At least she didn't knock on my door,* he thought with his eyes glued to his laptop, *and ask me if I had a good day.* But a couple minutes later, his Mom cracked open his door and asked if he had a good day.

"Are hot dogs and beans okay with you?"

Startled, he quickly fumbled to close the web page. Carole saw Reggie slam the laptop closed and stared at the white wall above his bed, looking embarrassed.

"You know Reg, if you were looking at porn, it can give you a warped view of things," his mom said.

"Whatever," he said, rolling his eyes.

"Look, honey, I know it's normal for boys to look at that stuff, but you can easily get the wrong idea on how to treat girls without forming a loving relationship.

"I know; you've told me that before," Reggie said without taking his eyes off the wall. Although he felt she was right, he said, "Hot dogs and beans are fine." As soon as she left, he put on his sweats, went into the living room, and plopped down on the couch. He turned on an old NOVA episode about 'The World of Insects' until he started to itch all over and switched to *South Park*.

"Dinner's ready!" his Mom called.

Slouching into his chair, Reggie started pushing the hot dog slices around the beans.

"Want ketchup?" she asked.

"No, Ma."

"Really? You used to always add ketchup."

Reggie looked up at his mom and asked, "These Wal-mart hot dogs?"

"All beef," she answered, "gluten-free."

"Can't you get those wieners like we used to get up in Crestview? They were pink, not red, and they had skin. They, like, snapped when you bit into them."

"I know Reg," she answered, "but we don't live there anymore."

"Yeah, I know. And it sucks! I feel trapped by all these stupid buildings and freeways."

"I know. I don't like the city either. You know that your dad had to sell the place so we could be okay." She immediately changed her tone: "How was school?"

"Sucked. Like always."

"Any cute girls yet?" she asked.

"Yeah, right Mom, all the girls are attracted to guys like me who look like freaks."

Looking at her son's finely chiseled face, the full lips and the gentle dark eyes framed by long lashes, she said, "You're crazy. You're a very good looking boy, Reggie, and you've got a big, gentle heart... once the girls get to know you..." She raised her hand in the air and snapped her fingers, "It'll happen just like that!"

"Yeah. Sure. Once they see through my hair," he smirked.

"That's who we're looking for!" she said, rubbing the top of his bushy head. "Got any plans for the weekend?"

"Nope."

"You always have a good time with Isaac at the Audubon Center," she suggested.

Reggie shook his head even though he actually already had plans to go to the center with Isaac. "Yeah, at least I'll get a break from that friggin' school, he blurted out, "You know I hate it!"

"You mean the kids?"

"Yeah, the kids. There are some major assholes there."

"What's wrong with them?"

"First of all, there's this Kevin kid who thinks he's such a cool dude—like he rules the hallways or something."

"What does he do?"

"He, like, pushes kids into the lockers—kids who aren't in his group. He tripped Isaac once, which really pissed me off."

"Did he ever do anything to you?"

"Not really, just called me 'half-breed' once."

"That's not very nice. I thought the school had all kinds of kids from all kinds of backgrounds?"

"It does, but he saw me talking to this girl..." Then Reggie stopped, knowing that his mom would want to know more about her.

"I just try to ignore him. But whatever. On top of that, most of my classes are really lame."

Reggie kept swirling the baked bean juice on his plate and pictured Jennifer, a girl in his biology class, who seemed really nice.

"You know how important it is that you get good grades," his Mom said. "Your dad will be asking this weekend."

"I know," he said, keeping his head down, thinking that was the hard part. His dad would probably be asking him about Algebra—the subject that *he* thought was so important. He could hear him lecture how he had to be good at numbers if he wanted to be a businessman—not a man who worked with his hands and never made enough money. Reggie was actually doing okay in school, but he wasn't doing it so he could become one of those suits slaving away in a cubicle.

"How's Algebra coming?" his mom asked.

"Jesus. Mom!" Reggie slammed his fist on the table. "Why do you always take his side—no matter what he says or does?" Seeing his mom's face wince then fall, Reggie immediately regretted blaming her. She put up with a lot; she even had taken a second job to keep things together.

After a long pause, his mom said, "It's tough in a new school, but I know you will find yourself. Things will turn around."

"Sure. Whatever."

"I'm sorry, honey, but I've got to head out to work," she said, grabbing her keys. She came back to kiss him on the top of his head.

Reggie smiled for the first time in the morning and said, "Don't forget the words to the Wal-mart customer cheer!"

"Oh, I won't," she laughed as she shut the door behind her.

At least I have biology tomorrow, Reggie remembered, as he headed back into his room.

****

Lupine-boy could not know what that collar around his neck would mean in the world of the two-legs. He was now almost a fully grown mountain lion and had the strong instinct to survive—to run away from danger. But now, Lupine-boy also now sensed an instinctual shove to find his own territory, to take a mate and father his own offspring.

One spring night his instincts pushed him in a new direction. Lupine-boy didn't perceive that on a high ridge above him, a larger male lion stalked him. Crouched and silent, the big cat waited for the perfect moment to shoot down on his young rival. Finally, the big cat leapt. In mid-air, his jaws and claws sprang open for the kill.

A split second before the big cat almost landed on the young cat's back to sink his two-inch daggers into his neck, the young cat jumped. The big cat tumbled and snarled, but only got in one good swipe at the young lion's hindquarters. Lupine-boy took off like a shot.

He sprinted down the canyon, jumped over high junipers and made incredibly sharp evasive turns that the heavier animal couldn't match. Soon he reached a hill looking down on the wide path that divided his forest homeland with shining dens of the two-legs. He saw and smelled the fast-moving lines of the growling beasts the two-legs rode in.

Death was right behind him, he knew this, but he also knew that it was possible that death faced him below, too. The young cat hesitated feeling the smooth path at his feet and saw two white eyes of one smoking beast roar past him. There. Now. He leapt behind it, running as fast as he could as another beast screeched and almost hit him. He made it half-way across, but a long stone barrier stopped him. He froze.

Lupine-boy could not go back. His heart urged him to leap again into the path of the beasts running in the other direction. A beast's two red eyes passed by him. He sprinted and leaped to the other side, successfully escaping the smoking beast. Looking up the hill, he saw a tall wire fence. He sprinted along the fence line to gain momentum and leapt. He felt his tail clip the top and he fell hard into a clump of sage brush. There, the mountain lion lay still licking his wounds. He stayed there hidden until next nightfall. Then he would slip out of the shadows.

CHAPTER TWO

Driving on the 101 to Encino, Joe Sartor shook his head remembering his encounter with the new juvenile mountain lion that had just crossed this freeway without becoming road kill. He had only months ago fitted the animal with a tracking collar and had given him a name: P12, for the twelfth puma or mountain lion they captured for their study. *I'll have to tell the Biology class about this miracle cat,* he thought. As he pulled into the high school parking lot, he wondered if these students would be interested in protecting this nearly endangered species.

Reggie Youngblood was the last student to make it into his seat just as the bell rang. He always waited in the hall to make sure Kevin was already in. Today was guest lecture day, and standing next to Mrs. Horton was a tall man with big shoulders. He was light-skinned, had a pointed jaw and looked a lot like his dad, except for his moustache. He wore a brown sports coat, jeans and dusty black hiking boots.

"Class!" Mrs. Horton announced in her booming voice, "We have been studying the genetics of fruit flies and how this little organism has been used by laboratory research scientists to understand how gene mutations arise and are passed down from parents to offspring."

Reggie remembered those lessons and thinking how boring and useless it seemed to him. How could anyone decided to become a scientist and spend every day looking through microscopes at little fruit flies?

Mrs. Horton continued: "Today I am pleased to introduce Mr. Joe Sartor, who is a wildlife biologist from the National Park Agency. Mr. Sartor is recognized as a world expert in capturing and studying large carnivores. I want you to pay particular attention to Mr. Sartor's talk when he discusses DNA analysis and how inherited mutations in inbred populations can affect their survival fitness. Now let's please give him a big welcome."

The kids clapped and Reggie wondered how a guy who works in the jungles and forest with wild animals could also be interested in genetics.

"Thank you, Mrs. Horton and class," Joe began. "Today I want to talk about lions, but not about African lions. The lions I'm talking about don't live in a pride with other lions and they don't hunt zebra." He scooted over and put his hand on a large piece of shaped cardboard sitting on Mrs. Horton's desk. "This kind of lion I'm referring to is a solitary creature who lives in the shadows and roams the hills at night and is rarely ever seen by humans."

As Joe slowly unfolded the cardboard cut-out, he continued, "This is our American lion, the powerful, independent, freedom-loving mountain lion." By this time, he had unfolded the full-body shape of the giant cat way beyond the sides of the desk to reveal the animal's long, sleek body. Reggie focused intently on the life-size photo and took in every detail of the lion's muscular shoulders—paws as big as saucers, sharp front teeth more than two-inches long, and a whiskered face complete with a nasty snarl.

Joe continued, "Some people also call this guy a cougar or sometimes a panther, but it's the same animal. He is lion and a big cat, and we use all those names for him, but his official scientific name is *Puma concolor*, meaning puma of one color." Gently stroking the back of the image, Joe described it as "a beautiful warm tan color with white on his chin and belly and dark brown on the tips of his ears and tail."

Awesome, Reggie thought, *I can see why this dude loves this animal.* Being a keen observer and lover of animals, Reggie was mesmerized by the picture of the mountain lion. It made him think of the leopard he had seen in the Los Angeles zoo. He remembered how it paced back and forth in between the boring corners of its enclosure like its spirit was broken. He could relate to the animal's feeling of frustration and isolation; how it felt when his dad would make him stay in his room an entire afternoon for being too wild.

The lights dimmed and the white screen lowered from the ceiling, and just like that Reggie's attention came back to the class. Photos of mountain lions came on the screen, the big animals running and leaping, and then one dragging a deer by the neck.

Joe said, "The mountain lion grows up to eight feet long and weighs as much as a grown man at 200 pounds. Nature has built him to be the ultimate predator. He can run at 40 miles an hour and leap 20 feet in the air to take down a deer twice the lion's size. He will often knock his prey down with one blow and then sink his two-inch long retractable claws into the deer's side so it can't escape. In the same exact instant, his massive jaws and curved pointed teeth clamp down on the deer's neck and twists it. The deer dies in seconds."

"Gross!" one girl gasped.

"Whoa!" the boys in the back yell.

"Go get 'em tiger," Kevin yelled as he pretended to claw the air with his big hands.

9

Reggie rolled his eyes as everyone looked around the room at everyone else. Reggie then looked over at Jennifer, down the row, holding her eyes closed like she didn't want to hear anymore. Looking at Isaac a few rows over, he could tell that he was disturbed at the fierceness of it all. Isaac was a sensitive kid and with his red hair and freckles, he looked kind of like a weakling. But he had a quick wit and a red-head's temper and he was the first and only friend Reggie had in his new school.

"I know this may sound cruel," Joe continued, "but the lion has no meanness in it; nature has given this animal the body, the skills, and the instincts it needs in order to survive—because it has no other means to obtain food."

I really get this animal now, Reggie realized. The lion knows what it wants and its brain signals every sinew and muscle to get it, in order to live. His weapons are his claws and teeth and he follows his nature—fast and with a direct purpose. It's not really killing, he believed, it's gathering its food.

Reggie not only became totally enthralled by the character of this animal, but also by how Joe understood it. Joe was, but wasn't like his dad. His dad knew a lot about animals too, but he's a hunter and respects animals in a different way; Joe *cares* about them.

Joe went on to explain how the mountain lion lived in North America long before humans did. How they lived in peace with the indigenous peoples, but not so much with the later European settlers. Reggie was surprised as Joe described how the early Spanish and English settlers feared and hated the mountain lion. *Why were the native people so different?* he wondered. He thought of his favorite picture book as a child; how Indian Chief Seattle considered animals his brothers and sisters. *Yeah,* he remembered, *even when my dad shot a ruffed grouse, he would thank the bird for giving its life. He must have been taught that,* Reggie thought, *by his Grandmother Wanchuat.*

Joe continued, "The early settlers killed thousands and thousands of cougars for sport, and by the late 1800s, virtually every mountain lion had been killed or had fled the United States, except for the mountainous West." A photo appeared, showing proud bounty hunters smiling over dozens of dead mature lions and their cubs draped dead over a fence.

As he was about to continue, Joe looked at the boy in front with bushy black hair and matching sparkling black eyes. The boy felt like he wanted to raise his hand. It was Reggie. "Do you have a question?" Joe asked.

"Sort of," Reggie replied, "Weren't these guys with guns predators, too?"

"You could say that. Good point," answered Joe.

Reggie glanced to his left and caught Jennifer's eyes and she gave him a nod and a smile. Only a second after that, he noticed Kevin who gestured to him like he was blowing him a kiss.

Kevin raised his hand: "What do you expect, though. I mean, these dudes were getting good money to have fun shooting wild beasts." Then he started to laugh. "I mean, man, I'd do it too."

Joe responded with an understanding smile. "Well, they *were* successful in killing off almost all the wolves and the grizzly bears in the West, even though we keep the bear on our state flag."

What a story, Reggie thought, wishing his dad could hear this. It was a real and happening story, not like those places and dates in history class. Reggie Youngblood had, for the first time in his life, felt a spark light up his brain. He felt a strong mysterious pull to *Puma concolor*. And this guy Joe, he thought, could lead him to the animal.

Next, Joe explained that the mountain lion is most threatened here in Southern California. "In the nearby Santa Monica Mountains," Joe said, "we know for sure there exists only two thriving lions. These are the two that we had captured and fitted with special radio collars."

Holding up a thick leather collar and pointing to a box underneath, Joe explained, "These collars contain GPS tracking devices that emit a signal that allow us to follow their movements and study their behavior." *That's pretty cool,* Reggie thought.

"Just recently," Joe continued, "a juvenile mountain lion from the San Gabriel Mountains made a daring and miraculous trip to this area. And in order to make it here, the lion had to cross over two four-lane freeways, the 101 and 405, both which carry over 300,000 vehicles a day. Up until this point," Joe went on, "all of them died trying to get across. But this young lion, is at an age where he has to find a new territory and his own mate, and he actually made it across. We collared and named him P12, but I like to call him 'Miracle Cat'."

If only I could be so brave, Reggie thought to himself; *and know where I'm going in my life.*

The bell rang and Mrs. Horton walked to the front of the class, her long curly hair bouncing on her shoulders. "Okay, everybody. We're going to take a couple minute stretch break, and instead of our regular lab period today, we'll stay here and go into Q and A with Mr. Sartor." The class immediately erupted in chatter.

Just as Reggie thought to go up and ask Joe a question, Joe headed out to the restroom. "Owww!" Reggie felt a sharp pain and a heavy weight on his foot. Kevin was standing on it with his back to the teacher.

"Why don't you go back to the mountains, half-breed?" Kevin snarled.

"Why don't you get off my fucking foot, dumb-ass?" Reggie replied.

Kevin then put his other foot together and all his 150 pounds on top of Reggie's foot so he couldn't stand up, so Reggie grabbed Kevin's arm and started twisting it.

"Smart comments, Reggie," the blonde girl said from behind as she bumped into Kevin's big shoulders, knocking him off balance. The weight lifted.

Kevin's ruthless eyes pierced through Reggie then he scowled, turned around and went back to his seat.

Reggie's face turned redder and he told the girl, "Kevin's always screwing around."

"Hi, I'm Jennifer. Pretty interesting lecture, hey?"

"Um. Yeah," Reggie said as Mrs. Horton announced, "Everyone back to your seats!"

"Well, Ladies and Gentlemen, it's time for questions and answers." Hands went up.

"I live in Agoura Hills," a tall girl with long bangs almost covering her eyes asked, "Should I be afraid?"

Joe sensed her natural fear of wild animals and responded, "Possibly an occasional lion might pass by the outskirts of your town, but because he is an animal of the remote woods, he very, very rarely enters into a town where people live."

"Don't lions eat people?" Kevin asked in order to get a few laughs, "I heard this kid up in Cupertino got his head chewed up."

"Not really," Joe responded, "Fortunately, in that case, adults were able to scare the lion away and the boy escaped major injury. They later killed the lion as a possible threat to other humans. These mountain lions do not hunt humans for food, but on rare occasion they attack humans."

"But why don't we just get rid of them somehow?" Kevin interrupted. With that question some other boys shouted, "Yeah, man!" in approval.

Reggie shook his head thinking what a stupid ass that Kevin is, like he can use a video game gun to evaporate all his enemies. Reggie raised his hand and asked, "Can't we share our habitat?"

A couple of boys in the back snickered at Reggie's question. When Reggie turned around, he saw Kevin mocking him by hugging himself, and then Kevin shouted: "Yeah, we can relocate them in your backyard, Reggie."

More laughter. Joe then held up his hand to get everyone's attention back. "You should also know that lion on human attacks are very, very rare. In California, since 1890, or in 124 years of record-keeping, there have only been 18 verified attacks on humans.

To compare, an average of 4.5 million Americans are attacked and bitten by dogs every year, and sadly each year about 20 to 30 people die as a result."

The students let out a collective, "Whoa!" *That ought to shut Kevin up,* Reggie smiled to himself.

Another boy near the windows wearing a bright red shirt raised his hand. "How do you capture them?"

Joe answered, "We usually use a leg snare. When it is tripped, it sends a radio signal to me at home. Most often it's in the middle of night, so I jump out of bed and into my jeep, drive fast and hike deep into the hills to find him."

What an awesome exciting job Joe has, Reggie thought to himself, *I'd be happy to jump out of bed for a job like that.*

"Once we tranquilize him," Joe continued, "we check his heart rate, take blood and saliva samples, measure and weigh him, take pictures, and then we attach the radio collar. The last thing we do is to give him a wake up drug, move away and let him slowly wake up and escape from his human tormentors."

Tormentors, Reggie thought, *Joe used the right word. You trap the poor animal so he can't move for hours as he tries to chew the wire off, then they shoot him with something that makes him sleep in the middle of danger, then poke and prod him before he wakes up in a daze. But I guess it's for science and for his own good,* he concluded.

The same boy in the red shirt blurted out, "Why are there so few lions?"

"Well," Joe paused, then answered, "We've lost several to car accidents, poachers, rat poison, and of course, lions killing other lions."

"Lions kill other lions?" the blonde-haired girl asked.

"Male lions fight other males over food and females. Right now in the Santa Monica Mountains we have one large dominant male with huge paws that we collared as P1, and this guy could and would easily kill P12. Female lions, on the other hand, seldom fight—they are totally focused on bearing and caring for their cubs. This is the natural order of things in their lives.

"Now, as you learned in Mrs. Horton's class, offspring of two *unrelated* animals are not very likely to get a harmful mutant gene from both parents. But offspring of *closely related* animals that each carry one mutant copy of a gene often will end up with two mutant copies and suffer the consequences. The small number of remaining pumas in our area means that unless we have new lions with new genes coming in from other territories, inbreeding will hurt the population.

Joe continued, "Inbreeding results when the dominant male has no other females to mate with, so he mates with his own grown offspring or grandchildren."

"So gross!" a girl in the back yells out.

Then Kevin let out a big laugh and shouted, "If I were the king, I'd want to protect my harem too."

Nobody laughed.

"Actually," Joe explained, "the result of this inbreeding can be disastrous for the next and later generations as the inbred cubs are more likely to have birth defects and be less able to fight off diseases."

Wow, Reggie thought, *I never was interested in genetics before, but now I can see how this plays out in real life.* Reggie then raised his hand. "Could that in-breeding affect more than their physical health, like their social behavior?"

Kevin laughed. "What? Like they don't say please or thank you?"

"Actually," Joe replied, ignoring Kevin, "that's a smart observation and a very good hypothesis for another research project."

Mrs. Horton stood up, gestured and thanked Mr. Sartor for his great talk. The kids clapped and then started gathering their things and heading out the door. Kevin, on his way out, gave Isaac his usual kick in the leg, and this time he looked over at Reggie, smiled and fake-scratched his neck with his middle finger. Reggie waited until all the kids left before going up to Joe to stick out his hand and thank him.

"Glad to meet you," Joe said.

"Uh, I really enjoyed your lecture. That was cool."

"Thanks," Joe said, "And I enjoyed your comments. You seem to have an uncanny understanding of our natural world."

"I don't know about that, but I did grow up in the San Bernardino Mountains and the folks at the Audubon Wildlife Rescue Center tell me I have a gift with animals," Reggie blushed. He wanted to say so many things, but also didn't want to be pushy. "Could I visit your office someday and learn more about our mountain lions?"

"Absolutely, and what's your name?"

"Reggie Youngblood, sir."

Then Joe handed Reggie a business card and said, "Reggie, you can call me anytime and check out our website." Reggie shook Joe's hand again and said goodbye and headed toward the door.

There in the hallway, stood Jennifer.

"I like what you said in class," Jennifer said, "You seem to have such a feel for animals."

"Thanks. Sometimes I think I understand animals more than humans," Reggie said.

"Ha! I know what you mean." Jennifer started to backpedal away and gave him a slight wave. "I'll see you Thursday, Reggie."

Reggie headed down the hall smiling, thinking for a moment that Jennifer might actually like him. Then he shook his head and said to himself, *'Yeah right, she had to save me from Kevin... How fucking embarrassing is that?'*

CHAPTER THREE

On the night before, high above the valley floor, another recent settler to Los Angeles started a new life in his adopted homeland. Lupine-boy, waited till dusk to explore the territory. Since he had killed a 100-pound buck and eaten it over a period of three days before he crossed the freeway, he didn't need to search for food. His nose was most attuned to picking up the scents of fellow mountain lions, both friend and foe. Lupine-boy kept raising his head and opening his nostrils in the hopes of picking up another whiff of that female perfume. It was a strange-to-him sweet and sour smell that enchanted him.

He climbed a hill where all he could smell were the two-legs. Approaching the sharp crest of the hill, he engaged his large hind muscles, and in two almost vertical leaps, landed on top. Looking down, he didn't see chaparral, but instead hundreds of dens for the two-legs lined up along black curving trails. The young lion saw odd trees with their straight-up-in-the-air trunks and only a round bush swaying on top. Behind the dens, he noticed small, same-shaped lakes behind some of them. He caught the faint smell of burned wood and meat as though a fire had recently swept down the canyon.

Winding his way around the dens, he heard the barks of strange sounding coyotes that sensed his presence. Lupine-boy dropped into a crouch with his hair raised on the back of his neck. Another loud bark and a two-leg shining a light toward him, shook his instincts to move away, so he bound back into the folds of the mountains without making a sound. Walking between the manzanita and yarrow of the canyon walls, he felt more at ease. He was thirsty so he followed his nose heading west where he soon came upon a large sweet water lake with a high cliff to one side. Here, he eagerly drank his fill.

Nose to the ground, he picked up the ever so faint scent of another male lion. Lupine-boy immediately dropped down into a defensive, ready-to spring and fight posture and gave out a low snarl. He processed the scent as old, but his instincts still made him shiver with fear. He lay there for a while to be sure, then fresh two-leg smells returned to his nose and he moved cautiously toward a flat treed area. On pathways among the trees were a cluster of large beasts standing quiet and not moving on their four round legs.

Nearby, he found another place where two- legs lived, but not in dens. He saw what looked like several large boulders spread apart over the ground, but they were not boulders. He saw lights in some of them and heard two-leg voices. Crawling up to a dark one, he smelled strange scraps of two-leg food and a box on legs that smelled of old fire. He slowly moved closer to the dark shape. The lion's sensitive whiskers felt its side. The surface was not hard and flexed when his nose touched it. Through the thin material, he felt warmth radiating outward and he could hear the two-legs breathing inside.

"Crack!" His pointed ears made a quick pivot. He froze. His eyes picked up a movement. A branch snapped behind him. Startled, he bolted in the opposite direction. After a few yards, he turned around to see a raccoon running the other way.

Heading further in the direction the sun set, Lupine-boy climbed a ridgeline and rested on top. There, where the stars ended, he could make out the vast flat span of the big water. He felt calm. Behind, he felt the soft glow of the sun on his fur and realized his long night would soon be ending. Below were two-leg dens dotting the hills with stars flickering inside. Closer to the big water, they became more dense, and at the end was a black path running along the shoreline with an occasional smoking beast running fast along it. Heading down further, he came upon a narrow gravel trail lit by the sun. He peeked through the crevice of the canyon.

She stood right there. All his senses immediately recognized a kindred spirit of his homeland—a magnificent doe—and his body shook with excitement. The deer had sunlight kissing her back as she foraged at the side of the trail. Her front hoof gently nudged the grass and her ears twitched as she chewed. Watching her carefully, the hair on the lion's back rose in anticipation. He began to stalk. He felt the skin and fur between his webbed toes, as his paws fell silently on the ground.

He crept quietly with intense concentration from hiding place to hiding place. His hind feet stepped softly into the prints of the forefeet to lessen any chance of snapping a twig and alerting his prey.

He slowly stalked with his head between his paws, belly to the ground, ears to the front and tail twitching at the tip. Soft. Silent. He got within a few body-lengths of his favorite prey. With his muscles wound and ready to pounce, he froze. Both animals' ears swiveled as they heard loud two-leg voices. The doe jumped down an embankment while Lupine-boy quickly moved higher above the trail. From a rock outcropping, he could see a group of two-legs *walking along; some tall and some small. The two-legs held a line connected to small white coyote that ran back and forth yipping at them. Lupine-boy waited for them to pass and then decided to follow them, staying hidden. The young lion stalked them silently from the bush above.*

The small two-legs entranced the young lion. They'd run and stop and jump and made squealing noises as they chased each other. They excited him somehow, and he moved in closer but remained carefully hidden in the cover behind them. He followed his all-powerful instinct to see without being seen. The two-legs didn't look to their backs or sides, so they had no idea he was there.

All of a sudden, both the two-legs and Lupine-boy jerked to a standstill. A piercing wailing cry shot up from the canyon. They all looked down to see a huge red beast hurling fast and screaming on the black path below, light flashing from its flanks. The fearsome, smoking wailing beast frightened the lion. His heart spurred him to scoot up a draw as the two-legs stood watching. He found a hole in some dense scrub and crouched down on a leafy bed. Then, calmly licking his paws, he watched the day breaking around him. Lupine-boy felt very tired, but he would stay here and wait for the coming night to fall.

CHAPTER FOUR

When the bus dropped Reggie off he was a little surprised to see his mom's old Subaru Impreza parked on the street. Unlocking the apartment door he found his mom at the kitchen table. "Hi Reggie. You look happy. Have a good day at school?"

Noticing that his mom seemed a bit in the dumps, he replied, "Kind of, I guess, but how are you? They let you go early at The Coffee Bean?"

"Yeah, it was a slower day today," she answered, "but it'll give me a chance to rest up before the evening shift at Wal-Mart, which would be a nice change. But I want to get back to that look on your face. School was just okay today?"

Not wanting to get into a real conversation, he simply said, "Yeah, pretty good."

"Want to tell me about it?"

Reggie ducked his head in the fridge. "Sure, but no more string cheese?"

"I'll pick some up at Wal-Mart tonight, there are Doritos in the cupboard."

Munching away, Reggie told his mom about Joe's lecture in Biology class.

She wanted to interrupt and ask questions, but it was so rare that her son talked with such enthusiasm about something. As a young child, being in nature was all that ever got him excited. She just let him talk and talk.

"This guy Joe is a wildlife biologist," Reggie explained, "and his job is capturing and studying mountain lions in the Santa Monica Mountains. I mean, how cool is that?"

Reggie's mom felt both delight and guilt over Reggie's burst of excitement. She knew how much he missed the woods.

"And the really cool thing was that he seemed to like me," Reggie continued, "He listened to me, said I asked some good questions and he even gave me his card."

"That's great, anything else going on?" she asked.

"Nope!" Reggie responded with a half-smile on his face, still picturing Jennifer. Reggie didn't want to tell his mom that a girl actually waited for him after class to talk to him, so he kept reading the back of the Doritos bag while he chewed.

Changing the subject, his mom asked, "How's Algebra coming?"

Reggie stiffened, threw down the bag of chips and shot back, "I'm so sick of talking about that class. You know what? I'm going to change."

After tossing on some sweats, he headed into the bathroom, took a leak, and then found himself staring at his reflection in the mirror. At 15, going on 16, he felt most people thought he looked young for his age. As he rubbed his face, his light brown skin showed no sign of acne and he thought it probably never would show the fuzz some of his classmates were developing. His nose was a little big, but straight, and his ears stuck out some, but he concluded he was an average looking dude. *Would I grow up and look more like my Dad?* he wondered. *Would I be able to grow a mustache like Joe?* His huge head of coarse black hair was his signature look and he liked how it matched the black of his irises, or were they his pupils? He could never remember. Then Reggie went back into his room and lay down on his bed, closed his eyes and soon started thinking about Jennifer.

He pictured Jennifer's blonde hair. It was short and spiked up straight like an all-around Mohawk. He wondered how it stayed up that way and wanted to touch it. She also had a row of small colored beads running down the ridge of each ear. He didn't pick up the color of her eyes because he mostly looked down during their brief chat in the hallway. But he really liked her ankle bracelets that had feathers on them and thought they must have tickled her feet when she walked. Most of all what he remembered, as he took in a deep breath, was her smell. A sweet smell not unlike the wild primrose he found in the woods that always heightened his senses. Just to be close to her for that minute gave him a feeling he never had before.

He opened his eyes, got up and looked into the mirror again. He put his hands on top of his head to push back that funny clump of hair that always stood up as the day wore on. It made him look kind of like.... *Yeah,* he thought, *like a friggin' half-breed.* He flattened it and rewound the band in the back and with a determined look, told his reflection, *'I don't give a shit about what that that asshole Kevin calls me—one of these days, someone is going to crack him in the face. And it might be me.'*

"Time to eat," Reggie's mom yelled, jolting him back to reality.

"Coming!" he yelled. Then, back to himself he thought: *'You know man, all she did was smile at me and say that she liked what I said in class. Then she took off. That's all you pathetic dork. It's never going to happen. Forget about her.'*

CHAPTER FIVE

It was early morning in Joe Sartor's bedroom, only a few days after he had given his talk at Encino High, when the phone rang before the alarm. After the fourth ring, Joe's wife Barbara called out, "Joe, you going to get that?" Barbara usually woke first to the middle-of-the-night calls that Joe often got from his work, as Joe was a heavy sleeper. He groggily picked up the phone expecting a message telling him one of his snares caught a lion, but instead it was Ralph Pena, a Santa Monica City-based conservation officer he'd known over ten years.

Joe rubbed his eyes as he listened, and then let out a loud "WHAT?"

Ralph repeated himself, "You heard me. There's a mountain lion cornered in downtown Santa Monica. I just got a call from the city cops."

Joe sat up. "Are you sure it's a cougar?"

"Haven't seen it yet personally," Ralph replied, "but the cops told me it's in a glass-enclosed courtyard in an office building on Second Street and that it's mighty pissed off. I'm driving there right now."

"Holy shit!" Joe said as he jumped out of bed, "You got your tranquilizer gun, right? ...Be there as soon as I can."

"Yep! I'll call you when I get there, 1227 Second Street. Hurry."

****

The young mountain lion cowered and shivered on the cold concrete as more and more of the two-legs arrived. His ears were pinned back with the loud wailing of the huge red beasts and his nostrils stung with the smoke of the black and white beasts. He moved as far back in the courtyard as he could, hiding under a large potted plant. It wasn't sagebrush, but at least it gave him some green cover.

Three two-legs started slowly approaching him with their short firesticks aimed at him. The lion panicked and tried to run down a path in the back, but he ran right into a glass wall and stumbled backward, confused. He tried again, but still couldn't pass through it. It was as hard as stone. He pawed at it furiously, but the path

21

would not open. The two-legs moved in closer, yelping loudly, and this time they were carrying long firesticks.

"POP! YOW! POP! YOW!" Fiery stings hit the lion's neck first, and then his back. His eyes burned. He tried to shake off the pain. Then he screeched at the attackers and ran to the other corner of the courtyard. They moved back. The lion crouched again. His tongue hung out panting for air. His heart beat in a frenzy.

****

As soon as Joe got off the phone, his first thought and worry was that it could be P12, the lion that meant so much to his study and to the small population's survival. Was he chased out of the mountains by big P1?

Joe told Barbara they had a mountain lion cornered downtown Santa Monica and he had to hurry.

Joe sped down the Pacific Coast Highway toward Santa Monica, which was still 20 minutes away, the whole time dreading the scene he might find. There were so few lions left in the mountains, and since he knew P12 was exploring the territory, there was a good chance it was him. There was also a good chance the lion would be killed before he got there.

About this time, Ralph Pena pulled his truck up to the police tape on Second Street. The police captain waved him over. "Hey, Ralph, glad you're here. The lion is getting pretty aggressive—I had my men shoot it with pepper balls."

Ralph shook his head as the captain lifted the tape to let him through and shouted to his men, "Here's Ralph, hold on he's got his tranquilizer gun."

Ralph found the big cat partially hidden and peering around a corner with no good target for a dart. As Ralph moved closer, the cat jumped to its right.

'POP! Whoosh!" The dart missed. The cat jumped to its left.

"Dammit!" Ralph yelled. "Stay still!"

'POP! Whoosh!"

"Got 'em!" Ralph yelled as he saw the dart stick deep into the cat's mid-section.

The cat howled and twisted his body. He bit at the dart as if it was an enemy lion attacking him.

"Alright! Good shot!" the cops yelled out.

"Just hold on, guys," Ralph said, "The dart will need at least ten minutes to take effect. "Don't agitate him, the drug can initially make these cats even more aggressive. We have to wait it out." Ralph picked up his cell and dialed Joe.

"Where are you?" Ralph said into his phone.

"I'll be off the PCH in about ten minutes. How's the cat?"

"I just finally got a dart into him, but he's still pretty upset—they shot him with pepper balls."

"Dammit! What the hell?"

"They were worried he might escape. There's a daycare nearby and lots of people are showing up to watch."

"Shit!" Joe said, "Be there as soon as I can."

****

The lion was now confused on top of being afraid, and there was nowhere to run. He snarled and lunged at the two-legs, hoping to scare them off. The two-legs turned around and yelled at some more two-legs behind them, carrying a large snake-like branch with a shiny head. One of the two-legs raised then lowered his hand.

"SWISHHH!" *A powerful jet of water hit the lion in the shoulder, knocking him over. He slid along the surface until slamming into a wall. He stood up in a daze, shook himself dry, but then he heard it again.* "SWISHHH!" *The water threw him, but he quickly caught his balance and charged at the attackers. They pulled back. Feeling he may have the two-legs on the run, he knew he had to fight. He snarled and showed his fangs. He lunged forward. This time the two-legs with their short firesticks did not retreat.*

"He's going to escape," one of the cops shouted.

"POP! POP! POP!"

The lion dropped.

"Fuck!" Ralph shouted.

"Had to!" one cop yelled back.

The crowd took a collective breath, and a mixture of cheers and moans broke out.

Then silence.

Ralph watched the lion take its last breath and bleed out on the concrete.

As the cops muttered amongst themselves, Ralph turned to the crowd and saw Joe running toward him with his gear.

When their eyes met, Joe already knew the end of the tale and shouted, "No! No, tell me I'm not too late!"

"Sorry Joe," Ralph muttered. "I got here late and had a hard time getting a dart into him. He came out fighting and... the cops shot him."

Shaking his head in disgust and failure, Joe asked, "Was he wearing a tracking collar?"

"Not that I could see," Ralph said, "but let's take a look."

Ralph introduced Joe and his credentials to the police captain and his men and they moved closer to the dead body.

"Why would he come into the city?" the captain asked.

23

Joe shrugged his shoulders and knelt next to the cat. It was a male about the size of P12, but no collar. P12 could have lost his, but as soon as Joe checked his ear and saw there wasn't a tag, or a sign of a lost tag, he knew it wasn't P12.

"Thank God," Joe said to himself. A huge relief descended down Joe's spine as he continued examining the limp body. It was a healthy looking male about three years old, Joe told the cops. "Probably a new juvenile coming down from the Santa Ana mountains, trying to establish new territory."

"But why downtown Santa Monica?" one cop asked.

Joe, still kneeling at the body, looked down at the cat's now vacant eyes and then looked up at the cop and said, "He was probably just lost."

After Joe called his team to come and pick up the lion for DNA analysis and burying, Joe thanked Ralph for doing the best he could. With a heavy-heart, Joe walked through the crowd carrying his gear and gun.

"How could they shoot the poor defenseless animal?" a woman in the crowd asked.

A guy joined in, thinking Joe was the shooter, "Shame on you—you shot it with pepper balls and hoses, what did you expect it to do?"

"Couldn't you have waited for the drug to take effect? It was cornered!" someone else yelled.

On the other side, a mom holding a small child asked the yeller, "What if it was your child at the pre-school next door?"

Joe shook his head, checked his watch, and called Barbara.

"No, I'm fine," he said, "Another dead lion, but it wasn't P12."

CHAPTER SIX

When Reggie got home Thursday afternoon, he plopped down on the couch and watched one of the National Geographic shows about how animals disguise themselves—bugs that look like branches and squid that change their colors. When his mom got home, they chatted about their days over their usual beans and franks.

"Another good day at school today?" his Mom asked.

"Not too bad," he answered, thinking how boring most of his classes were and how much he hated Algebra.

Then he remembered how Jennifer actually waved at him in the hallway, and she did it even in front of her girlfriends. "I like Biology, at least. Think I might get an A."

"That would be great," his mom said. "Oh! I only caught the tail end of it on the radio, but there was a story about a mountain lion shot in downtown Santa Monica this morning."

Reggie perked up. "Whoa. In the city and not the mountains?"

"That's what the news lady said. She was on a busy street talking to people who were around. Crazy, huh?"

"I'll have to check it out online," Reggie said. "Thanks for the heads up."

"Hey, you know we're on for Skyping with dad Saturday night, right?"

Reggie nodded, "Yep!"

She continued, "You're getting your report card Friday, right?" And with a pause, she added: "Hopefully it'll be better this time."

Reggie rolled his eyes. "Maybe."

"We'll have to tell him, you know," she said. "He'll be asking about Algebra. You know that will be the first thing out of his mouth."

Reggie dropped his head and ground his teeth. "Fuck it, mom, that's all he cares about. He doesn't even care about who I am!"

"Reggie. Come on. Cool it."

"No, Mom. I'm sick of it." Then he kicked over a kitchen chair, stormed into his room, and slammed the door.

Later that evening, Reggie's mom gently knocked on his door asking if they could talk. Through the door, he said: "Don't you get it? I'm tired about talking about school."

25

Sitting with his laptop on his bed, Reggie's eyes glanced at the algebra homework sitting on his desk; all those stupid numbers and formulas waiting to be struggled with. His mind was pulled by something else, however, and he read every story he could find on the mountain lion killed in Santa Monica. He was surprised by the lion's deadly journey, but he knew what had driven him. He almost felt like he was there, after he read what Joe Sartor said about the incident in one report. *Joe has an intuitive feel for these animals,* Reggie thought, but unlike his dad, Joe seemed to have a good feel for people too. Then Reggie remembered about the lion attack in Cupertino, so he Googled that and got a whole page of hits on California lion attacks.

Reading one Yahoo report, Reggie discovered it was a six-year-old boy who wandered away from a group of adult hikers when a lion jumped out of the bush and grabbed him by the head and started dragging him. The adults ran toward the boy shouting and the lion let the boy loose and ran away. The boy was okay physically, but thinking how scary that must have been, Reggie wondered if it would scar him mentally. The lion was later shot; a small sixty-five pound male juvenile.

The report puzzled Reggie, so he plugged in Joe's website to see if he could learn more. He spent the next four and a half hours (when he should have been finishing that Algebra homework) glued to the screen, absorbing everything he could about *Puma concolor.* Along the way he discovered that sometimes juvenile lions have not been shown how to hunt by their mothers. He also learned how they captured their prey. *So maybe this lion,* Reggie thought, *was a hungry lion, but a poor hunter. A lousy hunter like me,* thinking that's what his dad probably thought of him.

Reggie scrolled down to another lion attack story. This one occurred not far from his old home in the Los Angeles National Forest back in 1995. He read about a mountain biker heading down a trail who found a mountain lion running alongside his bike. He got off his bike to chase the lion away, but it bit at his tires and chased the biker down an embankment. The man fell down and the lion started biting at his head. The man picked up a rock and started hitting it, then threw more rocks at it and eventually the lion gave up and the two ran away in opposite directions.

Two days later, a 100-pound female lion was killed, a suspect in the attack based upon matching the lion's tracks. Reggie wondered if the female possibly had cubs nearby and considered the biker a threat. Whatever the cause of the attack, that biker was both smart and lucky, Reggie thought. He remembered reading on Joe's website that when you encounter a lion you should stand your ground and make yourself as loud and threatening as you can and if the lion should attack, fight back with all your might.

"Reggie!" he heard his mom yelling, "It's getting late, have you finished your Algebra homework?"

"Yeah mom, I got it!" he yelled, knowing his dad would kill him if he flunked it. He remembered it was only two days away when he had to face his dad on the screen.

Screw him, he thought and read another lion attack story. This one made Reggie feel sick when he read it. It was about a woman high school guidance counselor from San Diego who was not so lucky. Hiking in a local park in 1994, the gruesome scene surrounding the attack and the wounds on her body suggested a struggle to the death. Two hikers found her saliva-soaked backpack, her knit cap, glasses and a human tooth lying near a puddle of blood on the road and notified the authorities. Local rangers and a county deputy searched the nearby brush and found the woman's body; clothes torn off with distinct puncture wounds all over her back. The punctures were in sets of four and shaped in a box, indicating the four large canine teeth of a carnivore. Her scalp had been peeled back from the nape of her neck, which made the rangers believe she had been dragged by her head into the brush. Reggie could hardly read on, but the article finished by saying that park officials, federal hunters and local officers were quickly dispatched to find and kill the lion. That evening, they discovered the lion returning to the spot. They unleashed their tracking hounds and the 130-pound male lion was chased up a tree and shot.

Reggie's stomach churned with the news and he couldn't understand why the lion would attack that poor woman. He could find no answer, but he felt he could hear Joe's voice when he mentioned how incredibly rare such attacks really are. He then thought about how people kill other people sometimes for no reason at all. His dad probably killed people in Iraq that he didn't even know or know why he did. Reggie asked himself, why is everyone always at war?

Reggie then found a bunch of websites dealing with the relationship of Native Americans with the cougar, and he spent the next two hours immersed in Native lore. He became fascinated by how their relationship with the animal was so different than it is today. When he read about how the Cochimi Tribe of Baja, California believed the cougar had spiritual powers, he got really excited. He remembered his dad told him his Indian ancestors were originally from Baja. He used to talk about his Grandma Wanchuat who lived on an Indian reservation near San Diego when he was a kid. Surely, he thought, once his dad knew about this connection, he would be gung ho about him studying mountain lions. He loved nature too and these were his people; his dad would be excited about his new interest. *Right?*

As he researched, he signed up for a bunch of mountain lion and wildlife websites, discussion boards, and blogs, so he could keep up with what organizations and the public were saying. He thought Joe probably subscribed to all of these too. Maybe he could contact Joe and volunteer for his organization and somehow learn firsthand about the cougar. After another hour of reading, he went to bed and dreamt about the pictures he saw of the strange Native rock paintings of cougars and other animals.

CHAPTER SEVEN

By the time Reggie got to bed, Lupine-boy had already been traversing his new territory for eight hours, covering over 10 miles. Moving in a zigzag pattern, he stayed on constant alert for other lions and his next meal. He could tell when he was approaching the boundaries of his homeland by the sweet smell of strawberries on one end, and when he approached the fields on the other end, he found the smell of the tall four-legged animals that two-legs rode on top of. Then there was the boundary of the salty breezes from the big water and finally the boundary from the roar of the beasts on the wide path he once crossed.

Attuned to the scent of a dominant male, he knew if he smelled one he would be at risk, so he instinctively knew not to leave his scent as he travelled through the territory. Soon, he came upon a pile of urine-soaked debris that another lion had left to mark its presence. He bent down and touched the little pile with his whiskers, curled his lips, and opened his mouth to a grimace to learn more about who left it and what they were communicating. It was the fresh scent of the female that he first picked up when he entered his new homeland, the same sweet and sour perfume that stirred his body before.

But her scent also told him she was not in heat and may not be receptive to his sexual advances. He continued to follow the scent trails that she left behind in the scrub. A few hundred yards later, near an open space with buildings that humans visited, he picked up a strong lion scent with a foul edge to it. He slowly moved closer to the source, stopping every few body lengths with his ears and nose on high alert.

The scent was sour and heavy, not unlike the smell after eating a deer kill on the fourth day. But this was not a deer.

There, lying alongside a hillock, he could see the rear of a motionless animal: the long tail of a mountain lion; a male. As he moved closer, the smell of rotting flesh made him afraid, but curiosity pulled him in closer. When he first got a good look at the body, his instincts caused him to jump back in fear as the lion was a male about his age. The dead lion's head was cut off and missing, and its front paws were severed at the knee and removed.

29

Lupine-boy stood there transfixed for a long time. He could see no battle scars as if the lion had fought with another lion and the body was not eaten; there was only one round bloody spot near its chest. The blood beneath the headless neck had long since dried in the leaves, but he noticed the fur around its neck was ruffled and worn. He put his nose closer to shake off the cloud of flies laying eggs on the rotting flesh. Immediately he picked up the scent of something he knew intimately—a leather strap around its neck. Running his nose along the body he could pick up the smell of the sweaty oil from the hands of two-legs. He could not understand how this could be, but the danger came from the two-legs, and Lupine-boy darted up the canyon.

He continued on with his exploration, but with an even more heightened level of awareness. His slender, supple body glided over the landscape. With his keen night vision, he easily saw the best way to bend around rocks. His long tail waved independently, keeping him balanced as he navigated gullies. One time, his paw landed in a rock crevice followed by a shaking sound and a darting motion. Lupine-boy jumped in an instant, springing 10 feet in the air, landing far away from a large rattlesnake.

Feeling hungry, the lion kept his nose high for the nocturnal meanderings of his main prey. He got an occasional whiff of deer, as they seemed to be plentiful in the area, but he hadn't spotted a single one this night. Soon, though, his ears picked up a scratching and digging sound behind a thicket of sagebrush. Both ears pivoted to the front and then independently in opposite directions to pick up the strange sound. He moved very slowly, silently then stopping, waiting for a sighting of the target and a line of attack. Moving within no less than five body lengths from the source of the sound, his one eye peered around the bush.

There, unaware that his back was facing the jaws of his demise, sat a fat raccoon. He was furiously clawing at a decaying tree stump; splinters flew as he grabbed grubs and gorged himself with both hands. It had no idea that this would be its last meal. Lupine-boy, with head and body low to the ground, began the stalk. He drifted silently toward his prey, tail up in the air swaying rhythmically. As he got close, his body tensed and he shifted his rear leg muscles into power gear, raised his heels, and pounced. Just as the raccoon turned around, Lupine-boy clamped down on his head and the lion had his meal. He quickly ripped open its underside with a single swipe and eviscerated it, eating the warm organs first. Then he took a few minutes to lick away the blood splatters before heading off on the trail.

Lupine-boy decided to rest, so he lay down near a rock outcropping. Closing his eyes and taking in some light, but alert, sleep, he was awakened by a scritching sound. He opened one eye and found a little chipmunk sitting a short distance away, scratching its hindquarters. Lupine-boy kept his sleepy eye on the little critter and then slowly lifted his head and placed it on an outstretched paw in order to better watch the striped rodent with both eyes.

The chipmunk finally took notice of the lion and scampered into a crevice in the rocks. Lupine-boy grew tired again almost immediately, but as soon as his eyelids drooped, the chipmunk poked its head out of a crevice and gave the lion a teasing squeak. Since the lion had just eaten and the chipmunk wasn't even a snack, the lion felt an impulse to have fun. He jumped on the pile of rocks, sniffed the hole where the chipmunk fled and waited on top as still as a statue. Moments later, the chipmunk poked its head out below the lion and squeaked at his rear end. The lion jumped and spun around in the air, and then with a growl he took a big swing and fanned the air. Squeaking and swiping, the hide and seek game went on for several minutes until the cat lost interest and moved back through the scrub.

Moving up a canyon, Lupine-boy again picked up the fresh, sweet-sour scent of the female he smelled earlier. As it got stronger, he picked up another lion's presence in the air: a male. Soon, he found a line of lion claw scratchings on an alder tree trunk, so he put his nose to it and fully took in the scent. He could tell the markings were two or three days old, and that they were definitely made by a huge male. When he found a front paw print nearby in some dried in the mud, Lupine-boy placed his paw next to it and saw his was only half its size. He immediately feared this unknown, big-pawed lion, and so he quickly moved on.

A half-mile further on he quickly picked up another, but fresher scent of the big-pawed male. He knew Big-Paw was clearly posting warning signs all over his territory. Lupine-boy knew instinctively this was the most dangerous place he could be. This time, the young cat chose to follow the instinct to survive instead of the instinct to mate. Perhaps he would have another opportunity to find her. And hopefully, find her alone.

CHAPTER EIGHT

Carole Youngblood sat worried at the kitchen table. Her dark Latina eyebrows were almost furrowed together as she thought about her family. It was Saturday evening now on the west coast. Soon she and Reggie would connect to John in Iraq on his Sunday morning. In a way, she hated talking with him through that jittery Skype signal. It was good to see him alive, even if it was virtually, but she couldn't hug the real man. John was on his second tour with a tank brigade that often saw what the US Marine Corps called "hostile action."

Staring at the laptop screen, she was anxious to see those dark eyes darting above the high cheekbones on his beautiful brown face, but she worried about how he and Reggie would get along. He loved his son dearly, but was often hard on him. She hoped that he wouldn't remember to ask about Reggie's report card.

"BA DING!" the Skype screen lit up and after a few electronic spasms, John's face settled into a broad smile. She felt giddy seeing him there in his crisp fatigues, like the first time she saw her handsome hunk his National Guard uniform many years ago.

"Hi, Carole!"

"Hi, handsome!" she said as they both simultaneously touched their screens. Carole wanted to have some personal husband-wife time before she called Reggie to join them. "Honey. So good to see you," she said. "I miss you so freaking much."

"Miss you too, babes," he responded, "It's thinking of you that keeps me from going crazy around here." Even through cyberspace, he could see Carole's sensitive face twisting and worrying about him. "I haven't been on any dicey missions lately, if that's what you're wondering."

"I was wondering. And good to hear," she said, unsure if he was lying or not. He had become a good liar about these things. He even told her one time, right after his first tour, that he wouldn't tell her if things were bad, even if they were.

"Babes, tell me about you. How are you doing?" John asked.

"Oh, I'm pretty good, I guess," Carole sighed. "Having trouble sleeping and working a little too much, but I'm okay."

"I'll be home before you know it," he said. After a deep swallow, he asked: "And how's our big man? How's Reggie doing?"

"Oh, you know. Fine, from what he actually tells me," she said. Without letting John follow up with more questions about their son, Carole began talking about her new boss at The Coffee Bean, and how she's been really flexible with her schedule. Then she talked about the new apartment and how big it felt. After they discussed finances and John's plans to get a good job when he returned, Carole called for Reggie.

Reggie sat down next to his mom, gave the screen image a wave, and said, "Hiya, Dad."

"Man, you're looking big. Every time you look so big. How's it going with you?"

"I'm okay. Not bad," Reggie said nervously.

"How are you adjusting to the new place?" his dad asked. "Still liking your new room? Heard it's pretty darn big, from what your mom says."

"It's not too bad, but I miss the mountains and the woods back home."

"I know, me too, Reggie. I miss those woods like you wouldn't believe. But you know that we had to sell it, as much as it killed me to do it."

"I know," Reggie said. "Hey, when you get home can we maybe go back and hike the Horizon Trail?"

"Definitely," John said, his voice full of hope.

Thinking his dad is about to ask about school, Reggie jumped in, "Dad? Remember the last time we were up on Horizon Ridge when you were telling me about Grandmother Wanchuat?"

Reggie's father looked puzzled. "Um, yeah. I guess so."

"Didn't you tell me her ancestors came from Baja, California?"

"That's what she told me, yeah."

"What was the name of her tribe?" Reggie asked a little too eagerly.

"Oh, man. I don't remember, Reggie. That was so long ago, I was just five when I left the reservation. I'll have to think about it, but you're an American, so why does that matter?"

"Well," answered Reggie, "I've been researching about what the ancient tribes thought of the mountain lion and I came across some stuff about the Cochimi peoples from Baja, California and—"

His dad interrupted, "It could be they migrated north and blended with the Kumeyaay tribe. They were centered in the San Diego area where the reservation was. That's all I know, why are you reading about this?"

"I don't know. I'm interested in it. I found out that some tribes used to believe the cougars had spiritual powers, which I thought was pretty cool."

"So, is this mountain lion stuff part of your studies at school?"

"Sort of," Reggie answered, "A wildlife biologist came and talked to our class and what he was talking about got me kind of pumped up, I guess. He has this really cool job of tracking down cougars in the Santa Monica Mountains and Joe told us about..."

"Whoa! Whoa!" his dad interrupted again. "I don't get where you're going with this and what this guy is feeding you."

Reggie's mom sensed that both of them were getting frustrated and she patted Reggie's leg under the table, but the soldier in his dad didn't let up: "Mountain lions and hiking are okay for a hobby, Reggie, okay? But I need you to start preparing for a profession in life. You won't get anywhere in life sitting there listening and dreaming about lions with silly 'injun' superpowers."

"But Dad," Reggie said, "you love nature and *you* taught me everything I know about it. I love nature and that's why I like Biology class so much. I got an A in it, you know."

"That's nice. That's good to hear. But you're a big kid now and have to think about what you're going to do with your life as an adult." Then after a pause, his dad launched the bomb. "But how did you do in Algebra?"

Reggie looked away from the screen without responding.

"How many times have we talked about this, Reggie? How many times? Without good grades in Algebra, how are you going to get into college and get an MBA?"

The bomb finally hit its target and Reggie exploded, "I don't care about an MBA. I don't! And you want to know about my Algebra grade? I fucking flunked it!"

"Reggie!" his mom yelled, "You can't talk that way!"

His dad rubbed his hands over his cheeks to try to stay calm.

Reggie's mom jumped back in, "I know you're both upset about the grade. And believe me, I didn't know he was flunking that class until right now... But I just want to say that it's been hard, John. For Reggie in the new school and me working all the time, but we'll get a tutor if we have to. I'll work even more to afford it."

Reggie shook his head. There was no way he was going to let his mom work anymore than she already was. He felt terrible about exploding on his parents, and for the bad news about Algebra, but at the same time, he felt he somehow didn't care.

His dad finally removed his hands from his cheeks and spoke. "First of all, don't you *ever* speak to me that way again. You hear me?"

"Yes, sir," he mumbled.

"Good. But you know what, Reggie, you have some serious choices to make. You either take control of your life like a man, or run away from your life like a little boy. Which are you? Are you a man, or are you a little boy?"

Carole looked over at Reggie's reaction and saw that he was seething in that scary, teeth-grinding sort of way.

"I'm not running away from anything," Reggie said through his clenched teeth. He was shaking, but determined not to cry. "What about you, dad? You ran away and left mom and me to fend for ourselves in this fucking shit town. And I'm so sick of that patriotic duty crap you always say. You ran away." At that, Reggie stood up out of webcam range, but his mom put her hand on his shoulder and tried to hold him there.

"Reggie, how dare you!" His mom said. "That is so not fair and you know it." She pushed harder on his shoulder but couldn't get him back in the chair.

His dad licked his front teeth in anger. "You know what, Reggie? Go ahead and leave. I don't want to look at you right now."

Mom let Reggie go and he bolted to his room and slammed the door.

"Carole," John continued, "You've got to do something with him."

"I'm trying John," Carole nodded, "he was out of line, but it's kind of tough here going to a new school, new town, work and all, you know."

Carole watched her husband bury his head in his hands. He looked wounded by the friendly fire of his family; she felt sorry for both of them. She felt sorry for John because he was risking his life to keep his family afloat, though not together. She recalled how she had pleaded with him not to volunteer for that second tour. She thought about John's father committing suicide and worried that both her husband and son were unstable.

"Carole! Carole!" John called to her from the monitor. "I gotta go. Tell Reggie to put his nose in his books and that we'll talk when we get home. Seventy-two more days. That's it."

She nodded. "Seventy-two days. Take care of yourself, John. I love you."

"I love you too, Carole. Oh! And thanks for the boxes of Mallomars. They lasted about five minutes. Talk to you soon."

"Ding!" the screen went dark and Carole felt John leave her heart a second later.

Her thoughts immediately turned to Reggie. *Dammit*, she said to herself, *just when he was starting to find something that he was excited about and wanted to share, he got shot down.* Carole, grew up in a large Latino family with six brothers, had a better feel than John, for what boys went through. *Now,* she wondered, *how can I keep Reggie from going over the deep end without alienating John?*

Carole's phone rang. It was the Coffee Bean. "Sure, I can do another night shift. Be there in ten."

CHAPTER NINE

Tuesdays and Thursdays were the two days during the school week that Reggie dreaded the most; he had swimming class. Although Reggie was not athletic, swimming was the only sport he enjoyed. So, it was frustrating for him that he had to put up with what went on before they put on their suits and got into the pool.

The big shower room had long pipes running along two walls that sprayed fine jets of water that both tickled and stung from head to toe. The swim coach turned the shower on to warm it up while the boys got undressed. By the time Reggie got in, he and the boys were in a steamy fog. The high narrow windows let in shafts of morning light which glistened off the shoulders of the naked boys.

Kevin and his buddies used the cover of fog to bully the boys they called 'wusses.' They loved picking on Isaac. "Hey, homo," they called him, pointing at his small frame. "You've got such a cute ass."

On most days, Reggie and Isaac ignored the stupid comments, although Reggie wondered if this was just name-calling, or that they knew Isaac was gay. It didn't really matter to Reggie if he was, as they shared a mutual interest in animals and became good friends. Reggie always thought of himself as different and he could sense that feeling of isolation in others.

On this Thursday, Kevin hid a large bar of Ivory soap along his thigh as he slowly sneaked his way through the spray. Approaching Isaac from the rear, he made one fast upward jab and shoved the soap between his buttocks.

Reggie didn't see it, but he heard Isaac's yelp, which was followed by the loud laughter of Kevin and his friends. Knowing who, but not what was involved, Reggie turned around. He saw Isaac slumped down with his back against the wall. His legs were shaking and he held his hands in front of his face cowering under the blasting jets of water.

Reggie jumped in front of Isaac, faced Kevin, and asked, "What did you do to him?"

Kevin stood almost a foot taller than him, with more muscles and a lot more weight. Kevin smiled and held up the dripping bar of soap. "I gave him something all homos love, so bend over, pencil dick, and I'll give you your thrills too."

Reggie stood firm; he knew he didn't stand much of a chance, but he didn't care. "You know what, Kevin? You're an asshole!"

Kevin dropped the bar of soap and put up his fists. "Come on wussy show me what you got."

Water dripping down his face, Reggie elevated the dare with a 'come and get me' finger pointing and jabbing at his jaw.

Kevin hauled back his right arm and swung it at Reggie with his whole weight, but before Reggie could even duck, Kevin slipped on the wet soapy floor, made a 180-degree spin, and landed face down on the floor. He immediately turned over looking shocked and humiliated. Most of the other boys laughed, but Kevin's buddies shouted, "Get up and kill him, Kevin."

Others shouted, "Fight! Fight!"

Kevin struggled to get up as someone shut the water shut off. The coach ran into the shower room and pushed his way past the boys shouting, "Break it up! Break it up!"

Kevin, now standing, snarled to Reggie, "You're dead, Reggie."

The coach separated them and asked, "What's going on?"

Kevin turned and gave the coach an innocent shrug. The other boys stood there in silence like nothing had happened. Nobody, including Reggie and Isaac wanted to say anything.

"Kevin. Reggie," the coach said, "I'm still going to file a report—you two better watch it."

In the swimming pool, the tension seemed to ripple away with each practice dive, and Reggie gained some standing as he bested everyone in the butterfly. Later, Isaac found him in the lunch yard, where Kevin eyed the pair across the way like he was planning his next attack.

"Thanks Reggie, but I gotta ask," Isaac said, "how come you stuck up for me like that—Kevin coulda beat the shit out of you?"

"It's okay," Reggie mumbled as he wondered to himself, *why did I become Isaac's protector?*

"You know he'll be coming after you," Isaac warned.

"Thanks for the reminder. The guy thinks he's the dominant male in this territory or something. He's a wild animal."

The rest of the afternoon was uneventful. Reggie slugged through history and struggled with Algebra. In the halls, he looked over his shoulder, constantly feeling Kevin was stalking him. Luckily, English class took his mind off things; they discussed William Blake's poem, *The Tyger*. Reggie thought the words describing the tiger were cool, but didn't agree with many of the student's characterization of the tiger being evil. Eventually, the poem made him think about his fight with Kevin and what seemed to make him evil. *How am I going to deal with his next attack? Would I have to kill him before he kills me?*

Reggie then thought of his dad, who both killed people in war and built a beautiful house by hand, so he offered his interpretation to the class. "Maybe God put both beauty and violence in all animals," Reggie said. The teacher and the students were surprised by Reggie's comment.

****

When the school day ended and Reggie headed out the doors, he felt better as he sat on the esplanade to wait for the bus. Looking around, he noticed Jennifer sitting alone on the boulevard. She looked kind of lost—like the way he felt—but no way was he going to go over to her. But then she turned around and saw him looking at her, so she got up and walked in his direction. She wore one of those long sweaters, the breeze catching the sides like wings.

"I heard you almost got into a fight today," Jennifer said.

Reggie was surprised and embarrassed how the word got out from the boys locker room so soon. He didn't want to talk about that.

"That Kevin is a total jerk," Jennifer added.

Reggie thought all the girls in school thought he was this good-looking jock, so he said, "You don't think he's cool?"

"No way," she said, "He's so not my type. He's not anyone's type. Me and my friends think he's a total joke."

Beep! Beep! A car honked. Jennifer looked to the street and then back at Reggie and asked, "Wanna hang out sometime? Maybe we can get together some weekend?"

In shock, Reggie lost his voice for a second then said, "Um. Sure. I mean, cool."

Jennifer looked over to a silver Tesla and saw her dad gesturing for her to hurry. She reached into her backpack, pulled out a ticket stub from a Lady Gaga concert and wrote her phone number on it. Then she ran to the car, turned around, waved and yelled, "See ya!"

The bus pulled up at the same time Jennifer ducked into her car, and Reggie was beaming as he climbed in. He sat near the back and looked out the window, and his smile disappeared. There was Kevin, standing on the esplanade, staring at him with his beady eyes.

CHAPTER TEN

That night in Topanga Canyon, Lupine-boy picked up the sweet and sour scent of the female he had smelled when he first moved into the Santa Monica's. It was strong and fresh; she was near. Luckily, he did not catch the scent of Big-Paw or another competing male, so he thought this may be his chance. Anxious to find her, he began to run.

Reaching the top of a ravine, he finally saw her; she was barely half his size with a silky clean coat, a shade lighter than his. She stood below a California Valley Oak, twitching her tail. They locked eyes, but she did not move. It was like she expected him to know he should keep moving on, but he had no intention of going anywhere.

Keeping his distance at first, Lupine-boy made a wide circle around the young female. He kept his nose high in the air, always sniffing for another male. As he moved closer, he noticed she, too, wore a collar of the two-legs. The female dropped her tail and started a low growl as she nervously followed his movements. Lupine-boy knew she was not in heat, but he wanted her anyway. As he narrowed the circle, he began a proud stiff-legged prance, letting her get a good look at his full-bloom maturity.

She snarled loudly and showed her teeth. As he moved in closer, the female moved with him, but always keeping her hindquarters away from him. Lupine-boy then made a few short steps toward her. The female raised her back and growled at him to stay away, which surprised Lupine-boy and he pulled back and crouched down.

This, the female interpreted, was preparation for an attack because she screamed louder than ever and stood her ground.

After a few minutes, she realized he wasn't crouching to attack her and settled down to a throaty, but steady growl. Observing this, Lupine-boy did a surprising thing. He sat up on his haunches, and with casual grace, started licking his front paws. Then he yawned and preened. The tactic caused the female to stop growling and sit down and sniff toward the male. Seeing this as an overture, Lupine-boy started slowly stepping toward her again, but this time not in a stalking fashion.

She let him get within five feet of her before hissing and showing her teeth. The confident male kept approaching slowly, and finally reached out his nose to touch hers. Just as Lupine-boy hoped she was still going to let him mount her, she reared back, screamed, and with fully unsheathed claws, swiped at his tender nose. She missed by inches. The male, surprised but not deterred, sat down again; only a few feet from her in a ready-to-strike stance.

Lupine-boy was a picture of rejection, his ears lying on the back of his head. They now both sat eye-to-eye and began smelling each other. The pair then went from a dance to a conversation, sensing each other's smells, vocalizations, and body language. The female clearly smelled that he was a newcomer to the territory and from a different family. He could, in turn, smell that she was not nursing kittens.

It was then Lupine-boy smelled Big-paw on her body—a sour, almost bitter musk beyond her sweet. The older lion marked her as his territory. Deterred by this new information, Lupine-boy decided not to try to take her that night. She smelled somehow of fear—a Big-Paw reek that lay deep beneath her fur.

Lupine-boy left her shortly thereafter, but would seek her out again someday, knowing he would mate She-Paw someday.

CHAPTER ELEVEN

Reggie's Saturday morning trailed into Saturday afternoon when he finally woke up. He didn't sleep well, dreaming about fighting with Kevin. *More like nightmares,* Reggie thought as he stared at the ceiling. He couldn't get the dreams out of his head. There was Kevin chasing him in the mountains, catching him and biting him in the neck. He saw himself lying there bleeding to death in the dirt. *This sucks,* Reggie thought as he dragged his body out of bed, leaving the stupid nightmares under the covers.

By the time he made it into the kitchen, his mom was about to head off to work. "Good Morning, Reg."

Looking into the refrigerator he mumbled, "What's good about it?"

After a pause, his mom said, "I know you're angry at dad, but can we—"

"I honestly don't want to talk about it," he said before drinking right out of the orange juice container. He wiped his lips. "Can we just forget about it?"

She gave her son a long look. "I'll try and talk to him Reg." She then patted him on the back. "See you tonight, okay. Maybe we can watch a movie together or play a game."

"Maybe," he grunted.

After a peanut butter, jelly, and baloney sandwich, Reggie clicked on the TV and saw that stupid commercial for the 'cat brushing tower' with the ORDER NOW! 800 number flashing. He reached into his wallet and pulled out the Lady Gaga ticket with Jennifer's number. He took a deep breath, dropped the remote, picked up his cell, and pecked out her number.

"Jennifer?"

"Who is this? Reggie, is that you?" Jennifer's voice said. She sounded groggy, or maybe sad.

Calling her was a bad idea, he thought. He cleared his throat and said, "Yeah, it's me, but were you sleeping? If you're sleeping we can talk later or—"

"No," she said. "I'm just bummed out; my parents are at it again."

"Shit. Are you okay?"

"I'd rather not talk about it, if that's okay." There was a pause before Jennifer asked, "What you up to this afternoon?"

"Nothing, really. Just hanging out in my room."

"I was going to do some painting, but you wanna hang out?"

He nearly fell over and took a couple seconds to compose himself. He couldn't believe she wanted to hang out with him. "Sure. I mean, yeah. Where can we meet?"

They worked out the details to meet at a state park off the Ventura Freeway. The bus stop wasn't far from the park, and Reggie got there first and wandered around. The park was small and had some historic civil war regiment barracks that weren't open. The only other people there were a couple of moms and nannies wandering around pushing baby strollers. He found a bench away from the street so Jennifer's dad didn't think she was meeting someone.

Soon the silver Tesla pulled up. Jennifer got out carrying a wooden case and wearing a dark blue t-shirt and torn, acid-washed jeans. Looking around the park as though she was scouting a landscape, they spotted each other. Walking fast, they met with broad smiles, found a shady spot under a sweet gum tree and sat shoulder to shoulder.

"Thanks for inviting me," Reggie said. "What's up with your parents? I mean, if you don't want to talk about it, we don't have to."

"No, it's okay. It's stupid maybe, but they don't like my style or my attitude, I guess, and they definitely don't like my grades."

Yeah, I get that, Reggie thought as he noticed the two colors in her grey-blue eyes; it was like the blue was penetrating and determined; the grey acting soft and sad.

"Seriously? I always thought… You're not a good student?"

"Huh!" Jennifer chuckled, "The only class I do well in is art, where I can create and express myself."

"I know what you mean," Reggie mumbled. Then he looked her up and down and shook his head. "But what don't your parents get about your style? I think your style is awesome. I like the way you look." As soon as he said that last part, he looked away in embarrassment.

"Well, that's nice to hear. Thank you. I think you look cute, too." They took turns blushing before she continued: "I guess they think I'm some sort of a blonde goth girl who loves drugs, sex, and punk rock or whatever. They hate my hair and how I dress."

"I really like your hair. They're crazy. It's amazing the way you get it to stand up like that." Then, before he could stop himself, he asked, "Can I touch it?"

Jennifer laughed and then ducked the top of her head toward him. "Go for it. Be my guest."

He gently ran his palm over the flat top of the spikes. "Cool."

"Thanks," she said, looking up at him with her mixed eyes. "Want to see my tattoo?"

"You have a tattoo?" he asked.

"Yeah. I got it without my parent's permission. They were pissed."

A second later he watched her lift up her blouse and push down her jeans to the top of her pelvic bone, revealing what looked like a Monarch butterfly; wings spread on her smooth white skin.

"That's... awesome," he whispered, trying to remain cool. "Um, so does it mean something, or do you just like butterflies?"

"You know how they change. From caterpillar to butterfly. That's how I feel about myself."

"Have you changed a lot?" Reggie asked. "I didn't know you before."

"I've changed a lot, yeah," she said. "My parents always wanted me to be a little princess, and I was like that for a long time. But when I got older I said 'screw all that' stuff and became an artist. I'm an artist now. That's me being a butterfly."

"Cool. You seem so sure of yourself. I'm jealous."

She smiled at him. "It started a long time ago, so maybe I seem surer now. I drew a lot in middle school to escape and started reading art history books instead of Harry Potter or watching TV. Then I got into yoga and meditation, which really changed me."

Reggie kept silent and gave her a puzzled look. Art history books? Yoga and meditation? *Who was this amazing girl, and what was she doing hanging out with someone like me?*

"I know it sounds flaky," she said, "but for me, meditating provided a way to release my anxieties and open up a pathway to my art."

"I don't think it sounds flaky. I wanna know more."

"Well, meditating gives me space from all that crap about celebrity and material goods."

"Yeah, that's LA alright," Reggie said. "But how do you meditate? I mean, do you just like close your eyes and sit still?"

"Um. Well," Jennifer began, "it comes down to finding a quiet place and time to let go of all the distractions that make you crazy, like your parents, and get totally still in your mind and get into yourself."

"Seriously? You *are* a new age punker."

Jennifer laughed and without warning, gave him a quick punch in the arm and then flattened her back against a tree with her eyes closed. "No, I am serious about meditating. It works for me. Tell you what; I'll let you borrow my meditation guidebook. I'll bring it to school."

"Sure." Reggie said, still feeling her soft punch in his arm. "So, um, what kind of art do you do?"

She opened her eyes and reached for her wooden case. She started to leaf through several sketches and watercolors. "Want to see some?" Instead, Reggie's eyes focused on her ripped jeans. A large hole half way up her thigh revealed her creamy white skin with delicate light blue veins.

She broke his fix and said, "They aren't finished, but I think you'll like this one." She pulled out a colorful watercolor and held it facing her chest, pushing it in toward her heart. "It's sort of an abstract-impressionist piece I did right here in this park." She handed it to Reggie, "It's one of my all-time favorites." As Reggie gazed at the painting, the jumble of abstract shapes and colors framing an area of light drew him into the canvas. "When I painted it," she said, "I felt I was becoming one with the world."

"Wow!" Reggie let out. His fingers touched the dappled green and ochre edges of the paper. It stimulated his senses—how they were so alive like when he was in the woods. Then it reminded him of a page in that picture book his mom used to read to him as a kid—the young brave on horseback in the meadow of wildflowers. He always related to that Indian boy. He wished he had a way of capturing that feeling, creating something of beauty out of his own talent.

Jennifer watched his intense focus and admired his long, almost feminine eyelashes.

"You like it?" Jennifer asked, breaking his spell.

"Um. Yeah. I wish I could paint pictures like this. Makes me feel like I'm wandering in the woods."

"Exactly! You *do* get it," Jennifer shouted as she slapped him a high five. "That's one of the first watercolors I ever did after I started meditating." Then, she took a deep breath: "You can have it."

"For real?" Reggie said as he started handing it back to her.

"For real. Take it."

"Wow. Thanks a lot. I love it. I'll hang it in my room tonight."

Jennifer reached for her phone in her back pocket. As she did, Reggie looked at her small, nicely shaped breasts jutting upward. Jennifer looked at her screen and said it was her dad asking when to pick her up. She texted him: another hour.

For the rest of the time they talked about school, classes and people they knew. Reggie was too afraid to ask her if she'd ever dated anybody. Jennifer mentioned something about Monday and immediately she could see the dread come over Reggie's face.

45

"Worried about that asshole, Kevin, huh?" she asked.

"Yeah," Reggie said as he picked up a stone and threw it far into the grass.

"I got it!" Jennifer said, "Next week, you and Isaac can join me and my artsy friends for lunch in the yard, okay? Won't even have to see him."

Reggie's face brightened. "That'd be cool. I'd like that. But you don't have to, I mean, if you don't want to."

At the same moment Jennifer's dad's car drove down the street in the opposite direction.

"I better go," she said, and then she kissed Reggie on the cheek and gave him a close hug. Reggie felt her breasts against his chest and warmth rippled up and down his body. He was embarrassed by how attracted he was to her and he hoped it didn't show.

She broke the hug, grabbed her case, and ran to the parking area. In the car her dad asked her how the painting went. She told him it's going great. Reggie, with Jennifer's watercolor in hand, walked the six miles home.

CHAPTER TWELVE

When Reggie got home that Friday afternoon, his mom was still at work, so he grabbed a handful of string cheeses from the fridge and went to his room. He got some tape and hung up Jennifer's painting above his bed. *That old picture book,* he thought, *I wonder if I still have it?*

He went to his closet and pulled out a big cardboard box. It had the dump trucks and stuffed animals he played with and the books he read as a kid. Throwing all the toys over his back, his fingers felt a stack of picture books; *The Hungry Caterpillar, The Giving Tree, Bedtime for Francis.*

"Yes!" he shouted. There it was. He wiped the dust off of the tattered cover of *Brother Eagle Sister Sky.* There was the young boy with Chief Seattle in his regal feathered headdress. He plopped down on the bed and opened the cover and read the handwritten inscription.

My Johnny Boy, I love you and will always remember you. Grandma Wanchuat.

He read it, the whole time picturing his mother sitting on the bed and hearing her sweet voice. He loved that book.

Then he jumped on to the internet. He began studying Joe's California Carnivores website where it talked about the changing habitat that lions face in the region, when an idea popped into his head. Reggie searched the website for a contact form to ask a question. He wrote to the info@ address, hoping he might connect directly with Joe, and asked about the dangers of rat poisons to wildlife.

****

Later that evening when Joe Sartor got home, he felt the need to talk to Barbara. "I've been thinking lately." Joe said as he pushed away his dessert plate. "Thinking more about teaching again, you know mentor a young boy"

"Good idea," Barb shrugged, "You never did hear from Big Brothers?"

"Nah. When I called them a few months back, they said they just didn't have any kids in this area needing a mentor and I pretty much gave up on it." Then I got this email." Joe said as his voice rose in excitement. "There's this kid Reggie I met at the school lecture and he was real interested in my work and mountain lions. Good kid. One of the few really paying attention. Well, he emailed me today with a smart question and I'm thinking maybe he could volunteer at the office and I could mentor him a bit."

"That's a great idea," Barbara said, "I bet he would love that."

"PING!" Reggie couldn't believe it. Right there on his screen was a message from Joe's website. As he read it, he pumped his arms above his head: Joe just invited him to have a tour at his headquarters *this* Saturday. He quickly texted his mom at The Coffee Bean and got a tentative okay, but said that she wanted to meet Joe herself to be sure it was okay. Then he spent the rest of the evening pouring over Joe's website and learning everything he could about mountain lions.

On Saturday morning, Reggie and his mom pulled into the parking lot of the big government headquarters building where Joe had his office. Reggie rang Joe and he came down to the lobby to meet them. Reggie noticed his mom had a surprised look on her face when she saw Joe. It was the same surprise Reggie had when he realized how much Joe looked like his dad. They took the elevator up to his office and the three of them sat down to chat.

Once Joe filled them in on the volunteer program at the agency and how he thought Reggie could help with his study of mountain lions, Reggie's mom said, "Well I can tell that Reggie would *love* to help with all of that. How about if I let you guys get to it and get to work myself. Pick Reggie up at one, then?"

"One o'clock works for me," Joe said, shaking Carole's small hands. "I'll walk you out."

She waved him off and made her way to the door. "Not necessary. You guys enjoy yourselves."

Smiling at each other across the desk, Joe said, "Good to see you again, Reggie, and so soon."

"I know," Reggie said. "I've been doing a lot of studying about *Puma concolor*, and I want to learn more."

"That's a great attitude," Joe said. "It'll be fun sharing my love of these big cats with you."

Looking around the office, two things immediately stuck out to Reggie. The first was a big table behind Joe's desk filled with all kinds of electronic equipment, including three blinking and beeping monitors. The second thing Reggie noticed was a large framed photograph of a cougar mother nursing two cubs.

"You like the photo?" Joe asked.

"It's awesome. How old are those cubs?"

"Oh, maybe just about 6-10 weeks old. At that age they have baby-blue eyes," Joe said. "And they'll keep those brown spots on their golden fur for about six months. You might already know this, but soon the mom will supplement her milk and start bringing meat to her cubs, you know, introduce them to their carnivore natures. By the time the cubs reach a year or two, the mom will leave them to fend for themselves."

"After she's taught them how to hunt and survive, right?"

"Right," Joe said. "A mother has a pretty tough job teaching her cubs—the odds are stacked against their survival. The fathers don't help at all, so how well the mothers raise them will determine the success of the population."

"Yeah." Reggie mumbled, thinking about his own parents. He shook away the feeling and said, "The cubs have to have both instinct and learning in order to survive, right?"

"Right again, Reggie. You seem to have a feel for animals."

"I grew up in the mountains with not many people around, so my dog Hector and I became best buddies," Reggie said. "I used to talk to Hector because we spent a lot of time in the woods together and I took care of him, including the time I had to pull thirty-one porcupine quills out of his face!"

"Ouch!" Joe said, "I bet he didn't like the pain, but appreciated what you did to help. I used to talk to my dogs too, but now I talk to my lions on occasion."

"Really?"

"Ha. Really. But only unofficially, though. Don't tell anyone, okay?" Joe took another long look at the mountain lion photo and then turned his chair back to Reggie. "Didn't you also tell me you volunteered at the Audubon Center?"

"Yeah. I mostly clean cages, stuff like that, but we sometimes get to bottle-feed the rescued raccoons and opossums. Sometimes, my buddy Isaac and I get to feed mayflies to this injured owl we named Puddles."

"Puddles?"

"Yeah, because he gets excited when he eats and I always knew when he was going to pee all over Isaac's lap and Isaac would get so pissed off."

"Ha!" Joe laughed.

"Yeah, but the people at the center keep telling me I have this uncanny ability to sense what an animal is feeling or needing. I don't know if it's true or whatever, but it might be."

"That's pretty amazing, Reggie." Joe said. "My way with animals is more scientific and comes from years of study…though the more I work with them the better I understand them."

Beep! Beep!" One of the monitors started sounding and Joe ran over to check the figures crawling across the screen. He then looked through a stack of charts on the tabletop.

"You know what, Reggie? Let me show you how we monitor and track our collared cats. Pull up a chair."

Joe explained how the equipment worked and what they could learn from the tracking signals. "These GPS blips show us where the animal is roaming in the territory. Like now..." Joe pointed to a cluster of tracking points. "Here's my friend P12's signal, and our monitor is programmed to raise an alarm if we don't see the usual movement of the cat. We're getting a little concerned over P12 lately because it shows here that he's been staying in one small area for too long a time."

"What does that mean?" Reggie asked.

"Well, we don't know for sure, but it could mean he's mating with a female that we haven't collared or tracked, but we do know he's not with P13 because we have her sixteen miles away. You know, mountain lions are serial copulators, so they stay together for several days."

"What's that mean?" Reggie asked.

"Cougar mating, is what I mean. When cougars get together to mate, it takes place over many days, with each day containing fifty to seventy separate mating acts."

"Geez!" Reggie laughed. "So is that the only time males normally stay in the same location for that long a time?"

"Generally, yes. One time, I had the rare fortune to hear cougars mating. I was setting a snare when I heard what sounded at first like a pair of cougars fighting in the distance—screaming, yowling, it was incredibly loud and vicious. We know that they caress each other in foreplay, which is needed to induce an egg. Too bad I didn't have a recorder with me, but I stayed for hours, late into the night. In between the yowling were short, sometimes longer periods of silence."

"That must have been crazy to be out there and actually hear that," Reggie said. "What do you think the yowls meant?"

"Good question; I assume that there was considerable communication between the pair."

"You mean, like they were talking and stuff?"

"Well, we're getting into unknown and subjective territory here, but I believe they were responding to each other's dialogue; body language, smells, sounds, and so forth. We can't understand it, but they understand each other in their own language."

"Yeah! I totally believe they can communicate with each other," Reggie added, "I read that the Zuni Indian tribe believed animals could communicate with humans, too, like my dog Hector and I did."

Joe put a hand on Reggie's shoulder. "You know, as scientists, we can't prove that, but we can't disprove it either. So, you may be right."

"You know I read that many tribes, going back to the Stone Ages, believed there are Power Animals that have supernatural powers," Reggie said with growing excitement in his voice. "Even more amazing, these power animals can convey their traits to a human and empower them. I thought it was so cool that a person can discover his own Power Animal if he goes on what they call a vision quest."

Smiling broadly, Joe said, "I think some modern-day Native American tribes continue to practice vision quests."

Reggie looked at Joe and for several moments and seemed unable to speak. Finally, he said, "Really? That's so cool."

"Yeah. I think I read somewhere, they also call them spirit animals."

Getting even more animated, Reggie went on, "You know what else I read about? The Cochimi tribe of Baja, California believed the puma had spiritual powers. They refused to kill pumas when the Spanish priests, who ran the missions, told them to."

"They must have been brave people to defy the Spanish who stole their land," Joe said. "Those indigenous people were a lot closer to nature than we are today."

Reggie looked up at Joe, hesitating a bit, and then said, "You know, Joe, I believe my Tribal ancestors came from Baja."

"Boy, now *there's* a connection," Joe smiled.

"I think so, too, but my dad thinks..." Reggie paused for a second, and then in a softer voice, continued: "My dad says that I'm American now and to forget about that silly stuff about our Indian ancestors and whatever. He doesn't have much of a connection to his Indian roots.

"That's too bad," Joe offered.

"Yeah. My Mom told me he left the reservation with his parents when he was a kid. She told me his dad wanted to build houses in the LA area."

"That sort of explains it, I guess."

"Anyway," Reggie said. "I love learning about the mountain lions. Do you think they have an understanding of humans?"

"Sure, yeah. In a way, they have to. Over thousands of years living with the indigenous peoples, and then hundreds of years being with the Europeans, they've had to learn how to survive among us."

"And, what they learned became part of their instincts," Reggie mused.

"Exactly," Joe said. "It's almost like memories or stories passed along from generation to generation."

"So," Reggie said, "could it be that their ancestors are, in a way, alive in today's lion mothers? Like helping them teach their cubs how to live with humans?"

"You could say that, sure, but you probably couldn't prove that," Joe said as he looked from the monitor and then back at Reggie. "You know what, Reggie, all this talk has my instincts kicking in and I think we may have a real issue on our hands here. Look at P12's steady signal; his lack of movement is starting to get me pretty nervous. It's been several days since we tracked him near P13 and she's far away now. He could be injured from being hit by a car or maybe shot by a poacher, or, of course, another lion could have gotten to him and he's hurt. I'm starting to think I should get out into the field. Hate to do this to you since you just got here, but would you mind if I called your mom to come and get you? I promise we can get together again soon."

"No problem, Joe," Reggie said. He was sorry to have the day end so soon, but he understood that this could be a serious situation and he would hate to keep Joe from helping P12. "Just let me know what happens, okay?"

Joe grabbed his phone and then held up his hand to Reggie. "Will do, I promise."

****

Not far down the canyon from Joe's office, Lupine-boy had his own problems. For several days now he had an itching irritation around his nose, eyes, and ears, and he constantly scratched his head with his paws.

As the days wore on, Lupine-boy broke his skin with his claws, and blood oozed down his face. He lost patches of fur around his head and his ears leaked puss, which attracted flies that bit at him. Rubbing his head in the underbrush didn't help; it only brought further irritation to his skin.

Lupine-boy became lethargic and lost his appetite. He had no energy to find a meal, or even water. Without sustenance, he felt the call of death. He lost weight and the infections from the open sores entered his blood stream. He dragged himself along the canyon floor, dying of dehydration and starvation. It wouldn't be much longer.

****

Joe called his team, and with their radio antenna, receiver, and equipment, they drove to the nearest last tracking point on the road. There, they picked up P12's signal, and hiked down toward a densely treed section of a steep canyon.

Normally, he would not risk a crew to track down a lion that was not already snared or trapped, but Joe had the feeling that his favorite cat was in trouble. When the radio signal got stronger, Joe had the crew move cautiously so as not to surprise the wild animal. With binoculars scanning the canyon floor, one intern raised his hand and pointed. Moving super slowly now toward the cat, they found P12 lying down, chest rising and falling at a rapid rate: the animal was in serious distress. Taking out his blow dart gun, Joe moved closer in for the shot.

The dart's almost silent 'whoosh' and muted 'thud' struck P12 in the flank. The cat twitched and then raised his head, but quickly dropped it back to the ground. When Joe first saw him lying there, he knew P12 was in a bad way, but he was grateful to see he was still alive. Once the drug took effect, the team moved in. Lifting P12's head, Joe knew immediately what had happened to him.

The mountain lion had mange, and possibly worse. Scientifically, it looked like mange, usually caused by feeding on a carcass of an animal that consumed rat poison. Joe had seen that scarred and bloody head on two other mountain lions that died from mange. P12 was infested with thousands of almost invisible blood-sucking mites that feed on an animal's soft tissue. If not stopped, infection and dehydration, coupled with lack of energy and starvation, usually meant death.

Reaching into his medical kit, Joe found the medications that might have a chance to reverse the condition. First he applied the topical creams and injected him with Vitamin K. Then, Joe gave him this new drug called 'Revolution' to aid in recovery. After taking a few quick measurements, and putting on a new tracking collar, he took a blood sample to bring back to the lab for testing. After administrating the drug antidote, he left his favorite cat with a pat on the head and a silent prayer.

CHAPTER THIRTEEN

The Monday lunch meet-up with Jennifer and her friends ended up being a good deal for Reggie and Isaac. Very soon after Jennifer introduced her artsy friends, they were all sharing their lunches and some good laughs. Jennifer talked about the time she attempted to throw a pot in pottery class and it flew off the wheel and landed like a cow shit on the floor.

Reggie didn't see Kevin until Biology on Tuesday, and, except for the soccer champ's dirty looks and giving Isaac the usual foul kick on the way out of class, there were no problems. It wasn't until the end of lunch period on Friday when Kevin made his move.

Carrying his lunch tray, Kevin approached, wearing his NO FAT CHICKS t-shirt. Stopping at their table, he said, "No wonder you girls like hanging with these two. Cuz they're fags." That got a few chuckles from his buddies.

Jennifer immediately stood up and slammed her tray on the table. "Get the fuck out of here Kevin. No one wants to listen to a lame dickhead like you." Everyone at the table laughed.

Kevin smiled, ran his hand over his shaved head, and sneered, "You a fag, too, Jennifer?"

Reggie and Isaac both stood up. Before Reggie could defend Jennifer, Isaac said, "You're just jealous 'cuz you can't get a girl to talk to you, let alone sit and eat with you. Maybe you're the one who likes boys."

Kevin's beady eyes centered on Isaac and he tossed his lunch tray, including a cup of chocolate pudding, at Isaac. Isaac immediately scooped some pudding off his shirt and threw a glob at Kevin, who headed around the table to get at him.

No one noticed that Mr. Suarosky, the English teacher and lunch monitor, stood just a few yards away. He marched over to the table, grabbed Kevin by the shirt collar, and shouted, "What the heck do you think you're doing over here?"

Reggie said, "Kevin was doing his bully thing. The guy won't leave us alone. He's being a dick."

Mr. Suarosky, seeing Isaac wiping the pudding off his head, asked Kevin if he did that.

Kevin said it was an accident, but the teacher persisted, "Isaac, do you want to make a bullying complaint against Kevin?"

Knowing that it was a serious disciplinary school action and a lot of hassle, they looked at each other and Isaac said, "No, I want him to just leave us alone already. We're tired of it."

Mr. Suarosky gave Kevin a slight shove in the other direction and said that this incident would be reported to the office and that he would be watched closely from here on out.

After that day, Kevin seemed to keep his distance from Reggie and his friends. Reggie hoped that Kevin was starting to accept the school's authority, maybe even realizing a further incident might jeopardize his status as co-captain on the soccer team. But, in his gut, he believed Kevin had major aggression issues and would be back at it.

After most school days, Reggie and Jennifer would get together at the food court at the outdoor mall. Jennifer loved doing pencil sketches of Reggie, and he loved posing for her in contorted positions that made her laugh. Although they were becoming close friends, Reggie wanted them to become closer. He wanted to kiss her and put his arm around her and go out on real dates with her, but just couldn't seem to get the words out. Besides, her parents didn't let her go out alone at night, let alone with boys, so Reggie contented himself thinking and dreaming about her as a girlfriend.

The school year was coming to a close in a few weeks and Reggie wanted to make her his girlfriend before her parents sent her up north to camp. Reggie imagined kissing Jennifer's soft lips, feeling her close to him. One afternoon at the mall, he saw an opportunity as they walked past a quiet hallway near a storage area.

"Let's get a coke," he said as he took her hand.

Next to the vending machine, he put his arms around the lower part of her back. She did not pull away, but just said, "Reggie?"

He pulled her to him and just before he reached her lips, he closed his eyes. He didn't see if she had closed hers'.

He kissed hard. But it felt stiff to Reggie.

Then three sounds erupted.

The loud rolling rattle of a garbage cart being pushed.

The clicking sound of teeth coming together.

A muffled 'ow' from Jennifer's throat.

They pulled apart.

"I'm sorry, I just wanted to..."

The uniformed janitor glanced at the couple and smiled as she pushed the cart past them.

"It's okay, Reggie," she said as she wiped her lips. They walked back to the center court.

Jennifer must have felt massively embarrassed, Reggie thought. Or maybe she wasn't as ready as he was. Or, maybe she didn't really like him. *Whatever,* Reggie cursed to himself, *I so fucked that up. How's your lame ass going to fix that, half-breed?*

Back at school they carried on like nothing had happened. Neither Reggie nor Jennifer brought up the kiss and what it meant. Reggie didn't know what he was going to do. *She was the best friend I could ever have,* he thought, *but I want more.*

On the day of final exams in Biology, Reggie and Jennifer got to class early. Reggie noticed Isaac wasn't in his seat and neither was Kevin. Close to the bell, Reggie was starting to worry about Isaac and told Mrs. Horton he needed to go to the bathroom. He looked up and down the hallways and around to the corner lockers—no Isaac.

Heading to check the bathroom, the door swung open and an upperclassman ran out and Reggie saw Kevin holding Isaac up on a sink with his back to the mirrors, slapping his face.

Reggie ran with all his speed and pushed and knocked Kevin to the floor and yelled to Isaac to run. Still on top of Kevin, Reggie started pounding him in the face. A left to the jaw. A right to the nose. A left to the mouth. Kevin lifted Reggie with his arms and legs and in one swift move, threw him off.

Kevin got up, growled and grabbed Reggie by the shoulders and threw him against the stalls. Reggie slipped to the floor. Kevin kicked Reggie in the stomach and crotch like he was practicing goal shots. Reggie doubled up trying to protect his face. With a slight lull in the kicking, Reggie glanced up between his arms and saw Kevin grab something from his backpack. Kevin knelt down over Reggie and started punching again. Reggie felt the blows were now twice as hard. Painful thuds to his shoulders. Sharp cracks to the side of his head. Reggie felt blood trickling down his neck and knew he was being badly hurt.

"Whack!" he heard the door open and Isaac yelled, "Hold on Reggie, they're coming." Kevin got up, swung his backpack on his shoulders and pulled Reggie up to standing just as the teachers came in.

"Break it up you two!" the teachers yelled. They must have assumed it was a shoving match, until they saw Reggie's bleeding face. One of the teachers took Reggie under his arm and helped him to the nurse's station down the hall. The other teacher looked at Kevin's face which showed some red bruises on his forehead and cheek, but no blood.

"Are you alright?" the teacher asked, looking at Kevin's face.

"Yeah! He started it," Kevin said and wiped his nose and spit into the sink. The teacher escorted Kevin into the Vice Principal's office.

The investigation began.

Once Reggie got into the nurse's office and she saw the cuts on his head, she told Reggie to call his parents and that he should be taken to an emergency clinic or hospital. Reggie informed her that his mom was not allowed to use her personal cell phone at Wal-Mart and that his dad was in Iraq and there was no one else to call. The nurse tried his mom's number but could not get through. She called the store number and got a hold of someone from the office who said to hold the phone and she would find her supervisor. After a long, five minute hold, the nurse decided to call 911. While they waited, she cleaned and butterfly-bandaged the open wounds on his head and stopped the bleeding. She asked Reggie how he got the cuts. He only told her he got into a fight with Kevin, which she noted in her report.

When he got to the clinic, they tried again to get his mom, but they could not get through. They removed the old bandages, examined him closely and found that the cuts on his head did not require stitches, so they cleaned the areas and put on new butterfly bandages. His eyesight and cognition seemed normal with no indication of a concussion. The doctor probed his chest and although he winced in pain, there did not appear to be any broken ribs. Removing his shirt, they noted multiple contusions on his upper arms and shoulders. Afterwards, they summarized in the medical record the appearance of the bruises found. They were about five inches long and striped, just one inch apart in rows. Finally, after more examining and questioning, Reggie was released. He tried calling his mom several times, thinking he might catch her on break. But he couldn't even leave messages. When he finally got the Wal-Mart supervisor, he said she had left for the day. After an hour, the ambulance brought him back to school.

In the Vice Principal's office, Kevin was interrogated by two teachers from the disciplinary committee, Mr. Tremper and the security chief. Kevin's story never changed and he claimed that Reggie called him a fucking asshole and took the first punch. When Mr. Tremper asked what happened before that time with Isaac in the bathroom, he told him, 'nothing.'

The principal reminded him of the prior incidents in the pool shower and in the lunch yard and that if witnesses report that he had broken the school's policy on bullying or fighting he would be expelled for the remainder of the school year.

They also questioned Isaac, but he was very tight-lipped. Isaac told them that Kevin picked on a lot of kids and was unwilling to state why he thought Kevin picked on him. Since their initial review could not determine there was bullying and who started the fight, they chose not to bring in the local police at this point.

For now and until further notice, the principal told Kevin he was suspended for two days and the school would be calling his parents. Kevin requested that they not call his dad and stated, *'he will kill me.'*

****

By the time Reggie got back to school, it was last period. In the principal's office, Mr. Tremper asked Reggie to tell him about what happened. The principal was a very direct, no-nonsense man who towered above most of the students at six foot five and wanted answers. Reggie though, was feeling totally depressed about the fight and told him he did not want to talk about it and only wanted to go home. When Mr. Tremper pressed him to defend himself, Reggie only told him he was trying to protect his friend Isaac, from Kevin. When the principal asked him why Kevin was picking on Isaac, Reggie only shrugged.

Mr. Tremper respected Reggie's feelings at the moment, but also suspended Reggie for two days. He told Reggie that he had put a call into his mom to inform her, but hadn't been able to reach her yet. He reminded Reggie that his school would not tolerate violence and that Reggie would have to explain things to the disciplinary committee. Reggie nodded. The Principal gave him the suspension notice and told him to make sure his mom called back. Finally, he asked if he felt well enough to take the bus and Reggie nodded yes again.

****

Waiting outside at the pick-up area, Reggie watched the kids trickle out of classes and hoped he'd see Jennifer. Jennifer hoped she'd see Reggie and ran to him when she did. She gave him a long, swaying, 'she-cares-about-me' hug.

"Ow!" Reggie let out a short cry of pain, which he muffled into "*Oh,* good to see you Jennifer."

"Oh my God, you look really messed up!" she said as she looked back and forth at his bandaged forehead, then his eyes, then his bloody shirt, then back into his eyes. "Does it hurt bad?"

Holding her close almost made the pain go away. Reggie wanted to keep the hug so he said, "Bad enough."

"Here, sit," she said as she eased him into the bench. "You and Kevin, right?" she asked. "We heard the shouting in the hall and Cheryl said she saw Kevin being taken into the office—everybody's talking about it."

Reggie lifted his head, cracked a smile and said, "Yeah, he hurt me, but I got in a few punches too."

"Good—he's an ass, but are you expelled?" she asked.

"We're both suspended for two days, pending an investigation—my parents won't be happy."

"Was it over Isaac?" she asked.

"Yeah, I found Kevin slapping him up in the restroom."

"What did you tell the principal?"

"That I tried to stop him."

"You didn't tell him *why* he was hitting Isaac?"

"No."

"Come on, Reggie, don't you think they'll want to get to the bottom of this?"

"I suppose, but that's up to Isaac."

"Reggie!" she yelled, "you can't let Kevin get away with that—you might be expelled if you don't explain."

"I know," he said, looking at the floor.

Raising her voice even louder, she pleaded, "It's gay-bashing, Reggie—you have to tell them."

Reggie, looked torn, took a long time to answer and said, "Isaac doesn't want people to know."

"You're kidding me." Jennifer responded.

"No," Reggie added, "he told me he is very confused and I want to respect that."

"That's fucked up," Jennifer mumbled, shaking her head, "you'd be stupid to take the blame."

Reggie felt caught between her and Isaac, so he couldn't find words. A car horn sounded and they looked to the street and saw her dad's Tesla.

"Wait here," she said and ran to the car, opened the door and talked to her dad for a moment. Then she ran back to Reggie. "Come on, we'll give you a ride."

"You sure?" Reggie's replied, pointing to his head, "what's he going to say when he sees this?"

"Come on." She grabbed his hand and they ran to the car. Opening the back door, she slid into the backseat followed by Reggie.

"Dad, this is Reggie," she said.

Mr. Peters reached over the seat with a friendly smile and handshake, which quickly stiffened into shock when he saw Reggie's bandages, bloody shirt and anxious face.

"What happened to you?" he asked.

Reggie, figuring whatever he would say would not sound good, couldn't say anything.

His silence prompted Jennifer, "He stopped a bully who was picking on our friend."

Focusing on the bruises, Mr. Peters' said, "Only a fist fight?"

"Yes, sir," Reggie answered as Mr. Peters faced front and adjusted the rear view mirror to get a good look at the two. Reggie dropped his eyes, feeling like a criminal. Jennifer held and squeezed his hand in Reggie's defense and in defiance of her dad.

Mr. Peters drove off.

After a few minutes of silence, Mr. Peters asked, "Jennifer said Encino, right?"

"Yes, sir," Reggie said, "off of Dean Street—really appreciate it sir."

"No problem," he acknowledged then added, "What did you say your name was?"

"Reggie Youngblood, sir."

Following a long pause, Mr. Peters quizzed the two of them, "How long have you two guys known each other?"

Jennifer felt the irritation of parental nosiness and answered "Just a few weeks."

After another long pause, her dad asked, "Why was this guy picking on your friend?"

Reggie and Jennifer looked at each other for the answer. Hoping her answer might end the inquisition, Jennifer said, "Just because he's gay!"

"Not good," Mr. Peters said, "I hope that's not how these issues get solved at your school."

"Reggie and I don't want to talk about this anymore, dad," Jennifer's testy voice replied.

So until the car pulled up in front of Reggie's apartment, no one spoke.

"Take care, Reggie—I'll see you in a couple of days," Jennifer said as she rubbed his hair gently above the bandages, then looked to see if her dad saw her.

"Okay, and thanks for the ride." Reggie said as he exited the car with a quick wave. Mr. Peters nodded.

"I want to know everything," her dad said as the door closed and they drove off.

****

Reggie felt jolts of pain walking up the apartment stairs, but when he got to the door, the thought of Jennifer's touch made the pain go away.

Knowing his mom was working the evening shift, Reggie micro-waved one of those lasagna meals followed by half a package of Oreos.

He saw that the light was blinking on the home phone, so he listened to two calls from Mt. Tremper and erased the messages. He took two Advils, watched a little TV then felt really sleepy. By nine o'clock he hit the sack.

When he heard his mom come home and she knocked on his door, he made sure he was lying on the side with the bandages with his hair covering most of his face. She asked if he was all right and did he have supper. He stopped her by saying he wasn't feeling well, was really tired and would talk to her in morning. He knew he'd be in deep shit tomorrow, but he wanted to bury the whole incident. Besides, he felt he needed the sleep to be able to handle it. So he drifted off, feeling Jennifer's fingers rubbing his hair, interrupted by flashes of her dad's cold stare.

CHAPTER FOURTEEN

Reggie's wake-up alarm beeped longer than usual, so his mom knocked and opened his door. She gasped when she saw Reggie's hair had fallen to the side revealing his bandaged head and stains on his pillow.

"Reggie!" she screamed as she rushed to sit on his bed. "What happened to you? Are you alright?"

Reggie grabbed a handful of hair and covered the bandages and groaned out, "I'm okay ma, just a few bruises."

"What happened?" She asked.

"Got in a fight with Kevin—I'm not hurt bad." he answered, dismissing the gravity of it all with a wave of his hand. Then he asked, "Can I get back to sleep?"

Incredulous, his mom said, "No way, we need to talk."

Reggie responded, "I said I'm okay, mom, just tired. The nurse tried to call you at work, but we couldn't get through."

"Dammit!" she said as she shook her head knowing that her phone has not been working right for some time.

Then Reggie reached over to his night table, picked up the suspension notice, handed it to his mom and said, "Talk to Mr. Tremper first."

"Suspension!" she shouted, "Reggie what the hell?"

"Just call him ma and let me sleep a little longer."

Sitting there re-reading the note and shaking her head, she said, "Alright, I'll wake you up by ten o'clock," knowing that her afternoon shift didn't start 'till three.

Carole called Mr. Tremper as soon as she got into the kitchen. She was put on hold and grabbed a cup of coffee and held it with both hands shaking. Saying hello, the Principal first asked if Reggie was okay, then he apologized for not being able to get a hold of her. Carole was so embarrassed, she told him it was her fault. The principal described to Carole what the school knew about the incident so far. He told Carole that when Reggie and Kevin come back from suspension in two days, they will be interviewed by the disciplinary committee. Once they complete their investigation, they will be making their decision.

After Carole asked what they could decide, Mr. Tremper talked about possible expulsion of one or both of the boys for the remainder of the year with possible re-enrollment in the Fall, pending parental involvement and anger management counseling.

After that, Carole started feeling sick to her stomach and felt she didn't have the courage or the voice to ask any more questions. Then Mr. Tremper asked if there was anything Reggie told her or any circumstances at home that could have precipitated Reggie's actions. Not wanting to say anything until she talked to Reggie and his dad, Carole told him no, and thanked him.

Carole immediately dialed her husband in Iraq, knowing it was unlikely she'd reach him. His voice mail did pick up however and she left a message that it was urgent for him to call right back, but that everyone is fine. Keeping the phone on the bathroom counter, she jumped into the shower to clear her thinking.

At nine o'clock she woke him. "Reggie, I need you to get up now," she said firmly. "I put in a call to your father and we will need to agree on what to tell him."

Reggie got up, dragged himself into the kitchen and slumped into his chair at the kitchen table.

"How do you feel?" his mom asked.

"Tired," he replied.

"Who put on the bandages?"

"The doctor at the Urgent Care Center on Willoughby—he told me I was lucky the wounds were not deep and everything else was okay." They tried to call you from there and I guess your phone was on the fritz again, they felt they couldn't wait and just bandaged me up." When I called Wal-Mart, they said you had left for the day."

"I went food shopping, dammit!" she swore. "Look, I want to know every detail," she said, "now let me fix you something."

"Not hungry," he said while thinking he could go for a fried egg and cheese sandwich.

"I'll make you an egg and cheese sandwich," she said.

"Alright," he said as he put his head down into his arms on the table, groaned and hoped she would give him some time to wake up before the questioning began. Carole served Reggie and quietly watched him eat, giving him plenty of time to wake up. *Poor kid,* she thought to herself. She couldn't believe, although he could get very angry at times, that Reggie would ever hurt someone without a good reason.

She then told Reggie, "Mr. Tremper filled me in on what they know so far and the possibility that you may be expelled. There is no way we can keep this thing from your dad, he will want to know what happened and hear the truth from you." She went on, "But, we don't have to tell him everything, because we don't know how this will go down. He may call back anytime now and I'll talk to him first, but we can't let him get too upset—it might affect his alertness in the field, okay?"

"Okay," Reggie said, relieved that his mom was willing to downplay it.

"I need you to promise, Reggie, you will not argue with him," she added.

"Okay mom, I got it." Reggie agreed and thought, *thank God, that's the last thing I need right now.*

"Now, what happened?" she asked.

Looking his mom straight into the eyes and said, "That asshole Kevin was picking on Isaac so I stopped him, that's it!" Knowing she wanted the complete story, he explained the whole thing.

Feeling relief believing that her son was defending his friend and that this Kevin kid was the instigator, she asked, "Did you hurt him?"

"I got in a few good punches," Reggie replied, "but he got up and hit me hard—he's a big jock, you know."

Reggie's mom tried to get a handle on Isaac's involvement and asked, "Why was he slapping Isaac?"

Starting to feel frustrated and angry, reliving the whole thing, he answered gruffly, "Kevin is a bully mom, and he picks on anyone he thinks is different, including gays and half-breeds—Isaac never did anything to him."

"Isaac did nothing?" she asked.

"Maybe he called him a name once. You know, even if Isaac was gay, that's no excuse to hit him," Reggie answered.

Reggie jumped as his mom's cell phone vibrated on the table. "Now the damn thing is working," she said as she picked up the phone and gestured to Reggie to go to his room. She silently mouthed, 'I'll call you later,' and picked up the phone, noticing several messages she hadn't gotten earlier.

Pausing to find a calm voice, she replied to John's anxious questioning, "No, we're okay." Then Carole proceeded to give John an edited version of what happened. She downplayed the seriousness of the fight, that the other kid started it and that she believed that Reggie was only trying to protect his friend Isaac. Once Carole told him that Reggie was suspended, John demanded to speak to Reggie.

Telling John she'd go and get him, she buried the phone in her side, rushed to open Reggie's door and whispered to him, "Dad wants to talk, tell him the truth, then just listen and go along with what he says, promise?" Reggie nodded so she handed him the phone.

With a quiet voice Reggie said, "Hi, Dad."

"Are you alright Reggie?"

"I'm fine dad, it was no big deal."

"No big deal!" John shouted into the phone, "you could be expelled and have a permanent stain on your record, I hope you're telling your mom the truth about what happened." His dad continued, "If I find out you were at fault and they expel you— you're going to be in big trouble when I get home."

Carole could hear John's rant on the other end and could see a look of anger growing on Reggie.

"I told mom the truth," Reggie said defensively, "Don't you trust me?"

There was a long pause before his dad answered, "Who's this kid Isaac?"

"A friend, dad." said Reggie.

"If he was fighting there must be something going on," he continued, "is Isaac a troublemaker?"

Reggie's face reddened as the anger level rose, but he held back, "No he's not—I tried to protect him"

Dad shouted, "Alright, I'm proud of you that you tried to protect a friend. But this friend smells like trouble and I don't want you hanging around with him anymore, do you understand?"

The look on Reggie's face signaled to Carole he was about to explode, so she put her index finger to her lips then held her hands together like she was praying and pleaded with her eyes for Reggie to stay calm.

Furious but realizing his dad wouldn't know if he hung with Isaac or not, Reggie said "Okay" then shoved the phone over to his mom in disgust, grabbed his hoodie and headed out the apartment door.

Carole quickly jumped on and said, "I told him he could leave now, John—he's pretty upset too, but I think we'll be okay. I'm sorry to have bothered you about this, I guess I just panicked and I knew you'd want to know, but I will keep you posted, don't worry okay?"

John, apparently feeling reassured by Carole's handling of things said, "I'm sorry you have to handle these problems alone; I should be there with you when this stuff happens."

"I know and I've been thinking we ought to talk to his school guidance counselor, maybe they can offer some suggestions."

"You can give it a try, hang in there Carole. I'll be home in only sixty-eight days."

"I love you."

"Love you too, Carole, let me know what happens," John said, "good bye for now."

Carole clicked off, then ran to the window and saw Reggie in his bright blue hoodie running down the street.

****

Running off his anger and frustration, Reggie covered what must have been two miles of Encino sidewalks in twenty minutes. He could feel each footfall in his chest and his head pounded in pain, but he pushed past it. Finally getting winded, he turned around and walked to catch his breath. His cell phone sounded. Figuring it was his mom, he almost didn't take it out of his pocket.

"Yeah!" he shouted as he saw the call was from Jennifer. "Jennifer, thank God it's you," he told her as he ducked into the alley to talk. "How you doing?"

"Okay Reg, but I don't have more than a minute, my mom's waiting for me," Jennifer said. "How are you feeling?"

"I'm okay, a little sore in the body, but my dad keeps messing with my mind," he said, "he told me I better not get expelled and not to hang out with Isaac anymore—I don't think he believes me about what happened."

She paused for a moment to be sure Reggie was finished and said stammering, "Say, Reggie…"my…my dad, he doesn't want me seeing you anymore."

"What?" Reggie screamed.

"I'm sorry Reggie—he told me if I hang out with you…he thinks well, I'll get in trouble too, by association, he said."

"He hated my looks and my name didn't he?" Reggie responded, "Did he say he doesn't like gays too? What's with your dad?"

"Reggie, Reggie, he didn't say that. When he saw that you were in a fight, I…I think he's just afraid for me. Reggie, I gotta go, maybe we can talk when you get back, but we just can't meet anymore. I know that sucks, but I don't know what else to say."

"Goodbye, that's all." Reggie hung up.

Then he yelled to the top of his voice, "Fucking parents! That Fucking Kevin!" echoed down the alley.

Standing next to an alcove behind a store where they keep the trash bins, he spotted a can with long fluorescent light tubes sticking out. Growling with rage, he ran over to them picked a tube up and, one at a time, like a Javelin thrower at the Olympics, started hurling them against the wall. They made a satisfying crack and popping sound with each hit, shattering tinkling shards everywhere. Four more. Three more. Two more. And just as he hurled the last tube, a door opened and a man's head missed the shattering tube by a couple of feet. The man yelled at the kid in the blue hoodie, and Reggie took off as fast as he could down the alley.

Reggie only got two blocks when he heard sirens. *The guy must have called the cops right away,* he thought. He hung a left into the next alley and ducked down alongside a dumpster. The siren got louder and soon it reverberated even louder in the alley. *Maybe they weren't looking for him,* he thought. He hoped for a moment they didn't see him as the police car whizzed by him in the alley. But halfway down, the car screeched to a halt, with gears grinded into reverse. It burned rubber and headed back to where Reggie was hiding.

****

By this time, Reggie knew they got him. So he simply stood up as the car stopped. Both doors flung open and two cops with hands on their holsters came rushing towards him. They yelled at Reggie to put his hands on his head and face the wall. They frisked him, flipped him around and the Asian-American cop said, "Having some fun, kid?" The cop could see Reggie had a fearful, not defiant look on his face. He shouted at him to show his ID.

"I don't have it with me, sir."

"Where do you live, kid?" the cop asked.

"In Encino, on Dean Street,"

"Are your parents' home?"

"My Mom is. I didn't want to hurt anybody."

"Maybe, but you better hope it's just a vandalism charge," the cop said. "Get in the car."

At the station, they put Reggie into a holding cell and asked for his mom's phone number. While sitting there the anger had worn off and the shame took over as he realized he had gotten himself into deep trouble. *'Shit,'* he said to himself, *'you're a royal fuck-up.'* As he imagined how angry and disappointed his mom would be, a woman cop came into the holding area, unlocked the door and told him that his mother was here. When Reggie saw her, he knew she'd be mad—and she was.

Carole rushed in and grabbed him by the shoulders and said, "What the hell is the matter with you? You could have hurt someone."

"I was stupid," Reggie responded.

Carole shook her head in disgust and said, "We've got to figure what we're going to tell your dad!"

Reggie looked at his mom feeling like he used to feel before he cried, but held it back and held his head down.

The woman officer interrupted and told them that Captain Arnold will meet with them now to go over procedures. The Captain, whose head was shaved like a marine, introduced himself and explained how the janitor identified the kid in the bright blue hoodie and that when apprehended, Reggie admitted he did it.

67

Since he was a juvenile, he would probably go to Juvenile Court where his case would be heard. Then the Captain asked if Reggie had any explanation for what he did.

"No excuses, sir. I was just angry," Reggie answered

The Captain waiting to hear more, but after a long pause, Reggie's mom spoke up, "If I could sir, let me say that Reggie has been having a hard time at his new school and that with his dad being in Iraq, Reggie hasn't been himself lately."

The Captain's demeanor changed all of a sudden and he asked Carole, "Who's his dad with?"

"The 105th Armored Brigade," Carole told him.

"Fallujah?" he asked.

"Yes, how did you know?"

"Well, I was with the 32nd Infantry Battalion," the Captain replied "and knew some of the guys over there from that unit—we all had some rough going there." The Captain must have seen Carole's face drop having realized that her husband was still in the thick of it. "But I'm digressing," he said. "We will have to complete our investigation, see if the janitor and company want to press charges, file a complete report of the incident and determine the appropriate resolution."

Looking over at Reggie, the Captain asked, "Did you know that these fluorescent tubes contain mercury and lead and that when the glass breaks, poisonous gases are released?"

"No sir," replied Reggie.

"Yeah, most people don't," said the Captain, "you could have cut that man's face up and permanently blinded him too."

"I didn't mean to… to…" Reggie said as he looked for more words.

Then the Captain interrupted, and sensing that Reggie was remorseful asked, "You think you can control your anger and not strike out like that again, Reggie?"

"I think so, sir," Reggie answered.

"Alright," the Captain said, we will let you know if you will have to go to Juvenile Court and we may also have to notify your school." At that point Reggie and his mom looked at each other with mutual horror.

"Stay clean, Reggie," the captain said extending his hand "and thanks for coming in, Mrs. Youngblood." Then he added, "How much longer is your husband's tour?"

"Sixty-two days and counting," Carole told him as she thanked him for his understanding.

CHAPTER FIFTEEN

By the time Reggie returned to school after the suspension, he was fairly relaxed when the bus dropped him off. He and his mom had been over and over the fight incident and the tube-throwing incident and he was tired of all the worrying. Reggie knew he'd be meeting with the disciplinary committee and probably the Principal and his mom had called the school to arrange for a session with a guidance counselor. Reggie felt he just wanted to get on with it, but most of all he hoped he'd get a chance to talk to Jennifer.

Going right to the office to check in, Reggie was told by the secretary that he'd be meeting with the disciplinary committee at third period and meeting with the Principal fifth period, otherwise he'd attend classes as usual, but was not to have any contact with Kevin as that would affect any final decision. Reggie realized that meant he would miss Jennifer during Biology class, but figured maybe he could catch her after the last class before her dad came to get her.

****

The meeting with the disciplinary committee was uneventful. They questioned Reggie much as before and Reggie gave them the same description of the events he had before the incident. Isaac would not elaborate on the incident other than telling them that Kevin was picking on him. The committee chairperson informed Reggie that no other witnesses have come forward to bolster his story or to discredit what Kevin had claimed. They pressed him to be completely truthful and to disclose any information that could help the committee decide not to expel him. Reggie had nothing to add. Reggie was not only worried that Kevin would find him and beat him up later, but he figured he was finished anyway once the Encino police contacted the school.

The committee did not say whether or not they received notification from the police department, but Reggie couldn't be sure they hadn't or wouldn't. Before they released him, the committee chairperson went over the school policy on fighting and bullying and the zero tolerance part sounded pretty heavy to Reggie. He felt they were suggesting he would be expelled. They told him they had not made a final decision but expected to by the end of the week. What Reggie did not know was that all five members of the committee were in favor of expelling Kevin, based on his history. That same poll of the five members showed that three out of five, the required majority, were intending to vote Reggie out as well.

The meeting with the Principal led Reggie to believe that it was almost certain that he'd be expelled. Mr. Tremper made a big point that in most cases of fights between two students, both are deemed at fault, especially when it couldn't be proved who started it and why. Although they believed that Reggie was perhaps trying to help his friend, they had no firm evidence that Reggie didn't use unnecessary force. He also suggested that if they only punished one of the boys that might send a message to the student body that it's okay to fight if you're on the 'right' side. Mr. Tremper asked if Reggie had anything to say, Reggie declined. Finally, the Principal told him that they would make one last attempt to query the student body, by way of an announcement, if anyone had any information to share about the fight.

Then, he picked up the phone and called Ms. Jackson, one of the guidance counselors, and asked her if she was ready to see Reggie.

When Reggie got to her office, he knocked on the door and heard her say, "Hold on for a minute, Reggie—I'll be right there." Although Reggie never saw her before, the word among the students was that she was kind of weird and very young; having just received her college degree last year.

"Come on in," she said, giving him a friendly greeting at the door. She had sparkling green eyes, long blonde hair and to Reggie, was movie-actress pretty. Until he sat down, Reggie didn't notice her arm. He didn't stare, but unlike her left, her right arm was only as long as where her elbow would be. It had three dangling fingers that just flopped loosely when she sat down.

"I've been reviewing your test scores, grades and your file," she told him and, as she moved her working fingers through the folder said, "And, you're an anomaly."

"What's that?" Reggie asked.

"When your intelligence and test scores are in to top ninety-five plus percentile, but your grades are, well, at the bottom," she said, "it's puzzling."

"Um. Yeah, well, I'm a puzzle alright, with a few missing pieces," Reggie commented.

"I can relate to that," she said with a warm smile.

"Seriously though, Reggie, I find you amazing," she said with a half-smile, "Your math aptitude is very high... why do you think you don't do better in math?"

70

"Too many numbers," Reggie replied.

"Okay," she laughed, "But what about English?"

"Too many words," Reggie quipped and rolled his eyes.

Ms. Jackson let out an even bigger laugh and Reggie noticed that her eyes laughed too—just like Jennifer's did.

"So, I suppose, you find History too old?" she asked,

"No, just dead," he said with a smirk.

"But look,' she probed, "You seem to do okay in Biology."

"That's totally alive." Reggie responded.

"I understand that," she commented, "And I think it might be a clue to what inspires you."

Reggie didn't respond, but felt good that this woman would take the time to learn about him.

Looking through Reggie's file, she continued, "When I looked at your earlier interest inventories, you also rank at the top in conceptual thinking—what does that mean to you?"

"Ha. My mom calls it 'stare-itus'—a mental disease, I guess. My Algebra teacher used to say I was good at playing hooky when I was *in* school; day dreaming all the time. But that's when I get my ideas."

Looking more serious, Ms. Jackson said, "I think it's a real strength that you can apply to your chosen field—you can dream big you know. "I also note," she continued "that you haven't joined any extracurricular activities or sports, don't you like sports?"

"Too sporty," Reggie said, "you know all the competition, the cheering."

"Come on Reggie, you've got to have a hobby or something that excites you?" she probed.

"I used to like hiking in the woods with my dad and my dog," Reggie offered, "but that was before I moved to the city; can't learn much about our natural world with only Mexican fan palms lining the streets."

At that point, Ms. Jackson seemed to lapse into her own version of 'stare-itus' as she fell into deep thought, drumming her one set of fingers over the file.

For only the second time since they met, Reggie glanced over to her right arm and thought how she seemed accepting of her birth defect without embarrassment and how her personality made you hardly notice or care about it.

"Hey!" out of the blue, she blurted out, "I got it!—you could start your own school club!"

Although Reggie could feel her enthusiasm, he wondered what in the hell she was talking about.

"Do you plan on taking Environmental Sciences in the fall?" she asked.

"Probably," Reggie answered.

"Why don't you start a hiking club?" she suggested, "you know Mrs. Horton will be teaching the class—you get along with her don't you?"

"Sure. I mean, Yeah," Reggie answered, thinking of the only teacher he liked.

"Well, I know she belongs to the Sierra Club and is a real outdoorswoman—she might be willing to lobby for it, become your advisor and could help arrange school trips into the Santa Monica Mountains Recreation Area."

"Well, maybe. I already do some volunteering there for a wildlife research project," Reggie said, but thought it was a fantastic idea.

"I'll see if she's warm to it, okay?" she offered.

"Okay."

"Good."

Smiling broadly, Ms. Jackson closed the file on her desk and became contemplative before she gently asked, "How are you holding up with that mess about the incident the other day?"

"Not great," he said.

"Well I'm pulling for you and I hope you can stay in our school," she said.

"Me too."

"Oh, yeah, one more thing," she said as she handed him a sheet of paper, "Your mom had asked about other agencies and mentoring groups—here's a list I compiled for you; might not be a bad idea."

"Thanks," Reggie said as his answer caught her caring eyes and he reached out his hand to shake hers'. Without hesitation, she did a 'backwards' handshake with her left.

"Good luck Reggie, and it was nice to meet you," she said, "I'll let the office know you'll be down."

It was only a few minutes before the end of the school day when Reggie got to the office. The secretary told him he could wait for his bus, so Reggie went as far as the main doors where he couldn't miss Jennifer leaving and slouched against the wall. In a few minutes, he spotted her coming down the hall and they ran toward each other and hugged tightly.

Jennifer looked up at Reggie and asked, "Hey. Did you hear anything?"

"Maybe tomorrow," he answered with a sour tone.

"I feel so bad for you," she said with eyes starting to well up with tears. "And for us...I miss you."

"You think maybe we could find a way to meet before the school year ends?" he asked.

"I'm still grounded, but we can try—my dad's probably out there now waiting—he doesn't want us to even meet after school—I should go."

Reggie felt like he would never see her again, so without thinking, he gave her a quick kiss on the mouth. Jennifer was surprised, patted his cheek and said, "Bye," and ran off.

When he got home that afternoon, his mom was working again, so he made his own supper of scrambled eggs dipped in maple syrup, went into his room and plopped down on the bed with the 'Secrets of Meditation' book Jennifer had given him. *Maybe that will help me release some of my anxieties,* he thought.

After reading the first chapter, he got into the recommended sitting position with arms relaxed and hands facing upward. He couldn't come up with his own mantra to accompany his breathing, so he used their traditional *OHMM!*

The first few breaths did relax him and his mind stayed quiet for a while until he pictured Jennifer's worried face. Having read that he was supposed to simply let any thoughts or pictures go, he tried. But the thought of maybe not being able to see Jennifer again, kept repeating with each breath. Getting frustrated he opened his eyes and said to himself, '*Stop analyzing it, asshole, you love her—and you need to tell her that.*'

Then he picked up the book and read the chapter about 'Stilling the Voices.' Into the position again, he decided to lose the '*Ohmm*'—as it sounded to him too much like gloom. Anyway, the book said a mantra wasn't necessary. This time after six breaths, his mind saw pictures. He saw the principal, he shook his head at that image and closed his eyes again. Next he saw the stern looks of the disciplinary committee, which he quickly shook away and let his mind clear for two breaths. Lastly, he heard his dad's voice warning about getting expelled.

He jumped up and threw the book at the wall, knocking over his desk lamp. *Maybe I should try that vision quest thing,* he thought, *instead of this stupid meditation.* Disgusted with himself, he went into the living room and watched *Gorillas in the Mist* for the umpteenth time and fell asleep on the couch. He never heard his mother come home that night. He didn't feel when she put that red and black blanket over him. Next morning, his mom woke him up by placing milk and cereal on the coffee table. He sat up and she told him to have a good day, gave him a kiss on his bushy head and left for work.

Figuring this school day was his doomsday, Reggie sensed that his fellow tenth graders avoided eye-contact in the halls and in class. When he saw Isaac at lunch, they barely talked, but did chat about how well the barn owl's wings at the Audubon were healing.

After lunch, Mr. Suarosky came over to Reggie and told him that the Principal would see him and to go to his office before the start of fifth period. When Reggie got to the office, the secretary said go right in and Reggie was surprised to see Mr. Tremper smiling and actually reached out to shake Reggie's hand.

"Well, Reggie I'll get right to it. The disciplinary committee has voted to retain you as a student. Kevin will be expelled for the balance of the year, as he was found to be the instigating student."

Reggie was too much in a daze to immediately appreciate what the Principal was telling him. "Are you saying I'm not expelled?" Reggie asked.

"That's correct. At the last possible moment, one of your classmates—and we are keeping his identity anonymous for his own safety, came forward with some critical information."

Thinking it was Isaac coming out and telling them, Reggie asked, "What kind of information?"

"That Kevin was found to have brought a weapon to school and actually used it on you in the fight."

"What kind of weapon?"

"Brass knuckles."

Now the sharp pain and the blood on his head came back to Reggie's mind, and he said, "No wonder."

"Now, Reggie," Mr. Tremper said, "this information was not available to us right after the incident, so we did not involve the local police, but I want to tell you that that information, plus the medical records indicating your wounds and bruises, are sufficient for you to file an assault complaint with the local police, if you wish to do so."

"You mean, like going to court and all that crazy stuff? Like to put Kevin in juvenile detention?" Reggie asked.

"Yes. So you talk with your parents and we'll set up a time to meet and resolve this."

"I don't know, but will Kevin not be allowed back in school?"

"For the balance of the year that is correct, but it is possible that he could return in the fall if he completes anger management counseling and his parents agree to certain monitoring and controls. "But," Mr. Tremper continued, "If you were to press formal charges against him, we would not allow him back in school under *any* circumstances—that would be your call."

"Alright, I'll talk to my parents," Reggie said.

"Thank you Reggie and I'm sorry for all the trouble you've been through—this has been a very unfortunate situation. But know that you're in the clear now as long as you continue to follow school behavior codes. If you don't have any questions, you can go your next class now—Biology isn't it?"

"Yup!" Reggie said, thanked the Principal and headed down the hall still in a state of disbelief. Opening the door to the class, he saw Mrs. Horton wave him in smiling broadly and said, "Welcome back, Reggie."

Then Reggie quickly looked and saw Jennifer wave to him with a glowing smile. Then Isaac stood up and started clapping and most of the kids did the same. But before he sat down, embarrassed as he was, he had to check Kevin's seat to make sure it was empty.

Reggie wondered who the kid was who came forward with the information. He heard a rumor than another student saw Kevin afterwards and that he was beat up pretty badly by his dad. Apparently Kevin was very bitter about it all, especially not being able to win the soccer championship.

As soon as class ended, Reggie rushed over to Jennifer, but was stopped by Mrs. Horton who said she wanted to talk to Reggie.

"Can we talk next week, I gotta go?" Reggie pleaded.

"Okay," she said as Reggie headed out the door, "but so you know, I talked to Ms. Jackson...I like her idea of the hiking club."

Reggie turned around and said, "Great!" then waved out the door.

Reggie quickly put his arm around Jennifer and said, "Can you believe it?"

"You must feel good Reggie," she said, "I totally knew they wouldn't blame you."

"You know what this means?" he asked almost bouncing down the hall.

"What?" she asked.

He looked surprised at her answer, like she wasn't in tune with his thinking and said, "Well, so we can see each other again, now that I was found not guilty." He could see by the look on Jennifer's face she wasn't feeling what he was.

"I'm not sure, Reggie," she said, "I'll have to ask my dad if this changes things."

"Come on, can't he ever cut you some slack?" he asked.

"I'll try this weekend Reggie, but I'm not sure," she answered.

As they approached the exit doors, Jennifer held Reggie back with her arm and peered out the side window.

"He's here, Reggie, I gotta go—I'll try to call you when I can talk...see ya."

Looking dejected, Reggie stood at the door watching Jennifer get into her dad's car and drive off. Then he lifted his arm in the air made a fist and just stopped short of banging it into the wall.

CHAPTER SIXTEEN

Lupine-boy began his day soon after dusk and returned for the third night to feed on his deer kill buried in Rustic Canyon. As he approached the carcass, he saw that the leaves and branches he had covered it with, were disturbed. He froze for a moment. Fearing Big-paw or another lion may have found it, he quickly dropped his belly to the ground and slowly slid toward his kill on high alert.

Then he heard a rustling sound coming from a large patch of sagebrush above him. He tensed, and his powerful rear muscles became taught. His ears pivoted, and because the sounds came from multiple locations surrounding the sage, he knew it couldn't be a solitary, most always soundless, lion. The wind shifted and his nose captured the scent of a pack of coyotes. Lupine-boy knew they wanted to finish off the kill, but it was his kill and he was hungry.

Knowing there was some risk of being surrounded and attacked by the pack, he relied on the learning and instincts that were passed onto him. These coyotes were capable of killing him on the open chaparral. They could outrun him at long distances, and despite the lion's overwhelming strength in battle, his lung capacity was small. Lupine-boy knew he needed to fear them, but he also knew he was safe in this place. The oaks and the sycamores were everywhere, and in case the pack decided to attack, he could escape their jaws up a tree in an instant.

As the coyotes moved down the hill toward the kill, Lupine-boy slinked up the hill toward them. When the pack got within five of his body lengths, Lupine-boy jumped out of the brush, shrieked his most vicious shriek, swiped his sharp paw at the closest coyote, and sent him flying and tumbling down the hill. The rest of the pack ran back a short distance, turned around and bared their fangs and growled. Lupine-boy ran at them again—giving them an ear-shattering scream—and the pack high-tailed it up the canyon.

Lupine-boy returned to what remained of his kill. Exposed to the air, the meat was almost rancid, but he found a meaty shoulder bone and laid in peace enjoying his light breakfast.

Roaming the edge of Topanga Canyon, he soon picked up a fresh scent of another male lion. It was not Big-paw's signature, but it could be a new mature lion—one that he would have to fight. He followed the scent trail toward the direction of the sunset until he spotted the intruder. It was a very young, small cougar, having only lost its spots a short time ago. When the little lion caught sight of Lupine-boy, it ran up the nearest tree and climbed as high as it could and perched on a branch, shivering.

Lupine-boy lazily strolled to within a few body lengths of the tree and laid down for a catnap. As time passed, the young lion slowly climbed down, and not feeling threatened anymore by the big lion, scampered away. Lupine-boy followed. Now able to smell the youngster's fresh scent trail, he discovered it was a son of She-Paw from an earlier litter. Lupine-boy knew that cubs stayed with their mother until they were able to hunt for themselves, but this little lion was either lost or abandoned by his mom.

As he could not smell She-Paw, Lupine-boy followed the little one for a distance until he saw it head close to a wide hilly path of the two-legs with smoking beasts running up and down. He ran and chased the youngster away from the beasts, putting himself between the little one and the path. They continued to parallel the path until the young lion bolted in front of the older lion and shot across the wide path, making it in between two running beasts. Lupine-boy stood there for several minutes looking to see if the youngster would return, then headed back into the brush, trying to pick up She-Paw's scent.

****

It was almost noon Saturday after sleeping late and eating breakfast, when Reggie's mom reminded him that Isaac was coming over at one. His mom was in much better spirits after Reggie told her the good news the night before. He told her about the brass knuckles and that Mr. Tremper said that he could press formal assault charges against Kevin.

"As long as he's not back in school," Reggie told her, "I don't want to get messed up in that."

"It doesn't seem right that he should get away with it."

"I know, Ma. But getting kicked out of school and soccer seems like enough punishment to me."

"Let's think about it some more, but I will let your Dad know about the news."

Carole later called John and left him a message that Reggie was not expelled and arranged for another Skype session for Saturday evening.

When she reminded Reggie that she had also arranged with Isaac's parents to drive them to the Audubon Center, Reggie protested, "I super don't want to go!"

"Why not?" his mom asked.

"I just don't," he said not wanting her to think he might have something better to do—like talk with Jennifer.

"Do you have something better to do?" she asked.

"No, Ma," he answered thinking he didn't want to miss Jennifer's call and couldn't really talk when Isaac was around.

"Look Reggie, I haven't been able to do my turn driving you guys for weeks, and I promised Isaac's parents," she said, "besides if you get a call from her, you can always excuse yourself and take the call somewhere."

It took a few moments for his mom's response to sink in, and then Reggie said, "Who are you talking about?"

Carole considered for a moment revealing that she had heard him call out Jennifer's name in his sleep and had seen her name on that meditation book, but said, "Just in case someone else might call you, that's all I meant—you better get changed, Isaac will be here soon."

'Shit!' Reggie thought to himself as he went to his room, 'How in the hell does she know...guess I'll have to tell her sometime.'

When Isaac arrived, both boys went into Reggie's room. Following a fist bump, Reggie jumped and laid on his bed and Isaac sat on the floor alongside the bed and they started talking.

"I'm happy you're back at school," Isaac said, "and they kicked the asshole out."

"Yeah, on both accounts," Reggie confirmed, then asked, "was it you who came forward later and told them about your... your...?"

"My what?—that I'm confused about whether I'm attracted to girls or boys?" Isaac responded.

"No, I just meant...that if you told them why Kevin was bullying you—you know...being truthful about yourself."

"Does a label about sex say who I am?" Isaac shouted back, "Does everyone have to know? Does it mean I should get beat up?"

"I didn't mean to..." Reggie started to say.

"I know, I'm not 'normal' Reggie, he said, "but neither are you, so why do you want to say what I am. No, I didn't come forward— my shit is none of their business. I told the committee that you were my friend and you saved me from Kevin, what else did I have to say?" Isaac ranted.

Reggie stayed silent for several minutes, not wanting to argue as he empathized with Isaac. Then Reggie thought he heard a little sob, and looked down at Isaac who had his head between his knees and was shaking. He let Isaac continue to sob until he saw him lift his head and rub his eyes. Then Reggie asked, "You alright?"

"My parents think that I'm gay!" Isaac blurted out.

"Wouldn't they be okay with that?" Reggie asked.

"I guess so," Isaac answered, "My dad keeps saying: 'just tell us what you want—we'll always be with you.'"

"That should make you feel a lot better."

"Yeah. But it's much harder than that."

"What do you mean?"

"Coming to terms with everything about it. You know, you grow up listening to people, including my older brother, make fun of gays and folks still arguing they shouldn't have the right to marry, you...you kind of fear being, you know, defined by your sexual preference and being like an outcast."

After a long pause, Isaac looked up at Reggie and said, "My parents suggested maybe I could change to a better school. "What do you think, Reggie? What would you do?"

Reggie looked down at Isaac thinking, *why does he always look to me?* Then he reached down and put his hand on his shoulder and said, "Maybe it would be good for you, but I hope you don't leave."

Just as Isaac put his hand up to Reggie's to thank him, they heard Carole open the door and ask, "Are you guys ready to go?" All three felt embarrassed as the boys jumped up and silently got ready to leave.

Nothing but chit chat accompanied their drive to the Audubon and once they were there, Reggie and Isaac helped guide a kindergarten group through the displays. Then Reggie watched Isaac take care of his Salamander 'aquarium'. He always found it amazing how Isaac treated these tiny, silent, almost always in hiding, animals. Isaac decorated their glass box like a castle, making sure their habitat contained the exact natural materials they would encounter in the wild and keeping it sparkling clean. Reggie found the contrast with the habitat of his mountain lions intriguing; both of them cared deeply in their own ways about their favorite wild animals.

The salamanders were so delicate you could not handle them, but that didn't keep Isaac from feeding them one by one. Not just any food, either. He'd take Reggie out into the woods and dig into wet leave piles to find the particular kind of insects and worms they ate in the wild. And Isaac fed them in an incredibly intimate way. Grasping a worm with tweezers, he'd call his for his friends to come out of hiding. "Come on, Slomo," he'd say as he held the wiggling worm in front of its nostrils, patiently waiting for it to eat. 'Good Boy' he'd say when the slimy fellow chomped it down. *It was more than cute,* Reggie thought, *Isaac could be a great family man someday. Wouldn't it be great if all humans took such care of all living things?* The rest of the afternoon went by and Reggie never got a call from Jennifer.

Saturday evening's planned Skype call to Iraq for some reason was not going through. As Carole kept trying, Reggie hoped maybe he wouldn't have to talk with his dad about that school incident and kept thinking about what Isaac said and wondered if Jennifer was ever going to call. After Carole tried several times to get his dad on the phone, Reggie could see his mom was getting upset and worried, so he put his hand over the phone in her hand and said, "Let's just leave it alone—he'll call back."

****

Sunday. No call from Jennifer. Reggie tried several times to call her and she could not or would not pick up. Reggie's dad finally called back and when Reggie listened to his mom's side of the conversation, he sensed something was wrong. Carole held the phone buried in her neck and kept asking in hushed tones, *'You sure? You sure?'* When she went to get Reggie to join them, she told him that his dad was happy to learn about the school's decision, but that he couldn't talk for very long.

As soon as Reggie heard his dad's voice, he knew something was going on. His voice had a sort of forced muffled sound to it and he could hear the echo of voices like from a large room. When Reggie asked his dad if he was alright, he told Reggie he was fine, happy that he was cleared at school. He told Reggie he hoped he would have a good summer and would be home soon. Saying goodbye and handing the phone back to his mom, Reggie knew.

Carole knew too, but when she got off the phone, she told Reggie his dad was okay. Reggie told his mom he thought dad sounded okay too, but he did not tell her he heard the beeping of those medical monitoring machines in the background.

By Monday, no call from Jennifer. Back in school he expected to see her at lunch as usual on Monday, Wednesday and Friday, but also expected she'd be with her girlfriends. Isaac would be there too—not a good time or place to talk. When he met up with Jennifer in the lunch yard, she smiled and gave him a nice hug, but the two of them had to go along with the general conversation at the table and couldn't break away. After his last class he rushed to the exit doors only to see her getting into her dad's car. Although this was the last week of the school year and he was starting to feel panicky, he knew he'd see her in Biology class on Tuesday.

By Tuesday, Jennifer was already in her seat when he got to class. Reggie went over to her, touched her hand and asked if she was okay. She squeezed his hand, smiled and told him they'd talk after class.

"Are you sure you're okay?" Reggie asked after he rushed to her seat.

"Yeah, I'm okay," she responded with a half-smile.

"Did you talk to your dad?" Reggie asked as they walked down the hall.

"Not yet," She answered sheepishly.

"How come?"

"I was afraid of his answer."

Reggie sighed, put his arm around her and gave her a sympathetic side hug and said, "I'm sorry for bugging you, it's just that school's almost over and I want to see you this summer."

"I know Reggie," she said without looking at him, "I'll try tonight."

No call on Wednesday. At lunch Jennifer seemed more quiet than usual, but they feigned interest in what everybody else would be doing for the summer. When they got up from the lunch table, he asked in a whisper, if she talked to her dad. She only shook her head no with a frustrated look on her face. After the last period, Reggie had a meeting with Mrs. Horton to complete the school request form for the hiking club. He was unable to see Jennifer.

By Thursday, no call. After fourth period, Reggie rushed over to Biology class to find Jennifer wasn't there yet. He waited in the hall until after the bell rang, but Mrs. Horton told him to take his seat. A few minutes later, Jennifer came in and gave Reggie a crooked smile. Reggie worried the whole time as he sensed that her look meant things went bad with her dad.

After class, Reggie rushed to her seat and asked, "What happened?"

"Hold on," she said as she grabbed his hand and lead him out the door. "I couldn't ask him, Reggie," she said, "he and my mom had a big fight after supper and I knew it would be a bad time."

"Bummer!" Reggie responded, "Were they arguing about you?"

"Not directly," Jennifer replied, "they were arguing about my dad wanting to go to Australia for a summer vacation and my mom said no."

"What do you mean, not directly?" Reggie asked.

"Well I heard them screaming, my dad told my mom I'd be happier at the art school."

"Are you going away?" Reggie asked.

"I don't know, Reggie," she answered, "after the arguing stopped, I went to talk to my dad. My mom told me he left really pissed off and probably wouldn't be back 'till late and would probably be drunk."

"Will you see him tonight? Tomorrow's Friday." Reggie asked.

"Yeah. I know, I gotta' go to class," she said as she scurried down the hall.

No call on Friday either. Reggie was starting to feel desperate and heading into the lunch yard, he almost told Isaac to find a seat at another table, but didn't. When he first saw Jennifer, she looked sad and when they greeted, she seemed distant. While eating and avoiding the prying questions about what they were doing for the summer, Reggie couldn't stand it any longer. He stood up and rudely excused himself, and to the incredulous stares of the group, motioned to Jennifer to grab her tray and they moved to an empty corner at another table.

"Jennifer, what happened?" Reggie asked, "Did he say no?"

"We did get to talk, but we fought and I don't know what to do," she answered then put her hands over her face. After a few moments, she took her hands away and said, "I'm sorry, Reggie, this whole time has been so hard."

Just as Reggie reached over and put both of her hands into his and looked her in the face, the bell rang.

"Shit!" Reggie cursed as they stood up, "I know it's been hard, can we talk after school?"

"Let's try," she said. As they bussed their trays and walked into the building, she told Reggie, "I think I can call you this weekend as my dad's at a conference and my mom, well..."

"That would be excellent," Reggie said with an excited smile. As they hugged and separated in opposite directions, Reggie said "See you later." Then he wondered why Jennifer's 'See ya' response didn't feel excited or right. Soon both of them remembered that they had a 'last day of school' assembly during final period, so they weren't able to meet before Jennifer's dad came.

Saturday morning. Reggie was up at nine anticipating Jennifer's call. By eleven she called and said she could meet him somewhere for about an hour and a half starting at one, as her mom would be at the hair salon. Thrilled, but not thinking, Reggie suggested the state park where they used to meet. Jennifer was okay with that, but wondered how she could get there and return before her mom came home. Reggie told her he'd figure it out and get right back to her.

Checking the Saturday bus schedules in either direction, Reggie was surprised to find no buses would get the two of them there in enough time to meet and get Jennifer back. He could ask his mom for rides, but that would mean she'd meet Jennifer and that would open up all kinds of explaining.

'Ah ha!' he thought, I'll use taxis. He looked in his wallet and found seven dollars and then he found two more crumpled up ones and some change in his desk. He called Yellow Cab and was told it would cost about fifteen dollars from Encino and twenty or so one-way from Thousand Oaks. He'd have to hit his mom up for cash.

Anxious to get his plan underway, he knocked on his mom's bedroom door. "Hey, Mom," Reggie asked with a casual tone, "can I have fifty bucks?" As soon as he said it, he realized he didn't have a ready-made believable lie.

"Well I suppose," she said, "can I ask what you need it for?"

Reggie's mind raced through ideas like a donation to the Audubon or that new set of headphones, but knowing she'd know better, said, "For a taxi," then realized right away she'd never go for it.

"What do you need a taxi for?" she asked then added, "I can give you a ride anywhere up 'till six, when I go to The Coffee Bean."

Reggie knew the taxi idea was hopeless and let it out, "Can you pick up a friend in Thousand Oaks at around twelve and drop us off at that park near the 101 and pick us up later?"

"Sure, who's the friend?" she asked.

"Ma, can I ask you to not ask a lot of questions, just give us the rides?"

"Okay, sure it's okay with her parents?"

"Yeah, mom," Reggie answered, then called Jennifer to let her know and get the directions.

On the drive to Thousand Oaks, Reggie's mom didn't want to pry so she told Reggie, "We have an appointment on Monday to meet with the people from the Big Brothers organization—it looks like they've found a possible mentor for you."

Not much interested in that at the moment, Reggie responded, "Oh. Does dad know?"

"Yes and he said we should at least check it out," she answered.

"Okay, if I have to," Reggie said.

His mom added, "When I contacted the Big Brothers organization, I filled out a form indicating your interests in hiking the outdoors. Later, the man from the agency told me that they found a potential mentor who matched your interests."

"Sounds good, mom—turn left on Colonial Drive." Approaching the house Reggie told his mom, "It's the third house on the right, number 1604. And please stay cool."

Running to the car, Jennifer gave Reggie a quick hug as she glided into the back seat. Turning around, Reggie's mom greeted her, "Glad to meet you Jennifer."

"Good to meet you too, Mrs. Youngblood," she replied.

Looking in the rear view mirror, Reggie could see his Mom was watching them, but she turned up the radio to let them have a private conversation; which they did at a whisper level. Once they got to the State Park, Reggie's mom asked when they needed her to pick them up. Reggie checked the time on his cell and told her fifty-five minutes at the gate.

Standing side-by-side and waving as the car pulled away, the couple, finally alone, looked at each other. Over the weeks of growing friendship, they had come to know how the other was feeling just by looking at each other. When Jennifer looked at Reggie, his eyes opened wide like they were hoping—waiting for her words. When Reggie looked at her, her eyes turned down and he sensed her sadness.

"I'm sorry, Reggie," she said.

"Me too," he said as they hugged for a long time; feeling how each other's disappointment was comforted by their closeness.

When they finally parted, Reggie asked, "Wanna sit under that big sycamore again?"

"Um. Sure," she said, working up a little laugh, "but I didn't bring any of my art today."

Reggie laughed back remembering their first time alone.

When they sat down, Reggie began, "I'm going to really miss you Jennifer. When are you leaving?"

Surprised by the question, Jennifer replied, "First thing Monday, but how did you know really?"

"Once you told me your dad was planning that summer vacation," he answered, "I knew he wasn't going to leave you alone here. And, knowing how much your art means to you and how you talked about that art school in Atlanta, I figured I'd lose you for the summer."

"But we can call and stay in touch on Facebook," Jennifer offered.

"Yeah. Whatever. But it won't be the same. You'll have your art and I have nothing to do all summer but hang with Isaac."

"Well, you can critique my art," she suggested, "I'll post them on Facebook or email."

"That would be cool," Reggie responded.

Looking at his phone, Reggie told Jennifer they didn't have a lot of time left, but he felt he wanted to talk about how they first met, their friends and the school.

"Remember how Mrs. Horton always scrunched up her face and put her finger on her nose when she was thinking," Jennifer recalled.

"Ha!" Reggie laughed, "But she's pretty cool."

Reggie looked to the ground as he pictured the classroom and Kevin and his demeanor changed.

Jennifer saw Reggie's face change to serious and she asked, "I suppose you're still thinking about Kevin."

"Yeah. How did you know I was thinking about that messed-up sicko?"

"Just a guess," she said.

Reggie paused then asked, "Jennifer? Are you going to take Environmental Science next year? Mrs. Horton will be teaching it."

"I don't know," she answered.

Reggie looked at Jennifer knowing he'd soon have to say goodbye for the summer. She could see it in his eyes. Reggie wanted to kiss her and she knew it meant a lot to him, so she moved her head closer to him.

Reggie put both hands gently on either side of her face and he longed to show her how much he felt for her. He kissed her with all his feelings. Although Reggie did not feel her arms wrap around him, her lips were soft and wet and for a brief moment he lost himself in her. Then Jennifer broke it off and pulled back.

Reggie looked startled and embarrassed, so Jennifer put her hand to the side of his face and said, "That was sweet, Reggie."

"Seriously? You don't seem to want to really kiss me?"

"I do. I *want* to want you, but I don't know if I'm ready for that."

Trying to understand her, he said, "I won't hurt you... I promise I won't do anything you don't want to... I just feel like I want to be closer."

"I know that, Reggie, but it's me."

"You don't like me?"

"God, I do, but I'm not sure I know how to?"

Moving his body further away—thinking that she was going to tell him she didn't want to see him anymore—he asked, "What do you mean? Be honest with me, okay?"

She looked briefly into his eyes, then down to the ground and began rubbing her leg nervously. Then she looked up and said, "Something is holding me back, Reggie... Like I can't lose myself in you the way I think you want me, to... It's like my mind is fighting with the rest of me." Tears formed in her eyes. "It's like I'm all messed up inside... I... I don't know who I am."

"Jesus, Jennifer. You're the strongest, most independent-minded person I've ever known. I'm like totally confused right now."

She put her hand on the side of his cheek. "Reg, can I be open with you?"

Reggie nodded.

"I don't want to hurt you, or lead you on, but what if I'm gay?"

"Gay? What *if* you're *gay*?" he said raising his voice. "You don't know?"

"I don't. I'm really confused. You are the perfect boy and I have real feelings for you, but I'm also attracted to girls. Maybe it's just hormones. I don't know. I feel so stupid. But seeing how Isaac was struggling with himself, I realized that I need to get clear myself."

"Have you ever kissed... you know, been with a girl?"

"No, that's just it. One time I had sort of...like a bad experience."

"What was that?"

"There was this senior girl at a basketball away game and she came on to me really strong and it scared me," she said.

"Since that time, I've felt attracted to a couple of girls, but none of them have ever shown any interest in me that way, so I don't know. You know, I don't *want* to be gay and all that goes with that, so I'm totally confused."

For the first time in their relationship, Reggie felt like there was a jagged crack forming between them and he wanted to clear the air. "You've got to be one thing or the other, don't you?"

"You're supposed to *know*, I guess," she said. "But I haven't figured out my identity yet. I ... I just need time. That's why I said I wasn't ready."

"Jesus, Jennifer, what the hell am I supposed to do in the meantime?"

She looked down to the ground, searching minutes for a good answer, then looked up to him and said, "You could say goodbye to me for good."

Reggie was taken back by her answer. That was the last thing he wanted to do. He felt like he was going to cry. "Why didn't you tell me before?"

"Because I really like you and I selfishly didn't want to lose the best friend I've ever had. You might not know it, Mr. Youngblood, but you have an awesome personality and you're gentle and you're caring and you're not like most boys." She smiled a little smile at him. "Plus, we always have such a great time together."

He smiled back. "Yeah, we do, and you said we were soul mates."

"We still are."

"Do you think there's a chance for us if... if..."

"Reggie, I know this must be hard for you and I don't want to lead you on, but if you can give me the summer to try and sort things out."

Shaking his head, he said, "I don't know. This is just so crazy."

"Beep, Beep!"

"There's my mom," Reggie said, "we better go."

When they reached the car, their mood had changed. They spoke very little on the ride back to Thousand Oaks. The ride seemed to take forever to Reggie. When they got to her house, Jennifer told Reggie her mom might be home.

"Goodbye, Reggie," she said as she opened the door and gave him a quick kiss on the cheek. "And thanks for the ride, Mrs. Youngblood." She jumped out of the car and ran into her house without looking back. Reggie sunk low in his seat and closed his eyes.

"You okay?" his mom asked before putting the car in drive. "You want to jump in front up and talk?"

He sunk even lower in his seat. "No thanks. Just go."

On the ride home, his feelings were all over the place. The sadness he felt gave way to anger. Maybe Jennifer purposefully led him on? Did she? Would she do that? He thought for a moment. *No. I was so stupid; I could only see a part of her... What I wanted to see....What is wrong with me?*

****

When Reggie and his Mom got home, he went right to his room. His mom didn't bother him until it was time for her to leave for work. She knocked on his door and asked if she could come in.

"What's up?" Reggie said.

Knowing he wanted to be left alone, she said, "I'm going to work now—I left one of those chicken pot pies out for you to heat up, okay?"

"Um. Okay, Ma."

"Oh! And Isaac called, he said he got your voice mail—maybe he wants to go to the Audubon."

"Okay, I got it," Reggie said.

As Reggie's evening wore on, he became bored playing video games and watching American Family on the Comedy channel. He was thinking about Jennifer the whole time. Isaac tried calling twice and although Reggie didn't feel like talking to him, he picked up on the third call.

"Been trying to reach you," Isaac said.

"Um. Yeah. I've been busy," Reggie responded.

"How are you doing?" Isaac asked.

"Friggin' fantastic. How about you?"

"Hangin' in there. You don't sound too happy.

"Yeah. What's up dude?"

"Are you doing anything on Sunday?"

"I don't want to go to the Audubon."

"No, but I was wondering if I could come over."

"Nah! I don't feel like doing anything."

"I know how you must feel, but I was hoping we could talk."

"About what?" Reggie responded, a little irritated.

"Just to chat, see how you're doing. End of school. Maybe get things off your chest."

Reggie, figuring Isaac wanted to talk about his personal problems, was feeling preoccupied with his own. He really didn't want to talk, especially about what went on with Jennifer, so he said. "I just don't feel like it, Isaac."

After a long silence, Isaac said, "I hate to tell you this on the phone, but I'm leaving town."

After another long silence, Reggie said, "Where you going?"

"We're moving to Westwood," he answered.

"Where? That's fucked up!"

"Um. Everything just fell together, I guess," Isaac said, "our apartment lease is up end of the month and my parents found a more progressive school. And well, I agreed that a fresh start might be a good idea."

"Makes sense," Reggie offered.

Isaac's voice lowered, "And, Reggie, I wanted to also tell you that I told my parents I was gay and they were very accepting."

"That's good."

Isaac continued, "And I wanted to thank both you and Jennifer for accepting me and helping me find myself."

"Don't know about that, Isaac, but I'm happy for you," Reggie said, wondering why he seemed to attract troubled friends—gay troubled friends. *Maybe I'm gay too,* he thought for a moment. *I never felt an attraction to boys, but the way things happen, maybe I will.*

"Thanks," Isaac said, "How's things going with Jennifer? What's she up to for the summer?"

Pausing, Reggie figured he'd find out about her leaving anyway, but he didn't want to talk about the rest of it. "She's going away for the summer to an art school near Atlanta."

"No. Really?" Isaac said.

"Yeah. And if she likes it there she may not come back to Encino."

"Bummer or what?

"I figure I'll probably never see her again, that's all. She's got to get on with her life."

"Guess we all do. I'll miss you, Reggie. You've been a good friend."

"Yeah, I'll miss you too. Give me a call before you leave, maybe we can get together. Take care man."

"I will. Bye."

As soon as Reggie got off the phone, he felt mixed emotions. He regretted not meeting with Isaac and not feeling genuinely glad for him. *'Dammit!'* Reggie said to himself, *I'm envious...everybody's blowing this fucked up town.'* All Reggie could feel now was more alone and lost.

****

Joe Sartor didn't normally spend his Saturday nights in the office, although he sometimes made the short trip from home just to check in with the cats. It was almost eight in the evening when he noticed something unusual. Looking at P12's tracking point on the monitor, he saw that his favorite lion was roaming far beyond his usual territory, heading east.

By the looks of it, he was following Dirt Mulholland and currently signaling in Mandeville Canyon—somewhere near San Vicente Mountain. *Strange,* Joe thought, *and not so good, if he keeps moving in that direction. Damn mountain lion,* he cursed to himself, *he's pushing into very populous areas and soon he'll crash into the 405 freeway.*

The phone rang and it was Barbara asking him to come home so they could watch "Out of Africa" together.

"Be right there," Joe said and he soon left, but he didn't leave his worries in the office. *What in the world would possess P12 to go there?* He kept wondering on the drive home and throughout the movie.

****

High atop San Vicente Mountain, Lupine-boy could smell many two-leg tracks. The lion gazed all around at the distant mountain peaks, the moonlit big water and the wide swaths of land that were illuminated by the dens of the two-legs.

Lupine-boy pointed his nose in every direction to pick up the scent of She-Paw; he had been roaming every canyon in the territory for many nights, but had not caught a sniff of her. He knew she might be in hiding—deep in a den if she was nursing kittens—but there was no essence of pregnancy on her when they last met. He had to find her, and so he kept moving in the sunrise direction.

Winding around clusters of two-leg dens, he soon came upon a green rolling meadow with shallow holes filled with sand. Moving closer, he was startled by a strange gurgling sound when a whoosh of water shot out of the ground and sprayed in all directions. It felt cool on his warm fur.

After a big climb, he came upon a large white two-leg den and saw the wide paths of the smoking beasts—white eyes running in one direction, red eyes in the other. He felt the danger. As he moved down the hill, he spotted a tunnel underneath the wide path with no beasts on it. He slowly approached the opening and could see trees on the other side. He cautiously entered. Then he felt a vibration and heard a rumbling above him and sprinted to the

89

*other side. There, he began following a winding path of the two-legs
that only once in a while, had a running beast on it.*

****

After the movie and a midnight snack of blueberry-topped
cheesecake, Joe said to his wife, "Hey, Barb. I can't stop thinking
about where P12 is heading. Do you mind if I take a quick run into
the office and see what's up with him?"

"Sure," she said, "but don't stay long, okay?"

When Joe got to the office, he was shocked to find P12 had
crossed the 405 by the Skirball Center and was still heading east
along Mulholland—apparently making his way in between the
hill-top homes.

"Jesus Christ!" He cursed out loud. Then he thought, *this guy
almost got killed crossing the freeway into the Santa Monica
Mountains...Why in the hell is he... Crazy cat,* he thought. *No,*
shaking his head, *crazy miracle cat.*

Joe watched his movements for hours, knowing that cougars
can cover up to 20 miles in one night. He watched as the lion
climbed in and out of Dixie, Franklin, and Coldwater Canyons,
still heading east. *It didn't figure,* Joe thought, *P13 was nowhere
around there.*

By two o'clock, when his eyes started drooping, Joe noted that
P12 had already reached Mount Olympus. Tired, Joe finally left
for home.

****

*Weaving in between even larger two-leg dens along the winding
path, Lupine-boy reached a flat area where the two-legs had earlier
rested their beasts. Off in the distance, he saw a scattering of
lighted dens among the small hills, and beyond them, a huge
wooded area with almost no lights. This could be where She-Paw
travelled to as he could see a large lake and smelled sweet water
and the presence of mule deer. This was a place lions could live.*

*But, like other lands of the two-legs, it also had a barrier—
more double-wide paths carrying their smoking beasts. Being late
into the night, he saw there were only a few beasts running in either
direction, so Lupine-boy knew he had to risk his life again if he
were to find She-Paw.*

*Loping down into the ravine, Lupine-boy found a dark narrow
path hanging above the wide paths of the beasts and he crossed
over and dashed into the woods. Thirsty, he quickly moved to the
sweet water, but was soon stopped by a tall webbed wall. Further
on, he found a small creek to quench his growing thirst. He no
sooner lifted his dripping jowl from the water, when he smelled a
lion. It was not She-Paw; it was a male. It seemed close. Lupine-boy
scurried up a hillock to gain a vantage point for an attack.*

It didn't come. Remaining silent and cautious, he gazed into the distance and could see the impossibly tall lighted dens of the two-legs stretching across the horizon. The place glimmered, and at the same time frightened him—too many two-legs caused him to shiver. Not smelling the lion any longer, Lupine-boy headed north toward the large open meadow. The wind blew up and across the hills, so if that male lion or She-Paw was here, he would catch their scents. When he got to the meadow, he found row upon row of odd-shaped stones, mostly at his shoulder height. Some stones had fresh flowers growing around them, so he was delighted to take in their sweet softness.

Moving further toward where the sun rose, he caught the strangest mix of animal scents he could not place. Off in the furthest corner of the woodland, he saw a broad cluster of two-leg dens. With his acute hearing, he picked up a cacophony of nocturnal night calls. Birdsong. Coyote howls. The wails and screeches of animals unknown to him. Sensing that it was getting closer to sunrise, he headed back south and west to where he first caught the scent of the male lion.

Soon the wind shifted and there it was again. The lion scent was getting strong, fast. The male lions were heading toward each other. On high alert and prepared for battle, Lupine-boy spotted him sliding along the chaparral. The other lion saw Lupine-boy in the same instant. They now crouched and moved slowly toward each other, and when they got within 20 body-lengths, the local lion let out a warning hiss, but he did not give Lupine-boy the snarl before the charge. For several moments, they simply stared at each other.

Lupine-boy sensed that the local lion was possibly a few years older, but in battle would be an even match. Both animals tried to gauge the others' being—where he came from, his family, and how he lived. But mostly, each tried to assess their opponents' will and passion to fight. Each lion knew the risks of injury or death, but which one would make the charge would depend on posturing, threats, and what each of them had to protect.

The first clue that Lupine-boy picked up was that the other lion also wore a leather collar, so he knew he had met the two-legs. The second scent clue was also a familiar one—he had a scent similar to his current enemy, Big-paw. Instinctively, Lupine-boy let out a low snarl. No response from the other lion. The last scent clue that he took in made his decision to fight or flee. He knew She-Paw's signature intimately and he could smell none of her on the fur of this lion. She-Paw was not in this territory. Lupine-boy walked away.

As he left, he turned around on occasion, making sure he wasn't followed, then headed back the same way he came—crossing above the path of the beasts. Dawn would soon be breaking, so he needed to gain elevation and find a more remote wooded area away from two-leg places. When he reached the ridge of the first canyon, he looked back and saw quick flashes of light, but heard no thunder. He could make out a gathering of two-legs with the lightning-makers in their paws. They were noisily aiming them at some large, flat white forms that were added to the hillside. When the lightning struck them, the two-legs whooped and clapped their paws. Lupine-boy could see the flashes light up a strange white line of sharp and round shapes standing tall, but they held no interest to him and he took off.

Lupine-boy found a secluded crevice deep in the first canyon that did not smell of two-legs or their coyotes. He would head back home at dusk to where he last saw She-Paw.

****

Joe had a fitful sleep that night, waking up often and wondering about P12. His journey so far seemed purposeful, so Joe didn't think he was just wandering or lost. Looking at the clock, he saw it was only 5:00 a.m., but he felt wide-awake. He quietly got out of bed so as not to wake Barbara, put on his clothes, and was just putting a note that he had written on his pillow, when Barb said, "Let me know how he's doing, okay?"

Sitting in front of the monitor, Joe kept shaking his head. P12 was now tracking steady in Runyon Canyon, apparently spending the day there. He was alright. Joe was relieved, but he was shocked even more to see where the lion travelled that night. P12 had continued his eastern trek, made another miracle crossing over the 101 into the Hollywood Hills, and then into Griffith Park. Then P12 journeyed north into the Forest Lawn Cemetery, came close to the zoo, and looped back south and spent time near the Hollywood Reservoir.

What the hell was he doing there? Joe kept asking himself, tapping on his desk trying to bring up the answer. "Holy shit!" he yelled out. "Where was P22?"

He clicked over to another screen and found where the famous "Hollywood Lion" had spent his night. In his mind, Joe could picture that *National Geographic* magazine front cover featuring the brave, lonely cougar. Sure enough, there were tracking points showing that the twenty-second cougar Joe had collared was in the same location as P12 at the same time. *Absolutely incredible,* Joe thought. *Did he actually meet him?* He wondered. *Did they fight?*

Griffith Park was a scant 4,000 acres, totally hemmed in by roads and millions of Angelenos. There was plenty of deer to eat, but no female lions with which to breed. Joe wondered if P12 somehow sensed that and left. Then Joe had another *Ah hah!* moment—P13 was hanging out in Mandeville Canyon for the last several days. Perhaps she's nursing kittens. *Yes!* P12 was trying to find her, couldn't pick up her scent trail and must have thought she headed east. *These crazy, unbelievable, magnificent animals,* he thought as he picked up the phone and gave Barb the news.

CHAPTER SEVENTEEN

When Carole got home late, the light was off in Reggie's room, so she peeked in and was relieved to find him asleep. When she got up in the morning and knocked on his door, there was no answer. When she opened the door, there was no Reggie.

He must have gone early to the Audubon with Isaac,' she thought. *'Yes,* his backpack was not there, nor was his hoodie or favorite pair of Merrill hikers, so she went to check the refrigerator. She found that the bag of string cheeses that she had bought was gone and the cabinet showed a space where the can of Pringles used to be. She tried Reggie's cell—no answer.

She called Isaac's house and his mom answered and told her that Isaac was still asleep, but she knew they talked on the phone last night. In a couple of minutes, Isaac picked up and told Carole they hadn't made any plans for today. When Carole asked him if he had any idea where he would have gone, Isaac told her he didn't, but confirmed that Reggie seemed pretty depressed.

Carole next called the Audubon, but they weren't open till one. She began to fear the worst. She knew he was upset over whatever happened with Jennifer and worried he might do something crazy. She redialed Reggie—no answer, so she left a message to please call her back.

Starting to panic, she sat down and wracked her brain. *'Jennifer,'* she thought, *she is the key to this,* but she didn't have her phone number, didn't have her last name. Could she remember the house number on Colonial Drive?' *'Yes! 1604,'* she remembered. Going onto Who.com, she paid the one dollar and cross-referenced to the phone number.

"Hello, Mrs. Peters, my name is Carole Youngblood and I'm so sorry to bother you, but my son Reggie knows your daughter and I'm wondering ..." she continued when Mrs. Peters cut her off.

"Listen, my daughter has nothing to do with your son anymore, why are you calling here?" she asked.

Not wanting to sound panicked like she had no idea where her son was, Carole said, "One of their mutual friends told me they may have talked on the phone recently and..."

Interrupting again, Mrs. Peters got testy, "I doubt that, but I'll ask my daughter right now."

The phone went silent for a few minutes, then Mrs. Peters came back and speaking for Jennifer said, "My daughter hasn't talked to your son, but she said he's probably trying to find some peace of mind—Goodbye!" and hung up.

'Bitch,' Carole thought as she stared at the phone. She tried Reggie again—no answer. Looking at the time, she realized she needed to get ready for her eleven a.m. shift and that would make things more difficult. She'd have to explain her predicament to the register line supervisor, and tell her she needs to make calls in the hopes of reaching her son.

On her way out, she knocked on the door of the elderly lady on the first floor whom she often saw sitting near the window at the entrance. She introduced herself and asked if she'd keep an eye out for a bushy-haired boy in a blue sweatshirt and gave her phone number in case she saw him return.

Carole tried calling Reggie from the Walmart parking lot at 11:55 to no avail. By one o'clock, Carole was getting so upset she was making mistakes at the register. She turned on her red assist lamp and the supervisor came over. She pleaded with him for a short phone break and he gave her a firm five minutes. First she called the Audubon and they assured her Reggie wasn't there but would call if he came. Worried that maybe Reggie turned angry and maybe was in jail again, she dialed that kind Captain at the Encino police department.

"Ah! Mrs. Youngblood, sure I remember you and your boy—how's your husband?" he asked.

"He's okay, but my son's been missing since this morning and I'm worried," she explained.

"Well I'm glad to report, he's not here, but funny thing, I was going to call you on Monday. I wanted to let you know that the store where Reggie threw the tubes, isn't going to press charges—I think they knew they weren't supposed to leave those tubes in the alley." "And," he continued, "we will not refer the matter to Juvenile Court because of the boy's, well...circumstances—you'd be glad to know."

"Thank you so much, Captain, I really appreciate that, could you help find my boy?"

"Well, he'll probably show up, but we need to wait twenty-four hours before we start a missing child search, but I can let all our patrols look out for him, what was he wearing?" he asked.

"His usual blue hoodie and a backpack," she said.

"And bushy black hair," he said.

"Thanks again, Captain," she feigned a chuckle, "you've got my number and I've got to get back to work."

By this time Carole was a total wreck wondering what could have happened to her son. She couldn't get a handle on it. Reggie had never done anything like this before. There must be something terribly wrong. Maybe he was going to hurt himself, or do something crazy. She wanted to call John, but he would panic too and couldn't help. Back at the cash register, while customers were paying, what Jennifer had said kept flashing into her mind; *'Peace of mind...maybe he was trying to find some peace of mind.'*

At a few minutes after one, there came a knock on Esther Hollyfield's door in the Town of Crestline, high in the San Bernardino Mountains. Her dog was raising a bigger than usual ruckus and when she opened the door, Hector flew out and into the arms of their old neighbor's boy.

"Reggie Youngblood, what on earth are you doing here?" the surprised woman asked as she scanned the driveway.

Mustering as much casualness as possible, Reggie answered, "Good to see you again, Mrs. Hollyfield, I'm going for a hike—get some peace of mind. School's out and besides, I wanted to see my old pal Hector."

As Hector continued to nuzzle Reggie and whine, Mrs. Hollyfield asked, "Where's your mom?"

Wanting to characterize the trip as matter of fact, Reggie answered, "She's at work, I took a bus from Encino to San Bernardino, then another to Crestline and walked the couple of miles to your place. How have you and Mr. Hollyfield been?"

"Oh, we're good, don't get around much anymore though," she replied, then asked, "How's your dad doing? Coming home pretty soon I suspect?"

"He's good," Reggie answered, "he'll be back at the end of the summer. Would you mind if I take Hector with me up on the Ridgeline trail for a couple of hours?"

"Sure," she said, and then asked, "You'll be taking the bus back then?"

"Yep!" he replied then asked if she could fill up his water bottle, thanked her when she did, waved and headed toward the trailhead.

As soon as they started to climb and take in the woods, the attitudes and demeanors of both human and animal changed. With the rounding of each bend in the trail, the noise of the cars faded and the clean air became scented with leaves and bark and earth. Hector, although eleven years old now and much chunkier, romped over the ground like a puppy. He would stop every few yards, nose to the ground and take in animal smells that he remembered and still excited him.

With each step, Reggie became more attuned to his surroundings. He noticed how the sunny southern face of a granite boulder held blue star-shaped lichen and in its shadow, laid mounds of dark green moss. He caught site of a Stellar's Jay in the boughs above with its shimmering dark blue velvet crown. The bird made its *Shek! Shek!* call which seemed to Reggie to say *Yes! Yes!* As Reggie took in the whole of this tranquil world, the people and pieces of that mixed up world dropped away. He had long ago shut off his cell phone, leaving messages to linger. He wanted to get completely away from people. The trail ahead of him wouldn't have disappointments along the way or any barriers he couldn't walk around.

He knew the trail well. He knew when and where his destination—Ridgeview Rock, would appear; so he simply looked ahead, one sure step at a time. After climbing steadily for over an hour, Reggie heard Hector yelp and jump onto a side trail to the spot he and his dog and his family knew well. Ridgeview Rock provided an almost one hundred and eighty degree view of the mountains and valleys and forest canopy. At some six thousand feet, you could scan the horizon and feel you both commanded and connected with the planet.

Sitting with feet dangling over the rock ledge, Reggie and Hector shared the snack of cheese and chips, and he gave the rest of the water to his companion—chuckling as Hector's tongue stretched far into the bottle for the last lick. Resting, Reggie closed his eyes, but did not sleep. He heard the soft whisper of the wind through the pine boughs and felt it sweep the sweat off his skin. He thought of how the wind carried life to the forest animals; the scent of food, the fragrance of a mate and, the pricking odor of danger. *The wind in the woodlands carry me to another place,* he thought, *like I am home.*

He wondered how many varieties of trees there were and how the Douglas firs overhead had only one goal in their lives—to survive and grow to do one thing that was asked of it—be a tree. Sure, he thought, the tree breathed in carbon dioxide and gave us oxygen and housed birds and fed squirrels and played a role for all, but it was just being a Douglas fir.

As Reggie thought of his place among the trees, a picture popped into this mind. It was from that favorite picture book. It was the page where all the woodland animals stood in the forest and were looking out at him. *Looking at me to protect them,* he thought. He even remembered some of the words in that book, something like; 'I know the sap that runs through the trees as I know the blood that runs through my veins. The earth does not belong to us, we all belong to the earth.'

Hector put his head into Reggie's lap. Reggie stroked it a few times and soon drifted off to sleep. He found himself hiking with Hector, but not in the woods. Before him the trees morphed into strange looking cactus. They stood tall in the sand and their prickly arms pointed in all directions. In the distance he saw what looked like a village. He moved closer.

He could make out a circle of ghostly shapes dancing and he heard chanting, like the drone of some drunken men. Smoke wafted their way and stung Hector's nose. He backed off, whined and cowered in fear. But Reggie felt drawn to the people and took Hector's collar in hand and pulled him toward the ceremony.

As he neared, he could see native peoples. The older men who were chanting, wore long capes made of hair. The younger men, dressed only in loincloths, were digging into a fire pit. At first, nobody noticed Reggie as they removed large charred spikes from the pit and handed them to the women who stripped them of their outer layer and placed the flesh in a large bowl.

One old woman looked toward Reggie and beckoned for him to come. It was as though she knew Reggie was watching, but it seemed impossible, because she must have been blind. She had no pupils and both orbs were clouded over in blue and did not move. Hector growled and Reggie felt scared.

But the old woman smiled and held out her hands and gestured for Reggie to give her a hug. He went to her. She embraced him like he was one of her family, her people. Reggie felt comforted. She spoke, "Thank you for coming to say goodbye, Reggie."

Reggie pulled back, "How did you know my name?"

"You are my grandson," she said.

"But, but I never met you?"

"Ha!" she laughed as she pointed to his chest, "I am here, I am with you in your blood and your spirit—you do know me."

Reggie felt something stir inside him and he asked, "Why am I here, Grandma?"

"I wanted to see you before you left home on your journey to your new place on earth."

"Why am I going?"

"You are going to tell your new people not to forget us and our old ways."

"How will I do this?"

She pointed to his chest, "When you become a man, you will know. You have the gift inside you. The blood and the spirit of a great shaman who was your Grandfather."

"When do I become a man?"

"When you are one with the earth and the sky and you listen. If you watch, a powerful spirit will come to guide you. You must follow it." The old woman then gave Reggie a nudge to the arm and said, "Goodbye, Reggie. Take your dog and go now."

****

Reggie woke and heard Hector's bark at his side. Following his dog's stare down into a narrow ravine, he spotted a small group of mule deer standing alongside a dry creek bed. The deer were looking back up in their direction, ears swiveling to identify the sound. Soon the deer went back to their foraging and Reggie thought how content those animals seemed. Unlike humans with complex relationships, the deer had no more expectations for each other than to be a deer.

As they watched the does move away with the buck in the lead and a yearling following, he thought how much simpler it was to be a wild animal. *A wild animal's destiny,* Reggie thought, *was born within them. We screwed up humans have to create it. Or, maybe find it,* was his last thought as he got up and told Hector, "Time to go home, boy."

Heading back down the trail, his mind played slow motion pictures of Jennifer running into her house. Then he caught broken glimpses of that strange dream he had up on the ridge. *I never had a grandma,* he thought, *it must have been my Dad I was dreaming about.* He shook away those pictures only to hear his mom's angry voice upon his return. *Reality,* Reggie thought as he found himself detouring around a muddy section of the trail. He glanced down and abruptly stopped and stared. There were some large and very fresh paw prints. He bent over and recognized the four asymmetrical front toes of a mature *Puma concolor.* Snapping to maximum alertness, he did a three sixty scan and spotted Hector fifty yards away moving fast through the scrub.

Adrenalin pumping, Reggie yelled at the dog to stop and come, Hector hesitated; looking at him as if to ask why he would stop him from this excellent scent trail. A second call to come brought him back. Reggie pivoted slowly in a circle, eyes penetrating every rock outcropping and bush, but could not spot the animal. He remembered reading how rare it is for a human to ever see a mountain lion in the wild, but that it was much more common for the lion to be right there smelling, hearing and watching you.

Reggie felt for sure the lion was near and wished he could see him. Although he had felt an initial jolt of fear, he was no longer afraid for himself. He thought the lion's prey might be nearby, but he knew he was not the lion's prey. He also knew the lion was more afraid of him, but he still kept Hector close as he moved down the trail.

At the end of the trail and approaching his old neighborhood, Reggie watched in surprise as Hector ran to the door of his old house, not the Hollyfield's. Then Hector sat down and waited for Reggie.

"No, boy," Reggie corrected him and went over and patted his head, "that's not our home anymore, come on."

Heading down the road to the Hollyfield's, Reggie's thoughts turned sad about having to leave his confused friend Hector and the old place. But soon he saw Hector run and bark at the Hollyfield's door, and reality reappeared.

Mrs. Hollyfield opened the door and with an anxious look on her face yelled, "Reggie! perfect timing, your mom just called—she's on the phone."

Going into the house, Reggie hoped his mom wasn't going to take a fit when he picked up. On the other end, Carole was so relieved she found him and knowing that the Hollyfields were near, she did not take a total fit.

"Reggie, are you alright?" she asked.

"Fine, mom," he answered and added, "had a nice hike with Hector."

"Why didn't you tell me where you were going?" she asked, trying to hold back her frustration and anger.

"I thought you'd say I couldn't go and besides, I just wanted to be by myself."

"Jesus, Reggie, you can't just take off like that without letting me know," she said, but feeling herself getting mad, she added, "Did you get the peace of mind you were looking for?"

"I did, actually," he answered.

"Well, that's good Reggie," she continued, "you really had me worried you know, when I see you you'll get a piece of *my* mind!"

"Yeah, I'm sorry," he replied.

"Alright," she said, "I can pick you up around 7:45 after work."

"No, mom, you're totally not getting it. I'm going to get home on my own—the busses will get me there before you do," he argued.

"Okay," she said "see you then, can you put Mrs. Hollyfield on the phone for a minute?"

As Reggie handed her the phone, he said, "I better get going, Mrs. Hollyfield—good to see you again." He gave Hector a neck rub and waved goodbye out the door.

Staring out of the bus window on the winding, tree-lined road down to the valley floor, Reggie descended into a reflective mood. He looked down at the freeways and roads that wrapped around and choked the houses tight together. He saw how the gray-yellow smog encased the land and knew that the high cleansing winds were not there to carry it away.

He saw the cars following each other on the same path, but alone with their separate destinations. The contrast between nature and civilization was huge, Reggie thought. When he was in nature, everything came together and he felt somehow complete. When he looked at the city he saw isolation and felt he was being torn apart. Reggie then tried to do a 'brain dump' of all the crap that had troubled him there. He tried to carry his mind back to the woods, but he couldn't.

Soon the bus pulled into the San Bernardino station and getting off the bus he stepping around a couple of homeless guys and their shopping cart possessions. He bought his ticket to Encino and sat down on the furthest bench to wait for the bus and called Jennifer.

"Hi, Reggie, how are you?"

"I'm better... had a long hike. Thought I'd say goodbye. When's your flight?"

"Nine-thirty and I'm really getting nervous."

"How come?"

"I'm afraid about what I'll find at the school and about myself. I'm sorry, Reggie for dumping all this on you."

"That's okay. I know how messed up life can be sometimes. You need to sort things out."

"Thanks, Reggie, for being so understanding."

"You know, Jennifer, I was thinking. Remember when you told me you knew when you needed to become an artist?"

"Yeah?"

"Maybe your true nature will come out. Like your biology will tell you who you are."

After a long pause, she said, "Reggie that is so smart. You think that will happen?"

"I dunno, but maybe if you get involved with other people, you'll find out what's inside of you."

"God, Reggie you are a great friend. I won't forget you."

"I hope not," he said. He hesitated before continuing, not wanting to tell her what he truly hoped for. Finally, he said, "Can we stay in touch?"

"Of course! We'll talk on the phone and see each other on Facebook."

"Remember, you're going to critique my art," she said.

"I will. Gotta go, my bus just pulled up. Have a good trip."

On the ride home, Reggie was exhausted, mentally and physically, and he slept most of the way home. Picking up a double bacon-burger at Carl Jr.'s on the walk home, the smell from the bag and the twitch of hunger persuaded Reggie to consume it in four bites. When he got home he took a long shower and watched TV lying on the couch. When his mom came home, she sat down and hugged him for too long.

"Come on, mom," Reggie yelled, "I can't breathe."

"You scared the ever-loving hell out of me, why didn't you call?" she asked in a huff.

"I didn't want to talk to anybody," Reggie said trying to minimize the issue.

"Why didn't you text then, so I'd at least know you were okay?" she asked.

"I dunno I just didn't want to," he responded.

"I'm your mother, for God's sake, can't you tell me why?" she persisted.

Hesitating, knowing his mom wouldn't give up, he finally shouted out, "That's why, mother, I have to be more than your son. I'm just tired of everybody in my life pulling me this way and that way." Grabbing his breath he continued, "My only two friends are leaving town and I'm going to have the shittiest summer any kid ever had—is that enough reason to want to get away from it all?"

Reggie could see his mom's face change from frustrated anger to piercing sadness; her next words were, "But you could have told me that."

Reggie came back, "Look, I'm sorry, Mom. It's not your fault that I don't have any friends. I know you worry about me, but I'm going to be sixteen soon and have to learn how to handle things myself—I need to be my own man."

Carole sensed that her son, just then, had reached a milestone in his development and although it scared her, she knew he had to go there. She thought maybe that journey and hike on his favorite trail, might have had a good effect.

Reggie could see by his mother's attentive look that she seemed to understand him and said, "That hike with Hector helped me clear my head—helped me see things better."

"That's great, Reggie," his mom said as she ruffled his hair, stood up and did her finger snap, "Sometimes good things happen just like that." Reggie smiled for the first time at her caring face. Then he wondered if he could ever find a way to spend more time in nature. Maybe there he could discover what is in the wind for him.

PART TWO

CHAPTER EIGHTEEN

"Reggie!" his mom called following a knock on his bedroom door, "we've got that appointment at Big Brother's at eleven."

"Yeah, Yeah, I'll be up," Reggie responded with sleepy enthusiasm.

On the drive to the office, Reggie started wondering what he was getting into and asked, "Tell me again why we're doing this—I thought it was only if I was expelled?"

"No, Reg," his mom answered. "The guidance counselor thought a mentor would be a good idea and both dad and I think it could help."

"Help with what?" Reggie asked.

"As far as I understand it, these big brothers are supposed to be more like friends."

"I don't need any more friends," Reggie snapped back, feeling angry at himself; never being able to keep friends.

"Let's just take it one step at a time, okay?" Carole tried reasoning, "they told me this candidate shared a lot in common, and maybe you'll like him."

Reggie gave his mom an accepting shrug as they pulled into the office parking lot.

Stepping into the office, they were met by an older, pretty obese guy with a bald head and a bowtie and Reggie thought, 'no way!'

"I'm Bill Connors, the Director," he said, "welcome Mrs. Youngblood. This must be Reggie."

"Hi," Reggie squeaked out, while he shook his hand, relieved he wasn't the big brother.

Moving to a conference room, Bill explained how the process of matching and having 'brothers' worked and that after you meet and get to know each other a bit, it's up to the boy if he wants to go on a trial period of weekly meet ups with his 'big.'

Then Bill asked Reggie, "So, Reggie, if you want to give it a try, I'll invite him in and let the two of you chat—is that okay with you?"

"I suppose," Reggie answered with a 'nothing to lose' shrug.

When Bill returned to the room followed by the big brother, both Carole's and Reggie's eyes popped and jaws dropped to the conference table. It was Joe Sartor. Reggie's face lit up like the time he first saw a sunrise over Ridgeview Rock.

"Hi, Reggie." Joe said with a huge knowing smile.

"Hi Joe," Reggie said with a matching wide smile.

As Carole sat looking amazed, both Reggie and Joe rushed around the conference table to shake hands.

"Good to see you again, Reggie, and you too, Mrs. Youngblood," Joe said with a two-handed handshake.

"Seriously? You'd be my big brother?" Reggie asked.

"If you'll have me, I'd love to," Joe responded, "this way you can do volunteer work at the agency and we can also have free fun time together."

As Carole came to realize what was happening and saw the two together, her face changed from dumbstruck to awestruck. Her gaze got broken by Mr. Connor's declaration.

"I guess we got a match!" he said as he gestured all to sit. Reggie, still beaming, moved around and sat next to Joe.

"Sure looks like it," Carole added.

"Well," Mr. Connors continued, "then we just need to sign these papers and we'll be all set."

"How about a hike?" Joe asked, a moment later.

"Great!" Reggie answered.

"How about Saturday, Topanga Canyon—there's a lot of good trails there; I can pick you up at 9:00 a.m.?"

"Cool," Reggie agreed.

Carole said to Joe, "Thank you so much for doing this. I can't believe how this came together"

"Me too," Joe replied, "When I first met Reggie, I sensed we had something in common."

After they completed the paperwork, Joe put both Reggie's and his mom's cell phone numbers into his smart phone and then filled Reggie in on what to bring for the hike.

"I've got a good pair of Merrill boots—Ventilators," Reggie offered.

"Me too," Joe said, "They're the best for canyon hikes."

As they headed out the door and into the parking lot, Reggie asked, "How's P12?"

"We found him alive, but sick. We treated him and we're hopeful," Joe answered as he waved from his car door, "I'll fill you in when we meet, okay?"

"Okay, see you Saturday," Reggie replied.

After Carole pulled the car onto the street and into traffic, she asked, "What do you think, Reggie?"

"What do *you* think, Ma?" he answered, rolling his eyes.

"I guess"...she said snapping her fingers... "good fortune can come to you just like that." Then she asked, "Who in the heck is P12?"

"Our favorite mountain lion," he answered.

On Monday, starting his first week of summer vacation, Reggie was a bit more hopeful, having had the good fortune of connecting with Joe. But was it just luck, Reggie wondered? He remembered the time when he was hiking alone on the Ridgeview trail, when he thought he heard Joe's voice. *It wasn't like he was there talking,* Reggie thought, *but when you were in nature and got quiet, you felt more open to others and to new ideas. It was like that karma thing Jennifer said can come to you during meditation. Or, maybe like in a vision quest?* he wondered. With the thought of Jennifer, he realized he should call her to see how she was doing in Atlanta.

He got voice mail when he first called, but within a half an hour, she called back.

"Hi, Reggie," she said, "How are you?"

"I'm good," he replied, "How about you?"

"This Sayler's art school is really cool Reggie, I just got out of my photography class where we saw a movie about Vivian Maier, the street photographer— her images of people were so intimate." Jennifer must have realized she was getting carried away, so she asked Reggie what he was up to.

"Not much," Reggie answered, "Kinda boring actually."

"How are you getting along with your dad?" she asked, then realized that probably wasn't the best question to ask.

"Huh! Another bummer," Reggie answered, "My mom told me he got a concussion from a land mine exploding under his Humvee, but he didn't lose a leg or anything."

"I'm sorry, Reggie. Hope he'll be okay."

Not wanting to continue on that conversation thread, Reggie asked, "Where are you living?"

"Ho! I'm in a dorm and I've got these two cool roommates," she said laughing, "Terri is crazy but really nice. She's from Miami and Samantha is a farm girl from Macon who knits these voodoo wall hangings—they're a lot of fun. This school is filled with creative weirdos like me."

"Great," Reggie said, then not wanting her to think he was totally bummed out added, "Remember Joe? The guy who came to our Biology class? He's now mentoring me in Big Brothers and we're going on a hike together Saturday—I'm really excited."

"Sounds great. Reggie?" she said with a lot of commotion in the background, "I'm heading into my ceramics class now, gotta go...let's talk some evening, okay? Bye."

Reggie felt kind of like dissed by Jennifer with a little envy thrown in but it was softened up by his happiness for her. *I at least had Saturday with Joe coming up,* he thought.

On Saturday, Joe was at their door promptly at 9:00 a.m., and although Reggie wanted to head out right away, his mom wanted to chit- chat. She even offered Joe coffee, which he declined. After Joe filled Carole in on their hiking plans and when they'd be back, she gave up on her need to know more about him. She knew she'd still be at home when they got back and they could talk more then.

On the drive down to Topanga Canyon, Joe initiated most of the conversation. He already knew a fair amount of Reggie's background based on the agency's interview with his mom, but he wanted to hear Reggie's thoughts.

"Your mom seems really nice," Joe asked, "How's your dad doing?"

"Better, I guess."

"He'll be home soon, right?"

"Yeah, soon," Reggie said sharply, thinking his dad didn't know about Joe.

"You just moved to Encino recently, right?" Joe asked.

"A few months ago," Reggie answered in a sour tone.

"I take it you don't like it much." Joe asked—knowing Reggie used to live up in the San Bernardino Mountains.

"I hate it!" Reggie answered.

At this point in the conversation, Joe figured he better try a different approach. Big Brothers told him Reggie tended to be shy and had some trouble in school, but he sensed more was going on with him. *Maybe he just wanted to put all that stuff behind him and get on a new path,* Joe thought to himself.

"It's a tough adjustment to make," Joe offered, "but things tend to work out with time. Bet you're glad school's over."

"You got that right," Reggie nodded in agreement.

"Well, I'll tell you Reggie," Joe explained, "I've given a lot of talks in schools and I never met a kid like you."

Reggie perked up and said, "Thanks, I like Biology and your talk was the coolest," then added, "Were you going to tell me about P12?"

Joe then filled Reggie in on finding P12 seriously infected with the mange and possible life-threatening complications. As he described how bad P12 looked when they re-captured him and the medications they gave him, he could see worry coming to Reggie's face. Joe told him that P12 was ranging pretty well, so now they were hoping a trip camera photo might show he was in recovery.

"What did the blood tests reveal?" Reggie asked.

Joe looked at him in total surprise and said, "That's what I mean by very perceptive Reggie; that is the next important question alright."

"The blood tests revealed that P12 had traces of multiple anti-coagulant rat poisons. The poison in bait traps that homeowner's innocently put out to kill rats. It moves up the food chain as raccoons and bobcats prey upon sickly rats and get poisoned themselves. Then these poisons compromise the animal's immune systems, making them susceptible to mange."

Reggie asked, "You think P12 ate a raccoon or a coyote, and got poisoned himself?"

"Probably," Joe answered, "you know we found two other dead mountain lions that had mange and poison residue in their blood."

"I hope P12 is okay," Reggie said with his face turning grim, "People should know about this." As soon as he said that, he thought about how he didn't realize there were toxins in fluorescent tubes, then added, "People sometimes don't know how their actions can affect others and their environment."

"For sure," Joe added, amazed at Reggie's grasp and determination.

Joe's jeep pulled into the park entrance. Getting out, Joe noticed that Reggie must have forgotten his water bottle. Reaching behind the seat, he grabbed a box and pulled out an olive-drab insulated water bottle with a US Park Agency logo on it.

"I brought you a little gift," Joe said, "we can fill it at the fountain."

"Thanks," Reggie said, with a little embarrassment but a lot of appreciation.

Before they got to the trailheads, Joe said, "Let me show you my all-time favorite tree in the Santa Monicas—a huge California Valley Oak."

Situated on a hillock, the canopy of the oak enveloped the hill with its three-story high gnarled branches. Joe pointed out the bark, with its distinctive alligator hide surface and said, "The Valley Oak species is the largest oak in North America. I'm guessing this guy is at least 300 years old; growing here way before the Spanish arrived." Joe continued, "And some grow to be 600 years old. See these cluster growths in the branches—they're called galls and they provide homes for a tiny wasp." Then Joe grabbed a leaf and rubbed it between his hands, gestured toward Reggie and said, "Smell."

"Whoa! It smells so fresh," Reggie said with a big smile.

"Yeah," Joe said, "its leaves are known for their woodsy fragrance—kind of the essence of the outdoors."

Reggie was so blown away by the sensory experience of the tree, he sheepishly asked Joe, "Think I could take a couple of leaves home with me?"

"I'm sure the tree wouldn't mind," Joe said as he picked three leaves, patted the branch and handed them to Reggie.

Reggie was enthralled by Joe's knowledge and love of the tree. He thanked him then asked him, "How do you learn all these things?"

"By caring and studying, I guess," he said, "nature can teach us a lot about life."

When they got to the sign marking the trailheads, Joe said, "Let's take the Musch trail—lots of varied terrain and at this time of day we might run across some of my favorite woodland creatures."

The trail did some nice dips and turns over and around mostly Manzanita with its red boney branches. All of a sudden Joe looked down toward the end of a meadow and pointed.

"Look! There they are," Joe said all excited.

Reggie could see nothing really except for a huge rising cloud of dust, not unlike you'd see in the city when they used a leaf-blower on the sidewalk.

"You mean the dust?" Reggie asked.

"Yeah, they're right there," Joe said. "Move slowly, and keep the meadow grass to your right—we don't want to startle them."

Reggie looked puzzled as he followed Joe. He felt like they were stalking a white Rhino in Africa. *It couldn't possibly be a mountain lion,* he thought.

At the end of the meadow, Joe crouched down and put his index finger to his lips. They slowly peered around the high grass and saw what was happening. Spread all over the ground amidst a tornado of flying sand and dust, were the funniest looking little birds you would ever see—all taking a communal dust bath.

Dozens and dozens of adults and their brown-spotted babies were flapping their wings like landing helicopters. Instead of the sound of the whirling blades, the birds were all making this high *'Pip Pip'* sound like children screaming on a playground. Reggie couldn't help smiling as he watched the curved two inch long plume on the top of their heads bounce as they shook, rattled and rolled. Joe and Reggie looked at each other and both let out a belly laugh. The birds took that as an offense and they flushed up in the air then down again into the meadow.

The birds were funnier than anything Reggie ever saw on TV. "What were they?"

"The Valley Quail," Joe answered, "Our California State Bird."

"Heard of them," Reggie said, "But never saw them before."

"They're quite the social birds too," Joe added, "They hang out like an extended family. A male will travel around with two or more females and their chicks in a covey and he even helps care for the young."

"They're really cool," Reggie said as he contemplated the quail's more communal life compared to the often more separate family lives of humans.

The rest of the morning hike was just like that. Joe showed Reggie lots of interesting things about plant and animal life along the way, including geological formations, and even pointing out some early petroglyphs made by the Chumash peoples. Reminded of his many earlier hikes with his dad, Reggie remembered how much his father taught him about nature. Then the wounded deer hunting incident shot into his mind.

Joe was different, Reggie thought and toward the end of the trail he asked Joe, "Do you hunt?"

Joe told him, "I don't, why do you ask?"

Reggie paused before answering as he believed hunting was cruel, but did not want Joe to think his dad was a bad guy. His dad, Reggie thought, looked at nature as a place to play in and use—not to protect.

"Just wondering," he said.

Joe wondered if maybe Reggie was asking about his dad, who probably was a hunter.

"Hunters actually, can be some of our best allies in protecting the environment," Joe declared, "They love nature too and don't want it to disappear either." He continued, "Careful game management can also help maintain balance in nature. Overpopulation of deer, for instance, can mean starvation when food sources dwindle. Car accidents can kill the animal and humans too."

Reggie remembered how when his dad even shot a partridge or a rabbit, he would thank the dead animal. He'd bless it by placing some grass in its mouth. *At least he kept that Indian tradition,* he thought. Feeling a lot better about his dad, Reggie said, "That's a good point, and it reminds me of the role mountain lions play."

"Good point, Reggie," Joe offered as they reached the end of the trail and headed to the restrooms.

On the drive home, Reggie was feeling that some of the broken apart pieces of his life were beginning to come together.

"Did you enjoy the hike?" Joe asked.

"It was great," he answered, "Thanks for taking me."

"I enjoyed it a lot too," Joe answered, "how about next Saturday, after you do some work for me at the agency, we can do the Trippet Ranch hike."

"That would be great," Reggie responded and paused a bit before he said "Joe, can I ask you a question?"

"Shoot," he said.

"Why are you doing this?"

Reflecting for a moment Joe offered, "I got to a point in my career when I wanted to give back, I guess; maybe pass along my knowledge and love of nature to others—it's a gift my dad gave to me."

"That's a cool gift," Reggie said as though he just received it.

On the drive home they chatted about plans for the talk about public rodenticide use and how Joe would send Reggie a photo of P12 as soon as they got one.

When they got to the apartment, Carole had already made one of Reggie's favorites for lunch, tortilla soup, hoping Joe would join them. Joe agreed and the men ate like they hadn't in days. Carole noticed how glowing happy Reggie seemed with his new friend and how Joe treated him with such respect, letting him gush on about the trail and the discoveries they shared. She found out that Joe and his wife had been trying to have their own children and figured that must be a reason why he joined Big Brothers.

Carole couldn't help but compare Joe to her husband, looking alike and all, but their relationship was so different. Joe and Reggie were more like equals, listening and enjoying each other's stories and perspectives. As the two of them talked, laughed and high-fived, Carole wished to God John would listen better to Reggie and be more considerate of his feelings. She vowed to herself that when John got home, she would find the courage to get him to soften his approach with Reggie, without hardening his own feelings. *Damn,* she told herself, *I have to tell him about Joe before he comes home.*

After lunch, Reggie asked his mom if he could attend Joe's lecture next month on the dangers of rat poisons and Carole said yes. Reggie told his mom about the nice gift Joe had given him. Carole said she had seen the new water bottle. Reggie said, 'I really meant this gift," as he pulled out an oak leaf from his pocket, rubbed it between his hands and asked her to smell it.

CHAPTER NINETEEN

As the weeks of summer moved on, Reggie became more attached to Joe, further absorbed by nature and totally focused on mountain lions. He not only hiked with Joe every week, but he spent three-to four hours a week in the office as a volunteer. Reggie became adept at monitoring and recording the movements of the collared cougars and ravaged the agency's library—taking home every book about *Puma concolor*. The only thing Reggie couldn't do was to go out on field trips with Joe due to agency liability issues, but he told Joe one day he would.

When he had a break from volunteering or hiking, he thought about Jennifer—wondering if she was sorting things out. A part of him deeply hoped she would somehow get over her confusion and come back to him. A more realistic part thought, *you lame, naïve jerk, she's not for you*. Then, he got busy again, thanks to Joe. And despite being mentally caught in the lives of lions, something was still missing in his life. Something in his heart.

One afternoon, Joe asked Reggie if he'd like to get more involved than just attending tomorrow's public forum on banning rat poisons. Reggie jumped at the chance.

On the morning of the forum, Joe asked, "Since you know this material so well, how about if *you* present the portion about wild animal exposure?"

"Seriously?" Reggie asked.

"Seriously!" Joe answered.

Together they quickly went over the slides and photographs for that section. When the smattering of citizens and government officials showed up, Reggie wasn't at all nervous. Joe led off with the scientific segment and could see that Reggie's troubled issues with school and his dad were melting away. Reggie was energized and excited.

Finally the slide of an emaciated rat came up, and Joe introduced Reggie and gave him a nod. Reggie started, "So, once the rat ingests the poison, the anticoagulant causes internal bleeding and the rat dies a slow death within several days." Reggie could tell most of the audience nodded with satisfaction about getting rid of vermin.

"But unfortunately, many other small animals can also ingest the poisons that people put out." Then, slide after slide came up with photos of live, then dead woodchucks and cute chipmunks and the audience started letting out sad-sounding *oohs*.

"Even animals closer to home," Reggie proclaimed. As heart-rending photos of dead cats and dogs flashed on the screen, Reggie said, "Our pets too can fall victim."

"Then there's the secondary poisoning," Reggie continued as a slide of a dead raccoon came up, "as other wildlife eat the dead or dying rat for food. Here's a photo of a young mountain lion who became infected with mange and dehydration and died because of eating a dead rat."

By this time, the audience was wrapped in Reggie's hands. He could see they were taken in by every word he spoke. Reggie was hooked.

After the presentation, many citizens came to the microphone and spoke up for banning such rodenticides. A government guy—a Mr. Callahan, came over and congratulated Reggie and asked him if he could attend another important meeting on the subject.

Reggie first looked at Joe who smiled then said, "Um. Sure."

Joe looked at Reggie and felt he had just discovered his mission in life.

****

Reggie was feeling much better these days about his summer. His mom noticed how happy Reggie seemed. She too was in better spirits these days; despite the drag of two jobs and worry about John's health and return home. John told Carole for weeks now that the doctor's said he's almost fully recovered, but until Carole saw him and could be with him, she wasn't sure. The good news was that the Army would release him early from active duty and he would be home sometime before the summer's end. But Carole also worried that John did not know that Reggie was researching cougars. She had promised John to get him off that 'silly stuff'.

When Reggie first heard his dad would be home sooner, he said, "That's great, mom, have you told him about Joe yet? It's been weeks now and I don't want Dad to get, y'know, jealous."

"He's aware that you were doing a trial with a mentor," she said, hoping that would say enough.

"Mom, that's not enough," Reggie said, "you need to tell him I'm volunteering and studying more about mountain lions—I'm totally worried he'll freak out. He wanted me to quit bothering with them remember?"

"I know, I will," she said, knowing she shouldn't put if off any longer, but was fearful of John's reaction. She knew first-hand about John's jealous rages. She remembered how much it hurt when he accused her of cheating.

"You know if you keep putting it off," Reggie said, "dad may have a worse reaction when he gets home."

"I know, Reggie," she said," "I will next time we talk," realizing that Reggie's relationship with Joe and his dreams of the future could be in jeopardy unless she somehow smoothed things over with John.

****

The very next Saturday when Reggie was off hiking with Joe, Carole summoned the courage to call John and come clean about Reggie's new interest. She knew she had to get it out right away. John got angry right away.

"You mean that's the guy who was filling his head with that silly shit about mountain lions?" John shouted into the phone. "I can't believe this after you told me you'd get Reggie off that nonsense."

"John, please! It was just random that Joe was qualified and selected by the agency as a candidate to mentor Reggie and you should know that he has never been happier and more directed in his life."

"You're letting a stranger direct his life?" John asked with so much anger it wasn't a question. "I'm his father!"

"It's not that at all," she tried to explain, "Reggie's finding ...finding his own way."

"Shit, Carole," he yelled, "I didn't risk my life in this fucking war to hear my son's finding his way back into the woods like a dammed Indian."

Carole wanted to tell him he wasn't being fair to Reggie, but she heard the anger in his voice. She knew the jealous anger from before and she was scared for her and for Reggie, so she went mute.

"Carole, are you still there?" he asked.

"Yes, John."

"We'll have to straighten things out when I get home," he said in a more measured tone, "I need you to work with me on this."

"Carole?"

She held her breath. One part of her wanted to tell John to think more about Reggie's needs. The other part felt for John's circumstances. She knew she could not sway him now. *At least,* she thought to herself, *she told him about Joe now and would have other chances to explain things.*

"Carole?"

"Yes, John we'll talk."

****

When Reggie returned later that day from the hike and his mom had returned from work, the first thing he asked her was whether or not she talked to dad about Joe.

"Yes, I told him, Reggie."

"Good, what did he say?"

"Well, let's say he was less than enthusiastic," she replied to downplay his reaction.

"By the look on your face, Ma, he was more than angry. Did you stand up to him?"

"I told him that Joe was helping you."

"Was he okay with that?"

Carole could not come up with the words.

"You mean everything doesn't work out with just a snap of your fingers?" Reggie said.

"I will keep trying to work on him, I promise."

"You know, ma, I'm not going to let dad stand in my way anymore," he said walking out of the kitchen, leaving Carole standing there with nothing left to say.

****

Although Reggie was increasingly worried about his dad's return, he was determined to go his own way. He was, for now, dealing with that worry by immersing himself in what he was not going to give up. Reggie's favorite research subject was; Indigenous American Peoples and the Mountain Lion. He became very knowledgeable about Shamanism and Animism, where Native Americans believed that all nature is alive and every object and creature has its own soul.

Reggie knew many that tribes of the Southwest considered a vision quest a rite of passage into manhood for boys his age. A Shaman or Medicine Man would help the boy prepare for a journey. He'd go alone into the wilderness to connect with his inner self, just like Jennifer told him how mediation helped her. In a vision quest, he could either have an actual encounter with a Power Animal or have a vision of him; who would then become his guide and guardian.

****

Reggie knew he had to make his own vision quest. It would give him the strength to be his own man. He would talk to Joe.

On their next Saturday hike on the Backbone trail in Pacific Palisades, Reggie came right out with it. "Joe, would you help me prepare for making a vision quest?" he asked.

Turning around on the trail to face Reggie, Joe gave him a big smile and gestured toward some big boulders where they could sit and talk.

116

"Been reading about Shamanism, ay?" Joe asked, "Sure I'll help you but I'm no Medicine Man. What brought this on?"

"Nothing really," Reggie answered, "except this feeling that nature can be a bigger force in my life." Although he was thinking more about personal power.

"I don't know exactly how I can help, but don't you have any relatives on your dad's side who are more familiar with tribal customs who could guide you?"

"Nah. That's just it. Both my dad's parents are dead and didn't have any brothers or sisters. I never even knew another Indian, even back at my old school in the mountains."

"Yeah. It's really too bad," Joe offered, "Living in the city with all the pressures of school and growing up. What kid today has got the time and interest to connect with his family roots—computer games and action heroes grab all the attention."

"I care about it. Only problem is my Dad wouldn't be too happy if he knew about it, but he doesn't have to know if my Mom won't tell him."

"Are you thinking about the whole ritual? ...that total solitude thing ...the three-day fast ... the sweat lodge and all?"

"Nah!" Reggie replied, "My mom probably wouldn't go for that, but like an overnight by myself, to see what happens—I think if you support it, my mom will go along. I bought a guidebook and it covers the basics anyway."

"We can try, but I don't think she'll go for you spending a night in a sleeping bag on the forest floor," Joe said.

"I think she might," Reggie said, "As a young kid I used to sleep all the time overnight in a tent in our backyard—and it backed up to the San Bernardino forest. I know my way in the woods," Reggie said.

Joe gave Reggie an understanding nod, gestured up the trail and said, "Let's think about it."

A few yards up the path, Joe stopped in his tracks and said, "I've got an idea! There's our Agency lean-to cabin deep in La Tuna Canyon where we've done tracking studies—it's at the edge of a sycamore grove looking down at a well-travelled wildlife path leading to a spring."

Reggie's face was lighting up.

Joe continued, "The cabin's raised up on stilts with a door and a screened front so you can be in the woods, but totally safe, what do you think?"

"Cool," Reggie said as he shook his head, bouncing his mane of hair.

"I'll see if I can arrange for it next weekend," Joe said, "and talk to your mom ...by the way, when's your dad coming home?"

117

Reggie's face went from excited to surprise to trouble in an instant and he replied in a low voice, "In a couple of weeks."

By Wednesday, Joe had cleared access to the cabin and called Reggie to say they could both hike to it during the day on Saturday and he could pick him up Sunday morning. He told Reggie to lay it out for his mom, then he could talk to her afterwards if she seemed okay with it.

"Mom?" Reggie said, after she returned from her afternoon shift at Wal-Mart, "Joe arranged for me to stay overnight in a cabin this weekend in La Tuna Canyon and I'm really psyched!"

"Oh," she said dragging her 'all day standing legs' and plopping on the couch, "That sounds fun, have him call me and go over the details."

After Carole had a bite to eat and took a catnap, she woke up in a start and knocked on Reggie's door. "Did you tell me you were going to stay overnight in a cabin?"

"Yeah. Joe arranged it," Reggie answered.

"Will Joe be staying with you?"

"No, Ma that's just it. I'm going on a vision quest and you have to do it alone."

With a 'what the hell' look on her face, she asked, "What's that?"

Reggie pulled out a thin book from his backpack and plopped down a copy of 'Vision Quest: The Native American Journey to the Self through Nature.'

She thumbed through the book and stopped at a drawing of a Native boy sitting inside a ten foot circle in the woods There were drawings of grizzly bears and eagles floating in thought balloons above the boy's head, then she said, "I take it you're serious about this?"

"Dead serious," he said. "I have to do this, Ma. You were the one who encouraged me to honor my Native American roots, despite Dad's hang-up. And, you know how much being in nature means to me."

"Jesus, Reggie. I don't know. What's going to happen on this quest?'

"It's a rite of passage that boys have to go through to become a man and find a path in life. You know how important that is?"

She paused then said, "Yes, I do. But alone in the woods?"

"Ma, come on. You know I've spend many a night in the woods. I can handle it."

"What does Joe think about this?"

"He believes in me and supports me. It'll be in a safe, locked Agency cabin and he'll pick me up Sunday morning—there's nothing to worry about. Call him now, Mom, he's expecting you to."

Carole called Joe that night and found that he was, in fact, very supportive of Reggie's vision quest. He explained the location, the locked cabin and assured her he'd be safe. After the call, she went and told Reggie, it was okay. This time he gave *her* the crushing hug.

****

On Saturday morning, Carole found Reggie with a huge smile on his face, sitting next to his backpack with a sleeping bag rolled neatly underneath it.

"Good morning, Reggie, looks like you're all ready to go," as she noticed he hadn't left his dirty breakfast dishes on the table as usual. "You didn't have breakfast yet?" she asked.

"No, mom. Not hungry," he said.

After Carole made the coffee and sat down munching a piece of toast, she spoke, "What are you bringing to eat on your overnight?"

"Just water," he answered.

Staring at his crumpled thin backpack and figuring Joe must be taking care of the food, she wrinkled her brow and asked, "You're not bringing anything?"

"No, Ma, a vision quest requires fasting," he said.

Reggie could see the worry reappear on her face and Carole could see the intense determination harden on his. She wanted to hug him because he was her boy and because he was no longer a boy. "You sure you don't want to bring a can of Pringles?"

CHAPTER TWENTY

On the drive over to Tuna Canyon, Reggie told Joe, "Thanks for helping me and for convincing my mom it was safe."

"More than happy to—I know what this means to you."

Taking a narrow gravel road a quarter-mile in from the highway, Joe parked his jeep at the end marked by a sign reading; KEEP OUT Restricted Area - California Department of Water Resources. Handing Reggie a one-liter bottle of water, Joe said, "Better take this. It's quite a hike to the cabin and you may need it by Sunday."

It took them almost an hour hiking over rough terrain, with several climbs of a thousand feet, before they were able to descend deep into the canyon. The Agency had picked this remote location as the best area to do a survey of what the Santa Monica Mountain ecology might have looked like before development—and, there still wasn't a single house on any of the surrounding hills.

When they came upon an abundance of lush foliage near the canyon floor, Reggie knew they were near a source of water and the grove of sycamores. The cabin was hard to spot, on purpose Joe noted, but it had a great view of the path below where animal life could be viewed and photographed. The cabin was raised from the ground on stilts and had a screened-in front. They walked up the stairs and Joe unlocked the door and Reggie threw his backpack and sleeping bag on a lower bunk near the screened entrance.

"Want to hike down to the spring?" Joe asked.

"Thanks, Joe but I'd rather just begin my vision quest."

"No problem, but before I leave, let me show you the outdoor latrine area—it's some 150 yards behind the cabin. Make sure you use the shovel so you don't leave human scent."

"Will do," Reggie assured him.

On the way back to the cabin, Joe told him, "This area with the spring is very popular with wildlife—you're likely to hear a lot of activity from the nocturnal animals tonight. Lots of bobcats in the area, and if one should catch a hare, be ready for a lot of unholy screaming."

Reggie asked Joe, his voice filled with excitement, "Think I might catch a glimpse of a cougar?"

"Huh!" Joe laughed, "You'd be one in ten million humans who ever saw one free in the wild."

Joe then reminded Reggie to keep his cell on, handed him the cabin key and gave him a quick wave as he walked up the trail.

"See you tomorrow, 'round nine, and stay in the cabin after nightfall," Joe said.

That would be the last human voice Reggie heard for quite a while.

Scoping out the area around the cabin, Reggie spotted a young sycamore standing alone a few yards above the wildlife path. Although it had some sagebrush around it, he found a stick and drew a rough ten-foot circle around it for his vision quest. He pulled out his guidebook and reviewed all the preparations and rituals. He knew he couldn't take the full quest as his ancestors did, but hoped his shortened 'urban' version would work.

The first step in the process was to clear his mind of all human thoughts and simply take in the beauty of the natural surroundings. That was pretty easy for Reggie as he found delicate pink and white Yarrow and some Maiden-Hair fern at his eye level, both plants that like the wetter regions of the canyons. A black Phoebe lighted on a branch above him; a nesting female he thought.

Then he thought he wouldn't be able to relax and start his quest until he gave Jennifer a call and shared his excitement with her. Picking up his cell, he rang her and only got her voice mail, so he left a message to call back before nine Pacific Time. Then he cursed as he noticed his battery was low, so he shut it off and went back to his guidebook and nature.

He flipped to the chapter on singing a power song, the purpose of which was to wake up the Power Animal. *'No doubt my cougars are sleeping now,'* Reggie thought. He wondered what songs his ancient relatives would have sung, as all he could think of was the refrain from *Lion King*. Those lyrics; *till we find our place in the circle of life,* did seem to fit. He smiled to himself thinking of what the African boy lion Mufasa would think of his Western feline cousins.

Although Reggie understood he could be visited and guided by any number of Power Animals, he already felt, deep in his soul, that the mountain lion had to be his animal. Not just because of his love and appreciation of the creature he thought, but because of what he needed spiritually from the animal. He flipped back to the dog-eared page that first grabbed him when he read about the various Power animals and what they could provide a human. The Mountain Lion's totem and spiritual character was to help you become sure of your goals and purpose and to have little regret. *That's exactly what I need,* Reggie thought.

The guidebook also fascinated Reggie when he read about having 'out of body' experiences. These could come about after days of meditation and receptivity, where his spirit could actually rise up and connect with supernatural spirits. Although Reggie felt it was unlikely that he would have that experience here, he spent the next couple of hours in deep meditation, interrupted only by an occasional leg stretch and a pee break. During this time, Reggie did not receive a single vision, but he felt very peaceful and soon decided to take a hike in the waning hours of the evening.

Figuring he might as well check out the spring, he headed down the path. It wasn't a path really, but only bent down grass where much smaller animals tread—a path to a source of water and for predators, a route to find and catch prey. As he neared what looked to be the spring, he picked up the foul scent of rotting flesh.

Not wanting to get too close, he slowly approached a heap of leaves and branches. Nearby he found light brown patches of fur scattered around. No doubt it was from a cougar hiding a deer kill. He slowly backed away. He was not fearful, but cautious, knowing this was the lion's food. If he were a cougar and was discovered by the cougar who hid the carcass, he could be killed in a fight. He thought of what Joe would do in this circumstance. He picked up a large branch, with which he could, in theory, use to parry with the hypothetical beast.

As he walked back up to the cabin, he already felt the presence of his power animal. Knowing that the lion would probably come back to consume his kill, Reggie believed he might become one in the millions who ever saw a mountain lion in the wild.

Reaching the cabin just before nightfall, Reggie decided it was time to move inside. Sitting on the edge of the bunk, he re-started his vision quest. As his thoughts quieted, images started to blur across his projected mind.

Although he never saw an animal on the path below, his imagination brought forth a whole parade of wild animals: a badger, a fox, a skunk and several mule deer. The only image of a mountain lion that came into his mind was that of a photograph of P12's mange-ridden face.

At one point, Reggie fell asleep only to jerk himself awake as he almost fell off the bunk bed. Then he figured he might as well lie down. Using his backpack as a pillow and his sleeping bag as a mattress, he quickly fell into a deep sleep.

****

Late into the night, he came. The animal first caught the scent of the two-legs hiking hours and miles ago. So the lion moved slowly as he might be stalking prey, but cautiously as he might be preyed upon by the two-legs. The whole eight foot length of the mountain lion slinked over the rocks and slithered along tree roots like liquid fur. In the deep darkness of La Tuna canyon, all that any human could have seen of him were two green, moon-radiated eyes, advancing with intense single-mindedness. Once the lion got close to the cabin, he knew there was only the one two-leg.

Reggie could not see or hear that he was being sought out. Fast asleep, he could not know that animal that he wanted as his spiritual guide was steadily following his scent, and heading directly to the cabin.

At fifty feet away, the lion's acute hearing picked up the rhythmic inhale and exhale of the two-leg's breath. At twenty-five feet, the lion's acute night vision could see the rise and fall of the two-leg's chest.

On the ground below the raised cabin, the lion anchored its hindquarters with its tail and lifted its front quarters in one effortless ascension. It reached up and unsheathed its two-inch cluws and locked them on the outside lip of the cabin floor. At two feet from the two-leg's face, but on the other side of the screen, the lion's whiskers felt the warmth of his body. Although the lion could have cut through the screen and then through the throat of the two-leg in a single swipe, he did not. The two-leg stirred and the animal left as silently as he came. The cougar moved back down the path to the spring.

****

Only moments after the lion left him behind, the boy woke up. Reggie had no sense, vision or dream of the big cat's visit, but he felt empty or was it lonely. He turned his cell phone on to check the time. It was already 3:57 a.m. and no vision of his Power Animal. There was a text from Jennifer saying she was sorry she missed him, but that Terri and her were heading out to a party and she'd call him Sunday. Staring at the phone, Reggie noticed he only had ten percent battery power left, so he quickly shut the phone back off.

Frustrated with his lack of progress on his quest, Reggie looked down at the shadows on the moon-lit path. Nature was being filtered by the tiny squares of screen and he was lying in a comfortable bed in a cabin. *This was not how my ancestors would have made a vision quest,* he thought. If he was to experience or envision a Power Animal it had to be in their wild home, he was sure. So, he grabbed his sleeping bag, went outside and lay down on the ground next to the Sycamore. Here, in the circle of a proper vision quest, he felt the earth, he took in the stars and was connected.

****

Joe and Barbara didn't get back from visiting her brother in Fresno till 1:00 a.m. that Saturday night. At precisely 4:00 a.m., Joe woke up to a nightmarish feeling in his body. Was Reggie okay out there? He picked up his phone and tried Reggie's cell. Reggie did not answer and Joe panicked. He woke Barbara and told her he was worried about Reggie and might head out earlier.

It was some sixth sense that gripped and pulled at Joe as he dressed, grabbed a protein bar and drove to the office. *'Dammit!'* He cursed, he was halfway to Fresno when he remembered he should have checked the whereabouts of his collared lions again after he brought Reggie to La Tuna Canyon. Running up the stairs of the dark building and into his office, he flicked on the tracking monitor. He impatiently waited for the coded lights to blip on, showing the tracks and current location of each *Puma concolor* in his research.

"Son of a Bitch!" Joe shouted as he slammed his fist on the desk. There was P1, the old dominant male heading toward and now in Tuna Canyon and right at the location of the cabin. Grabbing his tranquilizer gun and his Sig-Sauer P230 pistol, he ran down and out to his car and screeched out of the parking lot.

****

The first sensation that Reggie felt was a soft tapping on the bottom of his sleeping bag. He moved his feet and waited. In a moment he felt it again. He opened his eyes and there were two mountain lion cubs, not more than a few weeks old, romping around his sleeping bag. They were spotted and their baby blue eyes shined as they chirped and swatted at each other. The first thought he had was *Holy Shit!* Then he worried where their mother was. Looking at the cubs again, he saw that they weren't really playing, but excited in a nervous sort of way, jumping in and out of the sage brush around him.

He heard a hissing and a deeper growl made by a mature lion. He could not see any large cats, even in the moonlight. It sounded like two adult cougars were very near. Then it got quiet and even the cubs lay frozen still in the bush.

He heard a loud scream and saw the shadowy outline of a mature lion run in front of him. This alerted the cubs and they scrambled after what Reggie presumed was their mother. Moments later there was a much louder guttural howl. He could not see the other cat, but he felt that it was a huge creature—almost monster-like in size and fierceness. Certainly not young

124

P12. The lion's snarl was combined with a caterwaul which had the ferocity to it that could only mean an attack.

More silence again. Reggie fought back the desire to run for the cabin. Then he heard some rustling off in the distance and muted screams. *Stay where you are,* he told himself. *Don't move.*

By this time, Joe was already hiking up and down the sharp ravines of La Tuna. He was wearing his LED light on his helmet, so he moved fast through the darkness of the canyon. But it would still take him at least an hour to reach the cabin and his heart was beating fast, from the adrenaline and from the fear. He felt the sweat running down his neck as he recalled the assurances he had given Reggie's mom about his safety. He had loaded both his tranquilizer gun and his pistol and was prepared to use the deadly weapon if needed. He had to get to Reggie and it seemed to take forever.

Finally, he could make out the crowns of the Sycamore grove near the cabin. Running at full speed to the cabin, he opened the door and let out a gasp. Reggie was not there.

He turned his head to light the surrounding area. At the base of a lone sycamore, he immediately spotted the bottom of a sleeping bag poking out of the sage brush and shouted, "Reggie!" as he ran to the spot. No answer. No movement. Joe dropped to his knees and shook the boy.

Reggie had fallen asleep and he groggily raised his head and said, "Joe? You're here early, what's up?"

"What's up with you sleeping in the open?"

"I wanted to have the best chance of having a vision. Wait till I tell you."

****

As the sun began to rise, the two started the hike back up to the car. Reggie had filled Joe in on his discovery of the deer kill, his decision to leave the cabin and why he did not answer Joe's phone call. Then Reggie told him about his vision, or was it just a dream? The more Reggie talked about it and thought about it, the more he became confused about its meaning. He wanted and expected to have a mountain lion of some kind connect with him somehow; give him guidance, talk to him even. But the lions in his dream did none of that.

Reggie gave Joe the details of the cubs, the appearance of the mother trying to corral them. He told him about the second adult, never seen, but heard loudly in all his fury.

Joe tried to help Reggie gather meaning from his encounter and asked, "What did you think was happening when you saw those lions?"

"When I first saw the cubs, I was delighted like seeing a litter of kittens in a pet store," Reggie offered, "but then they seemed afraid, so I felt afraid too. When the mom showed up, I was happy she was protecting them."

"And when you heard the other lion?" Joe asked, trying to determine what was real and what was a dream.

"I guess," Reggie paused, "I guess I wanted to get up and help protect the cubs, then I heard the big lion growl and it scared me, but I felt like I had to fight him off. Joe? What was really freaky about the whole thing was that I felt like I was in the lion's world not in my own world."

"What do you mean?"

"I was a friggin' lion, Joe! It was so real."

"Whoa! Reggie. It could have been just a bad nightmare. I worry that you might be taking this too far.

"I suppose, but I feel these animals are trying to communicate with me somehow."

Joe thought for a moment and said, "God, Reggie. I'm not a Shaman. I'm a scientist. There's been a smattering of research on intra-species communication, but this goes into the supernatural world and I don't know how I can help you."

"Sorry Joe, for being so weird. The whole thing just really felt so real and very bad."

"I hear you, but I've got to tell you something that makes this whole thing even crazier." Joe hesitated then spoke up, "And don't let it freak you out more, but P1 was actually in La Tuna Canyon last night—that's the reason I came here early."

Reggie turned and stared at Joe for a moment, then turned back and gazed through the windshield at the sky and didn't say another word the rest of the way home.

CHAPTER TWENTY-ONE

The plane carrying John Youngblood and his fellow Guardsmen and women of the 143rd Field Artillery Regiment was to arrive at Edwards Air Force Base at 16:42 military time. Reggie and his mom waited for the troop transport to arrive in the hangar with hundreds of other welcoming families. The hangar was festooned with balloons and a huge 'Welcome Home Heroes' banner. And children were running around with dripping ice cream cones and skipping through the popcorn on the floor. Outside, a full-dress parade band stood at the ready; the sun reflecting shiny spots off the brass instruments.

Reggie wondered why there was such a party atmosphere surrounding war. Sure, he was glad his dad was coming home, although Reggie worried about how his Dad's return might affect his work with Joe. His mom was very excited and told Reggie that there was a lot to be thankful for because most of the men and women of the 143rd were returning home together in one piece. Think of those who come home in a medical transport or worse yet, in a flag-draped coffin at Dover Air Force Base.

Reggie understood family, but never understood fighting these wars. People in Iraq and Afghanistan never attacked us, yet our government sends our people to kill them. *And we're supposed to be the superior animals?* Reggie thought. No one could give him explanations that made sense. 'No, these enemies were not trying to take our territory or resources.' 'No, we weren't fighting to dominate their territory.' *'Were we maybe trying to impose our way of life on people who were different?'* Reggie asked himself. No, would be the answer, but the explanations the government gave always had big words. Good feeling, must-be-right words, like *'protecting our sovereignty'* and *'our patriotic duty.'*

Just as Reggie could imagine hearing his dad say, *'When my country calls, I answer,'* he heard a woman shout and point to the sky, "There they are!"

The plane taxied the tarmac and stopped in front of the hangar. The band's cymbals clashed the instant the door opened and cheers came up as the soldiers deplaned. Spouses and relatives strained at the ropes and held back their children's cries of 'Daddy! Mommy!' As the soldiers all lined up in formation and

127

saluted to the National Anthem, Reggie could see his dad in the second row. Once the last beat of the band came down and everyone's national pride was stirred, the ropes were pulled away and mayhem ran its course.

Most of the soldiers ran toward their families in mass hugging and lifting of children. John Youngblood approached with a huge smile on his face, but he didn't run fast and Reggie perceived a look on his Dad's face like he had to concentrate on each step.

Embraces and kisses came before words. John held Carole to his shoulder while she sobbed. To Reggie, his dad's hug felt comforting on one part of his body, childish on the other. His dad's face and voice were strong when he asked, "How are you, Reggie?"

"Fine, Dad. Welcome home," he answered, glad that he didn't say anything about how big he's grown.

What really made Reggie feel happy was watching his mom. She kept grabbing her husband's face with two hands, looking at it then kissing him over and over again like she needed to see and feel it was really him. All the while, tears were streaming down her cheeks, blending with mascara—looking like a sad but very pretty clown.

On the drive home, it was close to supper time so Carole suggested they eat at John's favorite, the Outback Steakhouse, for prime rib. John said, "too noisy and too many people. I just want to go home."

Carole said, "I'll make mac and cheese with Canadian bacon, just the way you guys like it." When they got to Encino, John was not familiar with the neighborhood, so he asked Carole if she knew a store where they could pick up some beer. They stopped along the way.

Once they got to the apartment, John checked out the place. Looking out each window, he shut the blinds along the way.

When he got to Reggie's room, he asked Carole, "Why didn't you replace these old 'Lion King' curtains?"

"Maybe we could spring for them next month," Carole responded.

John must have sensed Carole's embarrassment, so he said, "Reggie's too old for that stuff, right Reggie?"

Reggie nodded, then his dad explained, "I never lived in a city with people in apartments so close to you, peering into your windows, but I guess I'll get used to it."

"You will, dad," Reggie offered, thinking he sounded a little paranoid, "After a while you won't even notice."

After his dad polished off three beers, he seemed to loosen up and he and Reggie talked about their good times together; fishing for sunnies at Big Bear lake, bowling at Christies and they laughed at the time they gave Hector a tomato juice bath after he got sprayed by a skunk. Before Carole finished supper, John asked Reggie if he wanted to arm wrestle, a favorite game of theirs.

His dad wanted to show Reggie the muscle mass he gained in eleven months in the field. Rolling up his sleeves, John said, "Show me what you got, kid."

Elbow to elbow, Reggie's arm almost met his dad's as they clasped hands. "You sure you're alright Dad?" Reggie asked.

"Didn't hurt my arms any. Ready?" his dad said as he tightened his grip. Reggie nodded.

They each put their forward pressure on the opposing arm, Reggie sensed, as he always did, that his dad's moderate strain was used to keep Reggie in the game. As in the past, his dad would let Reggie start pushing him down like his son was getting the upper hand, then he would strain back to make it seem like a real match. But *unlike* the old days, when Reggie would give his all and his dad would let him win, John snarled and slammed Reggie's hand down hard and shook the table.

Reggie howled. Carole jumped and John laughed. The pain and the shock of his dad's changed behavior hurt Reggie more in his heart than his hand. Carole could see that look come to Reggie's face, the look that, when he was a little boy, preceded crying. "John, what are you doing?"

John wiped the mischievous smile from his face and said, "In battle you have to be prepared for the surprise attack. Shit Carole, he's not a kid anymore."

"He's not one of your platoon buddies either, John! Now go and wash up you two, dinner's almost ready."

After dinner, Carole cleaned the table and although Reggie was still rubbing his sore knuckles with his feelings, he enjoyed watching his parents do the dishes. His dad would whisper something in her ear, then she'd give him a hip bump and he'd bump her back. Then he pulled the bow on her apron which dropped down and then she kissed him on the lips as if to say, *later.*

After the dishes were done, Reggie got the Monopoly game out of the closet. It was just like old times. The game was a short one though, as John began infecting Carole with his yawns which gave Reggie the on-board advantage. Reggie quickly bought up and traded for the cheap blue Connecticut, Vermont and Oriental properties and put hotels on them. Reggie yelped as his dad landed on them every time he passed GO and made him quickly declare bankruptcy.

Next morning, Reggie got up early, had breakfast and overheard his parents talking in the bedroom. His dad kept saying he was sorry—it'll get better. His mom kept consoling him saying, it's okay, it's been a long time. When they came out of the bedroom he didn't see their usual lovey-dovey playfulness that he always assumed followed a night of love making.

Carole had to work the afternoon shift that day. If John gave her a ride, he and Reggie could have the car to do things together.

"You guys could go on a hike," she suggested.

"Yeah! Dad." Reggie perked up, "I know a lot of cool trails in the Santa Monica Mountains."

John scratched his head as he looked back and forth at them and said almost stuttering, "I...I...don't think I'm ready to drive. I don't know the area either...I better not."

"Are you feeling okay?" Carole asked.

"Yes, I'm just a little nervous, that's all. Maybe after my checkup at the VA hospital on Friday, I'll feel more up to it."

"It's okay, dad," Reggie offered, "I've got stuff to do and we can play another round of Monopoly."

Later that afternoon, after Carole left for work, Reggie found his dad hunched over the kitchen table. At first, Reggie thought something had happened to him, but then he saw that he had his hunting rifles taken apart laying on the kitchen table. His dad barely squeaked out a word when Reggie asked him what he was doing.

Not looking up from digging into the trigger assembly with an oil cloth, like he was trying to rub out a stain, he said, "Just being prepared."

"Are you going hunting?" Reggie asked.

Now glaring at his son, he said, "No, but did you see all those creeps and weirdos on the streets yesterday? You can never be too cautious in the city."

Seeing his dad's attention return to that same spot in the trigger assembly, rubbing even harder, Reggie felt it was weird and told him he was taking a walk to the library. There, he spent a couple of hours poring over several books on wildlife conservation.

When he returned later in the afternoon, Reggie got another shock from his dad. When he opened the door, he felt a whoosh of air rushing by him. He saw his dad at the kitchen table. The draft caused the door behind Reggie to slam shut on its own. In an instant, his dad whirled around in his chair and pointed the Winchester .22 right at Reggie's chest. Recognizing his son, he lowered the rifle and yelled, "Jesus Christ, Reggie, you startled me!"

"Sorry, dad! The door slammed accidentally, I didn't mean to..." Reggie said, feeling a cold shiver of fear.

"That's alright, Reggie, I didn't mean to scare you. But I don't want you to ever tell your Mom about this and my guns. We need the protection now. Do you hear me?"

"Yes, Sir!" he said as he waved and ducked into his bedroom. Laying on his bed, Reggie thought about how his dad had changed. He wondered what horrible experiences he might have had in battle, the 'kill or be killed' thing. *Maybe he's like reliving those experiences,* Reggie thought. When he was home before going to Iraq, his dad certainly did have the final say-so in the house. Even when Reggie didn't get his way, he respected his dad's steady authority. Now, he feared his power—an unstable sort of power. *Is this what war does to a person?* Reggie worried to himself.

On Friday, Carole took John to the VA hospital and when they returned, Reggie knew they had been arguing. At supper, they continued the argument. Carole told John he had to take his meds with the meal. John told Carole he was not sick and left the table. He spent the rest of the evening in the bedroom.

This gave Carole the chance to talk to Reggie. John was diagnosed with Post Traumatic Stress Disorder, she explained, a result of the mine explosion under his Humvee in combat. Even with treatment, it might take years for the symptoms to pass. When Reggie asked about the symptoms, Carole told him that the doctor said that his dad would probably suffer from a whole range of them but that denial was the most serious one they faced now. Many returning soldiers, she explained, refuse to admit they have mental problems, which to them is a weakness, so until they become willing to undergo treatment, they make matters worse by burying the emotions of the trauma.

"What are some of those other symptoms?" Reggie asked, not wanting to tell his mother about the gun-pointing incident.

"The doctor said many things can trigger a 'fight' response like he had to have on the battlefield," she explained, "and sometimes just a loud noise can set him off." Carole continued, "Fear of strangers is another typical symptom, and I noticed right away that dad felt vulnerable. He seemed like he was on constant alert, waiting for the enemy to attack. We have to be prepared for a lot of mood swings and some could be violent," she added.

Trying to understand what his dad was facing, Reggie asked, "What are we going to do?"

Carole took a while to respond, "We just have to take it one day at a time, try not to upset him and be very patient. They say he won't ever come out of it without family support." Then Carole pulled out a white bag from her purse and told Reggie, "In the meantime, the doctor prescribed this anti-depressant that, after a while, should help control his bursts of anger."

"Okay, mom," Reggie acknowledged, "but how are we going to tell him about my hiking and Joe? I'm going tomorrow, you know."

"I'll handle it, Reg, we'll get through this."

That night, sometime around 1:00 a.m., Reggie was woken up by louder than ever shouting coming from his parents' bedroom. When he heard what sounded like furniture being moved, he got up and stood for a moment at his parent's door. *He's still bigger than me,* Reggie thought, *but I can't let him hurt mom.* Reggie stood there for several minutes, heard nothing more and went back to bed. He had trouble getting to sleep again wondering if they were fighting about him and Joe, but eventually he got back to a restless sleep.

When he got up next morning, he found his mom sitting at the kitchen table in her regular chair but at a strange angle, greeting Reggie with a not really 'good morning,' as she stirred her coffee.

"You alright?" Reggie asked as he went to the fridge for some OJ, "I heard you two arguing last night."

She wouldn't look up, but said, "We're okay now," in a not very okay voice.

Reggie walked over to the opposite side of the table, sat down next to his mom, and with worry in his voice said, "Mom?"

Carole looked up at her son and Reggie saw her left cheek, where only a couple of days ago, under the flag, were tears of relief and happiness. Now she had red and blue bruises in the corner of her eye.

"He hit you, didn't he?"

Carole nodded yes as she wiped the start of tears and said, "I pressed him too hard on taking the medications. I know it's his condition."

"Jesus, mom. I know he's sick, but he could really hurt you," and he put his hand on her shoulder.

Carole rubbed Reggie's even bushier bed-head hair, gained her composure and said, "I know, Reggie. And I decided for the safety of both of us, we should move into a motel for a few days. At least until he sees his therapist, maybe gets some new meds and things seem better."

"I guess...but how do you think he'll take it?"

"Very hard. But I think he has to know it is totally unacceptable and he could lose us if it happened again. He already feels deep remorse and promised to never do it again. But we have to make sure."

"Okay, it's good you're standing up to him. When are we going?"

"He's sleeping now, I'll start packing up a few things and we'll leave after you come back from your hike. Joe will be here in an hour. Have breakfast and get ready. When he comes, tell him I worked late and I'm still sleeping, okay?"

"You sure? I can stay home if you want."

"No, go enjoy your hike," she replied.

****

Reggie kept an eye open for Joe and ran out the door as soon as he pulled up. After their initial fist-bump greeting, Joe told Reggie he had some good news and told him to reach into his case and pull out a gift in the manila envelope. Reggie picked it up, undid the clasp and slid out a glossy eight by ten photo of a collared mountain lion. It was in full length surrounded by darkness with the animal's green eyes radiated at the camera's flash.

"Is it P12?" Reggie asked.

"Indeed it is," said Joe. "Looks a lot better doesn't he?"

Reggie slowly ran his finger along the photo of the lion starting with the head. He looked nothing like the mangy-faced creature in the previous photograph. He looked alert and healthy and his coat was smooth and shiny without a single pock mark.

"Check out the tail," Joe suggested. "See how full it is? When we found him with the mange, most of the fur on it was gone and he looked like a devil."

"Think he's all cured?" Reggie asked.

Joe nodded, "Well, he's on his way, I think."

"That's really cool. You must feel great how you helped him."

"I do" Joe replied, "the LA times interviewed me for a story. But how about you? Bet you're happy your dad's home?"

Reggie didn't answer right away, it took Joe's glance over to him to force a reply; "I am," Reggie said. "But he's got PTSD and I don't know what's going to happen."

"Geez, Reg, I'm sorry...I know that can be tough on returning soldiers and their families."

Reggie looked at the photo, "but I really don't want to talk about it now, okay, Joe?"

"No problem, but just so you know, Reggie, I'm here to help you in any way I can."

During the hike, Reggie had trouble taking in the trail worrying if his mom and his dad were alright. *I will have to try and stop him,* he thought, *if he tries to hurt her again, I will.* Joe could sense his mood and said little on the trail and on the ride home.

When Reggie got home, he saw the suitcases by the door. His mom and dad were sitting on the couch, holding hands. Reggie could tell they had both been crying. His mom said, "Hi, Reg." His dad said, "I am sorry what I did to your mom, Reggie. I promise to never hit her again. I will be going to see the therapist daily at the VA to get better. I hope you will come to trust me and come back home soon."

At first, Reggie didn't know how to respond, worried it sounded too much like he spent the day rehearsing it. Then he said, "Okay Dad. I believe you."

Reggie's mom gave his dad a quick kiss and said, "Be well." They grabbed the suitcases and headed out the door.

By the second day at the Motel 6, Reggie was asking when they would be going home. They left on the third day when his mom told him she had talked to the therapist, to his dad several times and felt they could go back. Reggie was happy.

Reggie didn't know what to expect when he got home, but his dad ran to the door and hugged both of them. He seemed calm and steady and very happy. Carole told them she'd get supper ready. His dad joined her in the kitchen and Reggie went to his room.

After supper, while his dad was watching TV, Reggie asked his mom, "How does he seem?"

"Much better." She said.

"Did you talk to him about Joe?"

"Yes, and he seemed to be fine with that," she whispered."

"That's great Mom. Thanks."

Later in the evening, his dad asked Reggie where he's been hiking. "Had a good hike up to the Nike Missile Site off Mandeville Canyon. It had a great vista," Reggie said, "Joe told me they chose that site because its location and elevation was ideal to protect the entire Los Angeles area from attack."

"That Joe fellow's a smart man, I hear," his dad commented. "Did he tell you that by the 60's Nike missiles were made obsolete by the Intercontinental Ballistic Missiles that could deliver nuclear weapons half-way around the world?"

"No, he didn't mention that," Reggie mumbled.

John then picked up the newspaper lying on the coffee table, handed it to Reggie and said, "You'll be interested in this article and picture of that lion that was sick with the mange." Reggie looked at the black and white photo in the LA Times which was the same photo Reggie had in color.

"Yeah, I know all about it," Reggie said as he reached into his backpack on the floor and showed them the photo Joe had given him. "Joe says he thinks he'll make it now. He's the one who treated him you know."

"You really care about these mountain lions, huh?" his dad asked then added, "I used to hunt them years ago you know, but never got one."

Reggie wanted to make the argument for protecting the lions, but he caught his mom's glance and sensed he better cool it.

"I know you did, but the thinking has changed in wildlife conservation these days."

"I suppose it has," John admitted.

Things went pretty smoothly the rest of the evening. John even agreed to go bowling. He and Reggie won two games each and Carole mostly threw gutter balls. Sunday was even better as John must have come to the realization Reggie was totally into hiking now. He suggested the family go up to their old neighborhood, visit the Hollyfields, and take a picnic up to Ridgeview Rock.

****

Carole packed a great lunch of fried chicken and potato salad, intentionally forgot the beer and managed to cover the bruise with make-up. John agreed to drive, telling Carole how he loved the winding road up the San Bernardino's. When they got to the Hollyfield's, Hector was three times as happy seeing all of his old Youngblood family and they had a great visit. It felt like great. John did not want to drive by their former home though, fearing it would bring up memories of how he lost it, so he let Reggie drive to the trailhead.

Reggie thought the woods seemed to soothe his dad even more than the drugs. They quickly fell back into appreciating nature together. They overturned rocks looking for newts and salamanders. They played their old 'who can name that tree game' and John was sure he'd stump Reggie when he pointed to what looked like a clump of birch trees in the distance. Reggie was smug and John was impressed when Reggie said they were white Alder. When they got to Ridgeview Rock and spread out the blanket and the picnic, each felt they were a family again.

Being in the woods was therapeutic to Reggie too. He thought about the night of his vision quest. Wondering what was and what wasn't real. He knew he had to go back again to find his power animal.

CHAPTER TWENTY-TWO

When Lupine-boy first heard the screams echo up Malibu Canyon, he thought it was two male lions fighting, perhaps over a deer kill, perhaps over a female. As a cub in his old homeland, he once witnessed such a battle. It was a battle to the death. The yowling and shrieking that accompanied that brawl, never stopped until the victor grabbed and held the enemy's neck, crushed its windpipe, and tore the vein. Then the throttle of death silenced him. This night though, the screams came in between long silences. Different.

Lupine-boy only encountered the scent of one other male in his many months roaming every mountainside and canyon in the area. This made him wary, but despite the possible danger to himself, he headed toward the sounds; curious as any cat. As he got closer, the two battle cries had distinct characteristics. One was louder and deeper suggesting the body mass of an older male, perhaps Big-paw. The other voice, although strong and fierce, seemed, by its volume, to be produced by a smaller animal, perhaps a younger male. Maybe a female? Maybe She-Paw?

The two lions were at it again when Lupine-boy reached a ridgeline above them. His acute night sight confirmed what he had heard. The large animal shadow circled the smaller, growling in what sounded like a sexual advance. Being high above and upwind, Lupine-boy now recognized their scents. He had smelled the old male's urine piles throughout the territory. He was the dominant male, Big-paw. She was She-Paw, the young female that communicated dark messages to Lupine-boy and previously resisted his advances. He remembered her scent and voice very well. He longed to meet her again and have her.

He could fight for her now with the likelihood of serious injury or with the older cat's determination—possible death. Suddenly the shapes and the sounds of the battle were stilled. The silence now stretched to a deadening—not even a rustle of leaves. Maybe it was a fight over a kill and the female lay dying, but what male would kill a potential sex partner?

Then Lupine-boy heard what he thought were mews. They were very faint but he knew the distinct chirps and mews of lion cubs. Could She-Paw have just bore him offspring? He heard a rustle

136

and saw a charge. A snarl then a scream. An attack. Big-Paw charged She-Paw. She reared up and struck him hard; clawing him in the face, and ran. He chased after her, but crouched down a few yards from her, finding her hiding in a thicket of sagebrush. Was she wounded?

Silence dropped over them again. After a long pause, Lupine-boy saw Big-paw move around toward She-Paw's backside, like he was looking for another line of attack. More silence. She-Paw did not move. Then, much to his surprise, Big-paw ran further away from her—up the canyon wall in Lupine-boy's direction. Did he give up that fight? Did he pick up his scent for a new fight? Lupine-boy was now on full alert; haunches tensed to spring, hair bristling on his spine—ready to take on the big old cat.

Then Big-paw changed direction again—moving further across the canyon. After another long period of silence, Lupine-boy thought he heard some muted cries off in the distance, but She-Paw still lay motionless in the thicket.

Hours must have passed as well as the sense of danger, as Lupine-boy saw She-Paw get up and move slowly toward a clearing. She was alive. He began following her. He got close enough to see she was limping on a rear leg, but otherwise moving steadily toward a rock outcropping.

Then she stopped. Lupine-boy watched as she sat for a while looking at the ground. Then she lay down and proceeded to move her head up and down in a licking motion like she was feeding. He slowly crept closer to get a better look. Then he smelled blood; blood that was not hers' or that of a deer kill. He moved one paw in front of the other in a slow crawl until he snapped a branch. He saw that she heard him. She quickly lifted her head and snarled in defense.

She reached down to the ground and picked up a spotted cub in her motherly jaws as if to protect it. Lupine-boy could see the cub was limp and dead. He then knew what the battle was fought for. Below She-Paw was another dead cub—partially eaten.

She dropped the cub and growled viciously. Lupine-boy backed off and once again left the female that he smelled months ago—the female that enticed him into the megalopolis. As before, Lupine-boy felt she was sending him a warning message.

CHAPTER TWENTY-THREE

Monday morning, things at the Youngblood's changed. His dad seemed fidgety and sort of on edge. Reggie watched John spill half a tablespoon of sugar before it got to his coffee cup. John told Carole he didn't sleep well last night and Reggie could see by looking at her, she didn't either. When Carole asked him if he took his pill, he looked into space like he was ten thousand miles away and finally told her that it was giving him nightmares and he wasn't feeling himself anymore. Carole suggested maybe it was time to make an appointment for the doctor recommended therapy, John got very irritated and told her he didn't need that and to leave him alone. Reggie could see his mom was quite taken aback by his dad's change of mood, but she didn't want to push it.

Soon after his mom left for work, the phone rang. It was Joe. He told Reggie about an important conference next month about funding for a wildlife corridor in the Santa Monica's. As they talked, Reggie knew that Joe's research findings made a strong case for the need to build a bridge over, or an underpass under the freeways so mountain lions could move more freely in and out of the mountain ranges. Reggie believed that this would mean greater genetic diversity among the lion population and ultimately better health and preservation of the species. Joe asked Reggie if he could attend. The important official from the Department of Fish and Wildlife that Reggie met, would be there. Reggie got the details, told Joe he'd like to make it and would check with his mom.

When he got off the phone, his dad was standing right behind him and asked who he was talking to. He knew his dad probably overheard some of the conversation, so he told him it was Joe.

"What did he want?" his dad asked.

"He asked if I could attend an important meeting next month about building a wildlife corridor."

"What the hell is that?"

Reggie proceeded to explain the benefits of a corridor...

"What, so we can have more mountain lions coming into backyards and killing people? Why are you wasting time with this? It's not going to get you anywhere in life."

"It's not like that, Dad," Reggie replied, seeing his dad getting redder in the face.

"Well, you seem to know everything don't you? Why would Joe want *you* there?"

"Important government people are going to be there and I'm ..."

"Government people!" His dad shouted, 'we're going to spend taxpayers' dollars on stupid shit like that? Besides, what has this government ever done for me and our people?" His rage continued after a short pause, "What is it with this guy Joe, inviting a school kid to something like that? What do you do with Joe? Has he ever touched you?"

"No, Dad, he's a good guy and he listens to me."

"Well, you listen to me, smart ass punk, I'm your dad, not Joe. I don't want you to see him anymore. You can go hiking with me, that's it! If he comes near you again, I'm going to pay him a visit, understand?"

Reggie could see that his dad was really pissed at him and knew that probably a lot was caused by the meds and the mood swings, but he could not let his dad rule his life any longer.

"Sorry, Dad, can't do that—it's my life," Reggie said in the calmest, strongest way he could.

John glared in disbelief at his son's disregard for his authority. He grabbed Reggie by the shoulders and slammed him against the wall.

"I told you, and hear me straight, you will never see Joe again, over my dead body!"

"We'll see what Mom says."

John pulled back his right arm, gritted his teeth and started to swing at Reggie's face. He could see the 'go ahead hit me' defiance in Reggie's eyes. Then Reggie raised his hands, clenched his fists and yelled back, "You better not hit mom again! We'll leave you for good."

John stopped his swing in mid-air, opened his fist and jabbed his finger under Reggie's nose, "Get out of my face before I kill you."

Reggie ran. Ran out the door and didn't stopped running. He didn't even know where he was going, just away from his dad. Kept hearing his father's words in his head, but didn't think he meant it. After a couple of miles of ignoring walk signs, several cars honking at him and one almost hitting him, he finally slowed down, caught his breath and recognized where he was. He found himself only a few blocks from the State Park where he and Jennifer first spent time alone together. He instantly missed her all over again, but he was sure she would not be coming back into his life. Sitting on the bench they shared, he pulled out his phone, saw that his mom had called, but he wanted to talk first to Jennifer. He wanted to know if she had met anyone and if she had figured out who she was.

"Reggie, how are you? I'm glad you called," she answered in her usual upbeat voice.

"Fucking shitty," Reggie answered, shattering the tone of the conversation.

"What's wrong? I thought things were pretty good with Joe then with your dad coming home?"

"I didn't tell you, but my dad has PTSD and he's not taking his meds. He freaked out about Joe, told me I couldn't see him and almost hit me. He's turned into like...like a monster."

"I'm sorry. What are you going to do? I wish I could help you somehow," she offered.

"Well, you did. Remember I told you I was going to go on a Vision Quest? I went last week. It's sort of an ancient Native American spiritual journey—like the meditating you wanted me to try. But instead of being in the now, it's like looking for a guide for the future—a power animal."

"For you, a mountain lion, I'm guessing," she said.

"Yeah, the lion symbolizes discovering your life purpose, but on the quest I had these dreams or whatever, that were kinda freaky."

Jennifer asked what they were about and Reggie described the mother and cubs being chased by this large male and told her it seemed very real.

"What did you feel like?"

"I felt afraid, and helpless, like I wanted to protect them, but couldn't."

"Were you in their space?" she asked.

"I felt like I was there, but I couldn't communicate with them. That big lion was powerful, but I sure didn't receive any guidance from him."

"Reggie, maybe there's message you need to listen to. Did you ask Joe if he had any knowledge about vision quests?"

"That's what's really weird," he said. "He told me that P1, the dominant male in the territory was actually near the place I had my vision quest."

"Holy shit!" Jennifer exclaimed. "No wonder you're freaked."

The way she understood him, the way they could talk about anything, helped Reggie feel calmer. Jennifer truly was a great friend. Wanting to catch up with her world, and at the same time afraid to ask about how she's doing relationship-wise, he asked,

"How's your art coming along? Have you done any more still lifes—I loved that one with the oozing avocadoes."

"Ha. Great, actually. I won a school award for a woodcut I did—a figure study of two heads. The art curriculum here is awesome and I've made so many cool friends."

Reggie couldn't hold back his curiosity about her possible romantic relationships any longer. He blurted, "You mentioned Terri a couple of times, but how come you never post his picture on your Facebook?"

There was a pause on the other end before Jennifer said, "Reggie! Terri is a girl! She's my closest friend. There are a lot of pics of her on my Facebook. She's the one wearing the owl-frame glasses and bushy black hair kind of like yours."

Reggie did remember seeing a picture of her with that other girl. They were arm and arm in a close-up—laughing and sticking out their tongues. The other girl's tongue was pierced with a black stud.

"Oh! That was Terri? The one with the tongue stud?"

"Yeah! Cool or what?"

"She's almost as cute as I am," Reggie kidded. Inside, though, he was filling up with sadness. They looked like a couple, a *couple*-couple, but he still felt too afraid to come out and ask her, so he said, "Jennifer? Are you ever coming back to school in California?"

"I don't know, Reggie, my parents have enrolled me in both schools and they have opposing views."

"That's crazy, what do *you* want Jennifer?"

"Honestly?"

"Honestly!"

After a long pause, Jennifer said, "I don't want to hurt you, Reggie."

"I think I know what you're going to say, and it's okay. You know you can always be honest with me."

"Reggie, with Terri and the school and everything else, there's just so much more for me here, but I will still come back to California to visit."

Reggie knew she was trying to avoid the subject that both of them needed to discuss and resolve. He took a deep breath and took the plunge. "Are you and Terri a couple?"

A long silence preceded Jennifer's answer. "Yes, Reggie. She's very sensitive and gentle and I love her and she loves me."

Another long silence, and Reggie said, "Congratulations. You worked it out and I am happy for you guys."

"Really?"

"Really!"

"Reggie, thank you for being an understanding friend. You know they say friends can be closer in some ways than lovers can."

"Hey! You're a great friend, too—gay or straight. I will miss you, Jennifer."

"You won't. I'll visit you. I promise."

"I'd like that. I better go. Keep painting and say 'hi' to Terri. Goodbye for now." Reggie clicked off his phone, looked up at the sky, and felt like he was going to cry. But the relief of it all kept the tears from forming.

Rubbing his face to shake it off, he grabbed his phone again and listened to the voice mail from his mom.

"Are you okay, Reggie? Call me. I'm here with your dad—he's pretty upset, please call when you can." *Click.*

Reggie called back. No answer.

Thinking of the incident with his dad, he called Joe.

"Hi Reggie, how you doing?" Joe asked.

"Not good, my dad's getting worse."

"Want to talk about it—I've got a few minutes before I head to a meeting?"

"Nah! Not really."

"Maybe you'll feel more like it when we meet on Saturday."

"Joe?" Reggie said hesitating, "I need to tell you my dad doesn't want me to see you anymore. He said *he* will hike with me. He told me he may have to pay you a visit someday."

Pausing, Joe said, "That would be a big disappointment to me, Reggie, but if that's what your parents want, I'll understand. I'd be happy to meet with him. If I can help you in any way..."

"Thanks. Maybe my Mom can turn him around," Reggie added.

"Okay, you let me know and if you can't make that corridor meeting next month, that's okay."

"Yeah, I'll let you know.

Joe?"

"Yes, Reggie?"

"Remember when you told me about your tracking of P1 to the cabin the night of my vision quest?"

"Sure, what about it?"

"Did you ever find some dead cubs?"

Pausing, Joe answered in a somber tone, "We did."

"When?"

"We did a pass through in Tuna Canyon with our mobile radio tracker and found the dead cubs the next week."

"Why didn't you tell me?"

Stammering for a good answer, Joe replied, "I...I didn't want to get you really upset about your nightmare and spoil your love of these magnificent animals, I guess. I'm sorry."

"What do you mean?"

"Reggie, it's hard to explain this kind of behavior on the part of cougars but the cubs were killed by P1."

"No!" Reggie yelled in disbelief.

"Sad, but it's infanticide—a fairly rare phenomenon, but sometimes cougars and even domestic cats, kill their young."

Reggie did not respond.

"Reggie?" Joe called out.

"Why would they do that?" Reggie asked.

"The 'why' can't be explained in human terms, but usually it's the male killing cubs sired by a rival male—you know how territorial the males are," Joe answered. "Mothers will sometimes fight the males to the death to protect their cubs."

"Did you do DNA testing? What did you find?" Reggie asked.

"We did..."

"And...?"

"The cubs had been previously tagged by us and we knew who the mother and father were and we did saliva testing on the remains and it was P1 who killed his own grandchildren."

"Grandchildren?" Reggie responded. "You've got to be kidding."

"Unfortunately not, Reggie"

"But his own grandchildren?"

"Our best hypothesis is that he wanted to stop the female from nursing and bring her back into heat."

"Geez!" Reggie responded, "Are you saying the female is, you know..."

Hesitating, Joe answered, "Yes, P13 is P1's daughter."

"Fucking monster! How could he do that to his own daughter?"

"Reggie, you know that's how it works in the animal world. Thank god she's okay. We've got her roaming her territory now."

"Joe? I gotta go. Talk to you later."

Reggie felt his stomach start to churn and the burn came into his throat—the feeling before he vomited. He bent over the grass, waited for it to erupt, but it was only dry heaves this time. After a few minutes his stomach settled and he tried calling his mom again.

No answer. As Reggie remembered, his mom was not working tonight.

He replayed her voice mail. She sounded alright, but what if she was covering up?

He started to run. *What if dad hurt her again?* He thought. *He was pretty angry.*

Ran through streetlights. Ran in front of cars. Made it home.

Could not see their Subaru parked anywhere.

Ran up the stairs and stopped at the door.

No voices. He opened the door.

"Mom?" "Dad?"

No answer.

Running into the bedroom, no one was there.

The closet door was open. He looked on the floor. His dad's gun case was unlocked and open. It never was unlocked. There was the .22 and the 30.06. His dad never let him see his gun case, so Reggie didn't know if any other guns were missing.

He tried calling his mom again.

She picked up.

"Where are you?"

"At the VA hospital with dad, are you alright?"

"I'm fine, what happened?"

"When I got home, I found your dad sitting at the kitchen table drinking beer with his hunting rifle next to him. As soon as he looked at me he started to cry. He didn't stop even after I held him. He was shaking and scared..."

"Did he say anything?"

"When he finally stopped crying he told me he almost hit you when you argued. He said he was a rotten father and should never have come home."

"He's really hurting, isn't he?"

"It even got worse," she added, "so I took him to the hospital. That's when you must have tried calling me back. They gave him some medication and he began to relax to the point of drowsiness; he's been sleeping quietly for some time."

"How did it get worse?"

"He got sort of paranoid, I guess. He wanted to bring his rifle with him. He kept saying someone was out to destroy his family. He had to protect us. And I worry, he might try and kill himself like his dad."

"That fucking war! He's got to get rid of those guns."

"Reggie!"

"No, Mom those wars—that's the cause of all of this, they fight to kill over there and they come back and see the enemy everywhere. Their minds get totally messed up!"

"Reggie, that talk doesn't get us anywhere," she scolded. "But you're right, I should have told the doctors about the guns."

"That's just the problem, Mom, no one talks about it—we're worse than wild animals."

"Reggie. Stop. Dad seems to be waking up. I'll call you later. Put one of those Marie Callender pot pies in the microwave okay?"

CHAPTER TWENTY-FOUR

Reggie's dad stayed in the hospital for over a week. He was confined to a special room and watched so he wouldn't try and hurt himself. The doctors put him on new drugs and he met with a psychiatrist daily. It might take weeks for them to take effect, the doctors told his mom. Carole visited him every day. The disability pay started coming in and she quit her job at Wal-Mart. The doctors reminded her that his condition was still volatile. That he would likely continue to swing between good and bad periods, even after he was released.

Reggie didn't understand what was going to happen to his dad. He only visited him in the hospital a couple of times and he seemed to be totally out of it. Hardly talked to him. *Was he feeling ashamed,* Reggie wondered? *Mostly drugged,* Reggie concluded.

His mom seemed somewhat relieved for the time being because he was kept safe in the hospital. On the other hand, she still carried a heavy load of worry. Reggie could see it in the way she spoke. Her eyes predicted the worse was still coming.

It was good that she had talked to Joe and told him what was going on and still wanted him to be a part of Reggie's life. Reggie would hold off on the Saturday hikes for a while, with his dad in the hospital and with school starting, but yes, she told him, Reggie could attend that wildlife corridor meeting next month.

Reggie still missed Jennifer. Even though he knew she had found herself with Terri, the thought that he probably would never see her again left a hollow feeling inside. *Maybe if I let her move out of my life completely,* he thought, *I can move on myself.*

****

Fall semester, day one, Reggie felt alone all over again like when he first came to the school. No Jennifer. No Isaac. But thanks to someone, no Kevin. He wondered a bit if Kevin was not allowed to come back and was at another school, but all that seemed in the past now.

After the welcome convocation and receiving his class schedule in his home room, Reggie perked up anticipating his Environmental Sciences class, taught by his favorite teacher, Mrs. Horton. When he got to class, he saw the new course book and was excited, there were two chapters on wildlife conservation.

Sitting in the same classroom he had in Biology, he couldn't help but look over to the corner seat where Jennifer used to sit. Two seats behind hers' was a new girl. She had long dark brown hair and dark eyes. She smiled a lot during class and her eyes seemed to sparkle like Jennifer's. Before the class ended, Mrs. Horton announced the first hiking club meeting and several kids in the class raised their hands when their names were called, including the new girl, Stephanie. *Good*, Reggie felt. The two smiled at each other when Reggie raised his hand. *She's not as cute or as exciting looking as Jennifer,* he kept thinking, *kinda plain-looking, but there was something about her.*

The new Hiking Club met during study period and Mrs. Horton laid out the framework for the Club and asked the students if they had any suggestions for the first hike. Reggie described a bunch of trails that he had been on and when Mrs. Horton asked him his favorite, he threw out the Parke Mesa Overlook Trail. Reggie told the group about the great views from Malibu to Palos Verdes.

Everyone seemed to think that sounded good. There were no other suggestions until Stephanie raised her hand. She agreed that the Overlook Trail was fine, but everyone should know that it has a 1200 foot elevation gain and some might find it hard for a first climb.

"Good point, Stephanie." Mrs. Horton said. "Do you have another trail in mind?"

"How about the Santa Ynez Canyon Trail? It's a more moderate climb and it's got a cool waterfall at the end."

"Reggie, what do you think?" Mrs. Horton asked.

"That's a good trail too."

"Everyone?" Mrs. Horton asked, and the entire group raised their hands.

After the Club worked on meeting plans, getting their parent permission slips, hiking gear, supplies and transportation, Mrs. Horton asked if anyone wanted to be an officer of the Club. Stephanie raised her hand and suggested that Reggie be President.

Reggie's face turned red and he said, "I don't know."

"Members?" Mrs. Horton asked. A boy in the back said, "Yeah he seems to know a lot about hiking."

"Reggie?"

"Oh come on Reggie, we want you," Stephanie said.

"Okay," Reggie said and they all clapped.

"How about Vice President?" Reggie asked, I nominate Stephanie."

"No way!" she said.

Then Reggie started yelling a campaign chant while smiling broadly, "We want Stephanie! We want Stephanie!" Everybody kicked in.

Stephanie won her 'election' too and that started their political and personal Hiking Club alliance.

****

By the time his mom dropped Reggie off on Saturday morning in the school parking lot, most of the Hiking Club members were already on the bus. Mrs. Horton checked Reggie in and before he sat down in the front, Stephanie gave him a big wave from the back. He noticed she wore a bright flower print shirt and had a big camera hanging around her neck.

When they arrived at Topanga State Park, Mrs. Horton announced that Stephanie agreed to be the club photographer and they all lined up around the Santa Ynez trailhead sign. Stephanie put her camera on a post, clicked the shutter release on delay and ran to get in the photo with everyone laughing.

Reggie immediately wanted to team up with his Vice President and Stephanie was more than happy to hike together. Reggie asked her right away, "I didn't see you in school last year."

"No wonder," she smiled, "I was in San Diego. My Dad took a new job up here and here I am."

"What do you think of it so far?" Reggie asked.

"We lived and hiked here when I was younger and I think I'm going to like this club."

"Me too, Mrs. Horton is great."

The pair then began sharing their knowledge of nature. Along the creek bed, Reggie pointed out some animal tracks to the group—opossum tracks. Stephanie asked him how he knew they were an opossum's and he told her to kneel down for a closer look.

As all the kids gathered around. Reggie said, "See the hind leg tracks?" as he pointed and traced one out. "Here's the large thumb that helps them to climb."

Stephanie and her classmates were impressed by Reggie's tracking skills and Mrs. Horton noted, "You've got a keen eye, Reggie, do you know what you call that thumb?"

"An opposable thumb," Reggie answered, almost bragging, as he held up and wiggled his thumbs. "Possums are the only non-primate that has them."

Stephanie then poked and twisted her thumb into Reggie's shoulder and kidded him, "You're such a smart primate, Reggie," and everybody laughed. *I like this girl,* Reggie thought.

Then it was Stephanie's turn to show her woodland chops when she pointed at a round-green-leafed plant, "Look, there's a marshmallow!"

Everybody gave Stephanie a puzzled look, thinking it looked nothing like the things they roasted over a campfire.

"Well, it's actually called mallow and it is very edible." To the amazement of the group, she plucked a leaf and took a bite.

"Yum!" Yum!" she said as she chewed and made an exaggerated swallow with glee. Knowing that most people don't like the fuzzy feel in their mouth and the taste of grass, she offered, "Who wants to try it?"

Reggie, wanting to take up any challenge Stephanie made, asked, "Why do you call it marshmallow?"

"Well, my dad, who's a botanist, told me they used to boil it to make the first original marsh mallows."

"Here, try it."

Figuring they named it and used it because it tasted sweet and fluffy, Reggie took the whole leaf, crumbled it up in his hands and popped it into his mouth. At first there was no look on his face as he chewed expectantly. Then he got a strange look; first in his eyes, then in his nose.

"Keep chewing Reggie," Stephanie said.

"Yeah, Reggie, Chew! Chew," the group chanted.

Getting red in the face out of embarrassment or pre-vomit, he spat the green glob out. "Disgusting! What kind of marshmallow was that? It tastes like a 'friggin' weed." The green juice dribbled down Reggie's chin as the hikers kept laughing their way up the trail.

"Are you mad at me, Reggie?" Stephanie said as she handed him her water bottle.

"Nah!" he said.

As they moved up the trail, Stephanie kept pointing out the names of various plants and flowers and snapping pictures, much to Reggie's amazement. At one point, lagging behind the group, Stephanie pointed to a shrub with delicate purple flowers drooping down in clusters.

She bent down to smell them, "Oh! My favorite sage. Smell it Reggie."

Inches from her face, Reggie smelled the flowers and her. She took his hand with her long delicate fingers and together up righted the hanging blossoms. They were soft. The flowers. Her hands.

"Can you guess the name of this sage?" she asked.

"No," he said not looking at or thinking about the plant only feeling what it felt like in her hand. *It was crazy,* he felt, *how the touch of a girl can pull you like a magnet.*

"What does the shape remind you of?" she asked.

"It kind of looks like a frilly vase my Mom keeps with her good dishes," he answered.

"Yeah! A vase...a pitcher—it's a pitcher sage," she said as she started pulling her hand away. She felt his tug to hold on a moment more. Looking at each other, they smiled and their hands parted.

****

Catching up to the group, everybody was in single file as they approached huge granite rocks, which both Reggie and Stephanie knew meant they were close to the waterfall. When they got there, most of the kids groaned in disappointment as the falls looked more like a leaking faucet.

The gorge below it though, was kind of cool "like a mini-Grand Canyon," Stephanie offered as she snapped some photos. Sitting on rocks around the muddy pool below, the club had lunch.

Stephanie shared her kale and cranberry salad with Reggie. He liked the cranberries. Reggie shared his string cheese and pepperoni slices with Stephanie. She liked the cheese.

Then she whispered in his ear, "I know this great hiding place along the trail, wanna go?"

"Sure," Reggie replied, "we're supposed to stay together... but hold on."

"Mrs. Horton!" Reggie called across the grotto, "Stephanie and I are done with lunch, and there's some wild blackberries Stephanie spotted on the trail. Is it alright if we go ahead and find them? We'll wait for you there okay?"

"Alright, stay there we'll be down in a few minutes," Mrs. Horton agreed as some of the members giggled.

The pair walked slowly at first and when they rounded a bend, Stephanie grabbed Reggie's hand and started running, "Up here, come on!"

Climbing up some huge boulders, she pointed to a narrow crevice in the rocks. "It's a secret lookout," she said. "They can't spot us from the trail."

They crawled in and sat next to each other. Soon, the pair could see the first kids coming down the trail.

"YOO HOO!" Stephanie called down and watched as they looked all around for the caller, but not up. The pair held back their laughs with their hands.

Then Reggie puckered up and blew a sharp whistle. The kids stopped in their tracks. Stephanie zoomed in for some good close-ups of the perplexed hikers. Reggie couldn't hold back his laugh any longer and one hiker, then another, pointed up at the two jokers in the cave.

"Guess we better head down. That was fun, Reg," she said.

"Yeah, it was. Can I call you Steph?"

They both had such a laugh he wanted to hug her, but then Mrs. Horton appeared looking up at them and yelled, "Where are the blackberries?"

CHAPTER TWENTY-FIVE

When the doctors at the VA hospital told Carole that John was doing better now and she could take him home, she didn't feel reassured. He was much calmer now, even gentle, but she worried that the drugs were just deadening his pain and anger. She remembered the doctors told her he could still have serious mood swings. They said by going back for psychotherapy twice a week, they could monitor his condition.

When she brought him home, John seemed genuinely happy to see Reggie, giving him a long hug. With tears in his eyes, he apologized for his bad behavior. Reggie felt better and hopeful, but worried about seeing him moping around the house, sitting dazed in front of the TV for hours. When he asked his mom if his dad was always going to be that way, she told him that he will have a flat affect for some time until he shows progress in therapy. *Flat affect,* Reggie thought, *he looked like those zombies on TV with no soul.*

Wondering what the therapy was doing for him, Reggie asked.

"Dad keeps going from being quiet to being angry. Is it just the PTSD and medications?"

"Not completely," she answered with some hesitation. His therapist, Dr. Rheinwald, told me he also had issues that went way back into his childhood. Stuff with his dad and all."

"Whoa!"

"Yeah. Your dad used to tell me how his dad would beat him, then blame the Brujo."

"What's that?"

"A bad shaman I guess, who would somehow pass along a curse through the generations. His dad thought he was cursed to be a failure and your dad used to wonder if the curse was passed along to him."

"Jesus, Mom. I didn't think dad believed in any of that old Indian stuff."

"Yeah, he always tried to make light of it, but I think when his dad committed suicide, it affected him more than he would admit. But hopefully, Dr. Rheinwald will help him work through those issues. We just have to keep trying to understand him and support him as best we can."

"I'll try." Reggie said. *Maybe I've got the curse of the Brujo,* Reggie thought.

****

Later in the week, something Carole told John really upset him. John had known that Reggie was no longer going on his Saturday hikes with Joe, but was pleased that Reggie's school hiking club was going well. That's when he remembered about that 'wildlife corridor' meeting that Joe wanted him to attend.

"Is Reggie going to that meeting?" John asked Carole.

"Yes, John, I gave him permission to go."

"What!" he yelled, "I told him to forget it."

Carole saw his flat affect turn into prickly anger and said, "John, please. Reggie told me he couldn't go, but I knew what it meant to him and you being in the hospital, I said he could. So you can blame me, I'm sorry."

"How could you do that?" his tone turning bitter, "you knew I didn't want him seeing that guy anymore...I trusted you."

"I'm sorry, John, it's not that I defied you, I stood up for *our* son...that meeting meant everything to him."

"What's a kid doing attending a government committee on a corridor for mountain lions?"

"John, this is where Reggie is finding himself, and he's already achieved a lot. Don't you want that for your son?"

John reflected for a couple of seconds, then said, "What has he achieved?"

"Let me show you," she said as she got up and went into Reggie's room and came back holding a newspaper.

"Look at this article. Reggie's appearance at a previous meeting has already influenced legislators to ban certain rat poisons that also kill wildlife."

Carole handed John the latest issue of Conservation News with a front page article including a photo of Reggie and Joe speaking at the conference. John looked at the photo for a long time, then started reading the article, but his focus kept moving back to the photo. Carole wondered if he was seeing a resemblance to himself and what he might say or do.

Pointing to Joe's picture, he asked, "Do you like this Joe?"

Hesitating, she answered, "Sure, he's a nice guy."

"Do you more than *like* him?" he asked.

She saw that his face was getting red and tense, and said, "Please John, I've only met him a couple of times with Reggie. You're not thinking I..."

John stared at the picture again and started shaking his head.

Carole stood up, worried that his new meds might be acting up and prepared for the worse.

153

"I don't know if I can trust this guy. I want to meet him face to face."

Carole sat back down and said, "No problem, John. Once you're better, we'll invite him over."

Next day, after Reggie left for school, John gave Carole a ride to work at the Bean and then came home. He pulled out that article about Joe and Reggie, noting the name of the Agency. He put on his camouflage shirt and pants, his blaze orange hunting vest, loaded his 30.06 rifle into the trunk and drove to Joe's office.

After he parked in the lot, he put his head down on the steering wheel. His head began to spin. He didn't know where he was. In the Humvee when the IUD struck? Then a park ranger in uniform walked by and startled John. Then he seemed to gain his composure and decided to leave the rifle in the trunk. He could come back if he needed it.

He found Joe's office number on the directory, headed upstairs and pushed open Joe's office door.

Joe immediately jumped up from his desk. Although he never met him, Joe recognized the face of the man who looked like him— Reggie's dad. Maintaining his relative cool from years of working with large carnivores, Joe said, "John?"

Taken aback by Joe's recognition, John said, "How do you know who I am?"

"Your son told me a lot about you; that you were a seasoned hunter. He told me you taught him everything he knows about nature and that you might pay me a visit someday."

John's aggressive demeanor began softening with Joe's welcome.

Joe reached out his hand and said, "Pleased to finally meet you. Have a seat."

John slowly moved toward the chair, sat, and then noticed the wedding picture on his desk.

"Good looking woman," John said. "How long have you been married?"

"That's my Barbara, we've been married three plus years now."

"Any kids?"

"No, but we'd love to have children someday, God willing."

Joe continued with his winning offensive saying, "You know John, you should be real proud of Reggie, he's so sharp and I'm convinced he could make a major contribution to wildlife conservation someday. Something that hunters care about too."

"Right," John replied but said, "but I'm here 'cause I'd like to know why you need a high school kid for a government meeting. It's during the school week, you know?"

"Yes, we'll need to get the school's permission as well as yours. But this is a great learning opportunity for Reggie." Joe went on to explain how Reggie's participation in the rat poison program really impressed an important State official and how Reggie's strong beliefs about the need for a wildlife corridor, could really have an impact.

"That's fair enough," John said, then he opened up, "I always thought that Reggie's love of nature was fine, but more like a hobby he could pursue outside of a career in business. Are you saying there is a potential career for him in this field?"

"Definitely," Joe confirmed, "I make a good living on very satisfying work. You know what's funny," he continued, "my dad wasn't too happy about my career choice either; he wanted me to have the secure life of an orthodontist like he was. As a kid we spent a lot of time fishing and enjoying nature and that's the field I wanted to be in. The last thing I wanted to do was poke around inside mouths all day. So I worked my way through college, got my Master's in Biology and never looked back."

"Yeah, well," John said, "you went your own way, something to say for that alright."

"How about you, John?" "Did you have dreams as a kid?"

"Shit, yes. I wanted to go to college and study geology—I was fascinated by how the earth was formed. My dad wanted me to join him in his cabinet carpentry business, Youngblood and Son. I didn't have enough guts to go my own way. I hated him for that and regretted it all my life."

"That's very unfortunate, John," Joe offered. "Sometimes family survival needs take precedent and life throws you a bad deal."

"Yeah. My dad's business failed." He paused, then said, "And he committed suicide."

Joe shook his head and said, "I'm sorry."

"Yeah, well I got away and at least my dad had taught me carpentry. Built my own house up in Crestview. Thank God I met Carole and we had Reggie. Anyway that's a long story, I better get going."

John stood up, shook Joe's hand and said, "You guys have a good conference then."

"Thanks," Joe said as John headed out the door.

When John got home, he took off his hunting gear, locked his rifle in the gun case, took a long shower and cried through most of it. He broke down several times during the day. When he picked Carole up and Reggie got home from school, both of them sensed that he seemed somehow different—less in a daze, but sadder.

155

At the dinner table, Carole asked John how his day went. He told them it went fine and that he had a good visit with Joe and that he *did* seem to be a good guy after all. Reggie and his mom caught each other's surprised and pleased expressions, then quickly went back to eating. After a while Carole couldn't hold back a follow up question about their meeting. John would only say that it was a short meeting and that he only wanted to know more about the wildlife corridor conference.

"And?" she asked.

"Both of us agreed it would be a good learning experience for Reggie," he answered. "And there's a meeting this Monday to prepare for the Conference. I'll call the school to arrange for Reggie to be absent both days."

Reggie looked at his mom, she smiled and snapped her fingers.

That was all. Cut and dry. And that was good. So they thought.

****

The next trail the Hiking Club decided on for Saturday was the Paramount Ranch Trail. The members chose it, in part, because that's where the studio filmed many of the old TV westerns. That Saturday when they headed up the trail, they goofed around on the grounds of the old movie set. Reggie got inspired by the saloon building and pretended to come out, guns blazing at the bad guys. Stephanie got a good snapshot.

The trail itself was quite nice and had a lot of diversity; oak savannahs, rolling grassland and the tall Sugar Loaf Peak which had excellent views of the surrounding mountains and canyons. When they reached the peak, all the kids wanted to stand at the very edge of the rocky ledge and pose. Stephanie obliged and took individual photos of the daring hikers.

Surprisingly, Reggie didn't watch Stephanie take the pictures—he found himself staring in the opposite direction. He was scouring the hills above the freeway like he was in a trance.

"Reggie, what are you looking at?" Stephanie asked. "Don't you want your picture on the ledge?"

"Sure," he said not turning around as he kept staring at the hills in deep thought.

"Reggie, come on," she said. "Are you alright?"

"Coming," he said as he walked to the photo op and sat down at the ledge.

"Reggie, why are you sitting? You look like some sorta guru or something."

"This is a special place for me and I'm taking it all in. Go ahead shoot my picture, okay?"

Click. Then Stephanie put out her hand to him.

"Now that's the last picture. Come on, the group is taking a snack break over by the mile marker."

Reggie got up, but instead of following her he said, "Let me stay here for a little while longer, okay?" as he turned around and looked down below the ledge.

"You're not going to jump are you?" She said as she looked back.

"Ha. Be there in a minute."

When the club members finished their break, Stephanie ran over to Reggie who was still staring below the ledge.

"Hey, Reg," she said as he jumped when she put her hand on his shoulder. "Here, I brought you a bag of dried cranberries."

He turned around with a huge smile on his face, took the bag and gave her a hug.

"Thanks for thinking of me Steph. I love these."

Soon the hikers were back on the trail. The dull roar of the freeway faded away. As usual Reggie tried to impress Stephanie with his knowledge of the fauna, including pointing out the difference between tree and ground squirrels. Stephanie took photos of everything he showed her. Climbing ahead, up a rocky hill strewn with gravel, Stephanie slipped. She let out a shriek, tumbled and fell hard before Reggie could catch her.

"Shit!" she yelled as Reggie jumped to help her.

"Here, hold on," Reggie said as her pulled her up, "you okay?"

"Oww! She cried when her left foot came down. She jerked it back up. "I think I hurt my ankle."

"You alright down there?" Mrs. Horton shouted from up top.

"Think Stephanie got hurt," Reggie called back.

"I'm coming down," Mrs. Horton said. "Wait there."

"Let's sit you down," Reggie said as he put his arm around her waist and coaxed her to sit on some large boulders on the side of the trail.

"Thanks, Reg, I feel so stupid."

"Hey. Shit happens. Right?"

When Mrs. Horton reached them, she asked Stephanie to remove her hiking shoe and sock so she could have a closer look at the ankle. She gently probed the area around the ankle bone.

"There!" Stephanie yelped and jerked as Mrs. Horton touched the sensitive spot.

"No broken bones, thank God," Mrs. Horton said. "I've seen this a lot over my years of hiking and unless it starts turning red and swelling up, it'll probably just be sore for a while.

"Reggie, would you stay with Stephanie here to rest for a bit? We'll continue up the trail to the five mile marker and loop back down."

Duh! Reggie thought as he looked at Stephanie, squeezed her waist and said, "Sure."

"Here, take these aspirins," Mrs. Horton said. "We'll be back about half an hour. She ought to be better by then."

As soon as the hikers left, Stephanie grabbed her camera and took a picture of her foot.

"You're something else," Reggie said, "You take pictures of every friggin' thing, what's with that?"

"I didn't tell you? I want to be a photojournalist someday."

"That's cool, what got you into that?"

"Um. I saw a documentary once about Dorothy Lange and other photographers who photographed the struggles people had during the Great Depression of the 1930's. I'd like to be as good as she was."

"What would you photograph?"

"Faces. I want to capture the stories that people's faces tell when they're meeting a challenge. Like not having a home ...losing a loved one at war. Not only sad faces, but hopeful ones too."

"That's beautiful, Steph. I admire you."

She turned and focused her camera on Reggie. *Click.*

"Cute faces, too. Like yours."

"Come on. Get real." Reggie said.

Click.

"Oh, there's that modest face," she teased and laughed.

He laughed. *Click.*

"Hey, how's the ankle?"

"It's not throbbing anymore. Would you rub it a little for me?"

"Um. Yeah. You sure?"

With the lightest touch Reggie could muster he ran the tips of his fingers over her ankle.

"Can you feel that? Does it hurt?"

"No, it feels good. You can rub it a little harder."

With the palms of his two hands, he began gently massaging her soft skin and looking back at her to make sure he didn't press too hard. One time he saw her eyes were closed.

"Reggie, can I ask you something?"

"Yeah?"

"Have you ever gone out with a girl?"

"Um. Sort of, once. She's gone now."

"You broke up?"

"Sorta," he mumbled again, not looking up.

"Guess you don't want to talk about it, huh?"

Reggie nodded.

"You can rub my whole foot, if you want."

Reggie began to run his hands up from her toes, along her heel and up to the top of her ankle and back again.

"My leg is a little tight too, how about if you put those magic hands to my calves?"

'*Oh my God,* Reggie thought as he began massaging. *Her leg is so smooth. So soft. So long. I want to go all the way up to her shorts.*'

"Mmm, that feels good," she said as she put her hand on his neck and stroked it gently.

Geez, Reggie thought, *this is driving me wild* as he felt the bulge growing against the tight fabric of his jeans.

Stephanie put her hand on his chin and pulled him up toward her.

"I like you, Reggie."

"I like you too," he said feeling weak.

She pulled him up closer to her and lightly, tentatively kissed him softly on the lips, hoping he'd want more. Reggie looked into her eyes.

Melted into her lips.

Full mouths wrapping. Deep. Wet.

Wheeew! Reggie felt like he was soaring.

Stephanie made a soft moaning sound.

Reggie pulled away. "Did I hurt you?"

"No way, kiss me again."

Holy Jesus, Reggie thought, *I super don't want her to stop.*

Off in the distance, they heard voices.

Reggie broke the kiss. "We better stop."

"Um. Yeah," she said as she looked into his flushed face and patted his head. Reggie kept his hand on her waist.

After a few moments, Stephanie spoke, "Reggie, can I ask you something else? What was that up on the peak when you were like staring into space then looking down below the ledge? It was kinda weird."

"Sorry, I was thinking I need to go on another vision quest and think this would be an ideal place to do it."

"What's a vision quest?

"It's an ancient Native ritual. You go alone into the woods and try to discover your power animal."

"Power animal?" she asked.

"Yeah, well, connect with the spirit of an animal that will guide you in your adult life."

"I suppose you're questing for a mountain lion?"

Reggie looked at her startled and said, "How did you?..."

"Know?" she said. "I checked you out. One of the girls, Leah, who was in your Biology class last year told me you were into them, big time."

"Guess I am. That's why I was looking into the hills. That's where a young lion risked jumping over the freeway to find a new life. His name is P12."

"You sound like you're close to that animal?"

"Yeah. Sometimes I think I'm too close," he said as his face turned worried and he pulled his arm from her waist.

"What do you mean, Reggie?"

Staring at the ground, Reggie let out, "It's complicated, hard to understand."

"Tell me," she said.

Giving her a fearful look, he said, "Last time I did a vision quest it turned bad—it got violent."

"Whoa. Violent? What are you saying?"

Looking up the trail they saw the hikers coming down.

"It just got freaky that's all...kinda messed up my mind...like I was going mental. I didn't know if I was a human or an animal."

"Oh my God, Reggie, that's scary. Why would you want to do another one?"

"I dunno, it's like...like I have to. Maybe I'll go on one tomorrow. I'll tell you about it later."

"You better," she said as she punched his arm and laughed.

"Well, well," Mrs. Horton said, "looks like we're all better— that ankle doesn't even look red. Help her up Reggie, let's see if she can walk."

Stephanie let out a small 'Ouch' as she set her foot down. With Reggie holding her arm, she hobbled out a couple of steps then cracked a forced smile. "Just a bit tender," she said, "I think I can make it back alright."

The trail was mostly narrow on the return, so the group had to take it single file, 'Indian' style. Reggie told Stephanie to go ahead in case he had to catch her falling again. As Reggie watched her walk, he wished he had his hand on her waist again, so he could feel her hips rocking.

Reggie's eyes stayed glued ahead on Stephanie.

Her bouncing ponytail.

Her long legs.

Her beautiful rocking hips.

Every once in a while, she'd turn around and they'd give each other a knowing smile.

On the trail back, Reggie didn't feel the trail. His legs floated up and dropped down like they weren't even touching the ground.

****

160

When Reggie got home, he told his mom he had to go on another vision quest.

"When?" his Mom asked.

"Tomorrow," Reggie replied.

"You're *not* staying overnight!"

"I know, Mom—just during the day. I found this area near where P12 entered the Santa Monica's. There's a nice spot below a ledge where I can sit and take in nature.

"You'll have to ask your dad."

"Can I say it's okay with you?"

"You can as long as we know exactly where you'll be and stay in touch by phone."

To Reggie's amazement, once he told his dad his plan for Sunday and that he had his Mom's approval, his Dad went along. *Maybe it was the drugs,* Reggie thought, *he didn't remember he told me to forget about the old 'injun' ways.* He even told Reggie he knew of vision quests from his grandmother and wished he had the opportunity to take his own.

Reggie was totally surprised by his dad's first ever positive comment about his background, so he asked, "Your Grandma taught you about Indian ways?"

"Well she tried to. Grandma Wanchuat was a very wise and kind woman and her husband was a Shaman of the tribe, but he died before I was born. She used to babysit me and told me stories about her ancestors and tribal traditions."

"What were they? What do you remember?" Reggie asked with great excitement.

"Well, to be honest with you I didn't understand a lot at only five years old, but I remember when she told me stories about animals that talked. A frog I remember, I used to believe her. That's when I got into trouble with my dad."

"What kind of trouble?"

"I'd come back and tell my dad about what she told me and he'd get mad at his mother for filling my head with crazy ideas. He'd tell me that these old Indians couldn't tell the difference between the real world and the supernatural world. I think that's about the time he decided to take his family and leave the reservation."

"Why did he leave?"

"He got fed up with the poverty and booze and drugs on the 'rez' as he called it. He didn't want his son growing up there, getting caught in that."

"I thought he was a great carpenter?" Reggie asked.

"He was. Self-taught. Built most of the homes on the rez, but half the time he never got paid for it, so that's when he decided to take his skills to the LA area and start his own business. Funny, he hated what the white man did to his people, but he wanted to be like them and make money. Then his business failed and he..."

"Killed himself?" Reggie said.

"Yup. That's the story of the Youngblood's. He was a bitter man and I think he passed along some of that bitterness to me. I wonder how my life would have been different if I stayed on the rez and listened to my Grandmother."

"Did she give you that book about Chief Seattle, when you left?"

"Yeah. I know it was one of your favorite books. I let your mother read it to you—it brought up too many bad feelings for me."

Reggie looked at the sadness in his Dad's eyes and said, "Thanks for telling me that, Dad."

"No problem, Reg. Now how about I give you a ride up there tomorrow? I can hike with you to the spot and pick you up there by, say six in the evening?"

"That would be cool, Dad."

Reggie was a happy camper. *Joe must have really turned his dad around,* he thought. That night, Reggie had a restless sleep, excited about the possibilities of his coming vision quest.

****

On Sunday morning, when his dad dropped him off at Sugar Loaf Peak, Reggie put in that call to his mom to make sure the cell connection wasn't blocked by the mountains. His dad told him he'd be back at six and to have a good day.

As soon as he left, Reggie climbed down underneath the peak to the thicket where he still had a broad and solitary view of the canyons and hills. At first, he took in the beauty of the place, just as the vision quest book suggested. He watched a 'red-tail' circle and bank around the up-drafts that were formed by the heat of the mountainsides and the shade of the valleys. When the hawk finally dove vertically and disappeared among the oaks, Reggie figured he was probably clutching a squirrel in his talons.

To get in a receptive mood to discover his power animal, he thought about P12. That brave young cat who made it over the freeway. He could almost see him crisscrossing every square mile below him; searching for food or a mate, avoiding humans or another male. Every once in a while he heard hikers on the peak above. One group apparently decided to have their lunch above him as he got a shower of orange peels—their bright orange ellipses decorating the grey-green sagebrush.

Throughout the morning his quiet mind tangled with his lively mind and he thought about Steph, his mom and dad, Joe and then back to Steph again. Getting hungry, but also needing to pee, he hiked further down to find an even more wooded spot and he looked up at the peak to check the line of vision before unzipping his fly. Heading back up to his spot, he sat down and opened his backpack. His mom made him two fried egg and baloney sandwiches, so his growling stomach convinced him to ignore the fasting and he devoured them, gulping them down with Gatorade.

Trying to get back into a meditative state, he dozed off and soon a slight smile came to his face. He first pictured Steph sitting next to him. Running her fingers through his hair and combing it. She piled it even higher with her fingers and laughed. He let his hand flow to her shoulders where he slowly pulled her toward him and they kissed.

It was almost a butterfly kiss. A very soft feel that fluttered from his lips and moved to the bottom of his throat. She wrapped her arms around him and...

He woke, shook his head and took a long drink of water.

Then he lay down and soon returned to stillness. *More dreaming. This time it started in school with Steph and him walking in the halls, holding hands like they were going out. Kevin was walking deliberately toward the pair and when he approached, Reggie guided Steph behind him and asked Kevin what he wanted.*

"Your slut of a girlfriend," he said.

Then Reggie pounced on him. Grabbed at his throat. Held and locked on it tight—not with the claws of a lion, but with his thumbs digging into his Adam's apple. Kevin began gagging and Reggie could see his eyes bulge out. But it wasn't fear in Kevin's eyes—it was adrenalin. Kevin kicked him between the legs hard and Reggie buckled and lost his grip on his neck. Then Kevin raised his knee up hard into Reggie's chest, knocking his air out. Bent over, the pain wracked him up and down.

Reggie knew he would be killed if he didn't fight for his life.

Kevin thought he had Reggie finished and wouldn't face him again. Kevin laughed. Reggie kept his head down, sprung with his hindquarters and rammed him in the stomach. Kevin fell to the floor. On top, Reggie grabbed his hair with both hands and slammed it hard on the floor, and growled like a demon. Again. A thud and a crack. Again. Kevin's eyes rolled back into his head like a child's doll—getting duller and duller with each slam. Then Reggie saw the red begin to ooze over the black and white tile. A lion would finish him. Reggie slammed his head one last time. He felt the head loosen. Did he?

Reggie got up. Steph was standing there crying, her hands covering her face. Reggie took her arm, and said, 'Let's get out of here'...

... When a mayfly landed on his nose and he swatted it, jerked up and rubbed his face awake.

'What the fuck?' Reggie cursed out loud, *'I come out here to discover a power animal to guide me on my life's journey and I dream I'm turning into an animal?'*

He looked at his phone. Only 4:30. *I'm out of here, he thought, this vision quest thing is all fucked up. My mind only fills up with killing. How can I make it stop?*

He called his dad, who was surprised it was so early, but was glad to know everything was alright.

In a hurry to get away from that freak-out place, Reggie started walking back to the trailhead and parking lot to meet his dad.

On the hike back, he kept seeing Kevin's dying eyes and hearing his skull cracking. When he pictured the oozing blood again, he buckled over and dry-heaved to the side of the trail. Only bringing up a burning yellow sputum—that made him gag again.

Despite how much he despised Kevin, he thought he could never do that thing. Or could he? He wasn't sure anymore. He *felt* like he could and *felt* like he would. These fucked up vision quests, become real—that's the problem, Reggie thought. When he had a vision that he saw a male lion chase after a female and her cubs, it felt very real.

Joe verified that P1 was in the area of his cabin that night and that they later found the dead cubs. *Can't be, can't be,* he told himself. *But what came first, the dream or the event?*

Howls of laughter came up the trail and Reggie spotted a troop of boy scouts. When the leader stopped and asked him how far to the peak. "About a mile up," Reggie said, feeling his feet firm to the ground, waken to reality. When he reached the trailhead, his dad wasn't there yet, so he sat on a picnic bench, pulled out his phone and ran through his contacts, asking himself who could he talk to about this.

He wanted to call Steph, but what was he going to say? That the vision quest had him killing someone because of what he said about her? If he told his mom she would worry and obsess about it. He couldn't dare tell his dad in his condition. Maybe he could ask to see a counselor at school on Monday. Joe? He was always understanding and had a good feel for people's needs and problems. *I wish I could ask a Native American who's been on a vision quest, but where? No way,* he thought, *I've already cheated, doing a half-assed version. Maybe I should just stop freaking out.*

The old Impreza pulled up and Reggie walked quickly to the car, opened the door before his dad came to a stop and threw his pack into the back seat.

"Everything alright, Reggie?" his dad asked.

"Yeah," Reggie answered looking out the window.

"Have any visions?"

"Nope."

"You sure you're alright? You don't look so good."

No answer.

"You called early, so I ..."

"I'm okay, dad, just an upset stomach, that's all."

For the next half an hour, Reggie didn't say a word until his dad talked about his own father.

"You know, Reggie, when I was a kid," his dad began, "you didn't talk to your father about things like feelings and personal problems. My dad thought you had to buck up to everything." He continued, "I know we've never much talked either, but if there's something you want to get of your chest, I'll listen. Maybe I can help you."

"Thanks Dad, but I don't want to talk about it," Reggie replied, thinking of how his attempt to connect to his Indian background did not seem to be working for him. He started feeling even more freaked out thinking about his father's bitterness and the suicide. "Please, Dad. I don't feel very good."

"Okay, okay. I'm sorry."

Reggie looked over at his dad and could see that he genuinely wanted to reach out and listen, but he said, "Maybe when I feel better, we can talk." Reggie could see that his dad felt rejected, but there was no way he could tell him about what was making him sick.

When they got home, Reggie told his mom he wasn't feeling well and no, he didn't want to eat. After his Dad nodded to confirm his feelings, Reggie grabbed a can of Dr. Pepper and spent the rest of the evening in his room. He didn't even return Steph's phone call, knowing she'd want to ask him about his vision quest.

That evening, Carole could see something was terribly wrong. She asked John, "What's going on with Reggie?"

"I tried to get Reggie to talk about it," John said, "but he got really angry. Never seen such fear and anger in his eyes."

"What do you think caused that?" Carole asked.

"I was telling him how my dad and I never talked—that's when he blew up. It was stupid of me. It probably brought up bad things in his mind. How me and my dad fought and the suicide."

"Oh God, John," Carole said as she took him into her arms, "This scares me."

"Me, too," he said. "Maybe he'll be better in the morning."

In her mind, Carole hoped that meeting for the wildlife corridor conference with Joe tomorrow might brighten him up.

CHAPTER TWENTY-SIX

First he smelled her, then he heard her. Lupine-boy had been coming back often to Topanga Canyon where he first met her. He hoped he would soon find the young She-Paw in heat. On this night, he quickly picked up her invitation—a scratching containing the pungent promise of sex. Luckily, he did not pick up any scent of Big-Paw, his rival, her master. So, he followed the primordial obligation of his species and began his pursuit of her. Reaching a ridge overlooking the canyon, he heard her call. It was a caterwaul, a much louder version of the same call he heard his small cat cousins make from the yards of the two-legs.

Like a simultaneous cry and scream, it shot sharp through the canyon mist and echoed against the rock ledges like a dozen she-devils. She-Paw advertised her readiness and location, and he knew it was meant for him. He would answer the call.

He moved quickly down the ridgeline, along a dry creek bed, and into a dense wooded area. Then he saw her; sitting near a stand of sycamores. She-Paw recognized him and let out another caterwaul, this one with an even higher-pitched vibrato. Feeling the impulse in his loins, Lupine-boy jumped at her. She snarled and reared back like she did when they first met—a warning snarl that surprised him. Even though Big-paw wasn't near, she gave him a message of fear.

He approached her again, this time more cautiously, anticipating they could rub heads, or maybe he would even be allowed to lick her face. She gave him a low growl and then moved back nervously and bent down into the crouch of female submission. He pounced on her back with the furor of an attack, held her with his forepaws, and rammed his hindquarters into hers. In less than a minute, his jaws firmly—but carefully— grabbed at her neck, and he growled at the climax of his first conquest.

Resting for a few minutes still atop his lioness, he entered her again, this time more powerfully than before. She let out some growls as her body shuttered from his pounding. Lupine-boy remained faithful to his species that day and continued his short but frequent and vigorous couplings. He was now Lupine-lion.

Lupine-lion became more familiar with his new partner over the hours, but She-Paw still did not take to his instinctual attempts at neck rubbing and licking during rest periods. She would snap and snarl and even produce an 'ouch' sound whenever he attempted foreplay. She communicated with Lupine-lion in cougar language and he desperately tried to understand her.

When he was on top of her, he certainly could smell Big-paw on her fur. But Lupine-lion could also smell something more, something strange below the clutch of fur. Were his animal instincts—passed down to him for thousands of years by his ancestors—telling him that he must act in a way to preserve his species? For the moment, Lupine-lion only acted upon the immediate instinct to mate, and he did that with total abandon. Lupine-lion did not perceive, in his current single mindedness, that the sounds and smells of mating awakened the acute senses of another male cougar. Still miles away but moving fast, Big-paw was on his way to recover his possession.

Early on the second day of their affair, following a few hours of deep sleep, She-Paw was startled awake by what can only be called a sixth sense. She couldn't have smelled her old master's arrival who approached silently upwind from the couple. But she alerted Lupine-lion with her defensive hissing alarm call.

Jumping into a fighting stance with his heart beating fast, Lupine-lion saw Big-paw. The old master stood on a hillock only 50 lion-lengths away. The low morning sun was at his back, giving the animal the golden glow of a forest god. Although Big-paw stood perfectly still, taking in the situation and his line of attack, his shadows moved ominously, wrapping around the trunks of the sycamores, and surrounded the pair.

She-Paw slowly moved away from Lupine-lion while hissing and twitching in fear. Lupine-lion, though, no longer felt fear. He had taken the female from the old lion and now she was his. That's when he 'heard' a simple and direct command from his paternal ancestors: Prepare to fight and prepare to die. He let out a loud yowl, a message that announced, "This is my territory, and I dare you to take it."

Big-paw yowled back, bared his teeth, and began to march toward the young lion. When he got within 10 lion-lengths, he moved to the left and toward the female so the offender could get a good look at him. Lupine-lion could now see the big cat's assets. His fighting weight was at least a 50-pound advantage. His paws were huge, his claws were long. His head and body were covered in scars from previous battles that he had no doubt won. Then there was the swagger; Big-paw paraded back and forth as if he could bluff the young cat into not taking him on. Lupine-lion stood his ground. He faced and followed his enemy, hissing at him as if to say, "YOU should be afraid."

By this time, both males were in full view of the female. Her maternal instincts compelled her to view the competing males and select which one best fulfilled her obligation to the species. She had to choose (or be chosen by) the strongest, most vital male who would pass along good genes to her kittens to help ensure their survival. She knew her old master well, having already fathered their offspring. He had proven his strength in battle. So, there must have been a much more powerful knowing that caused her to make her next move.

Out of blind fear, or perhaps out of blinding courage, she snarled at Big-paw and moved around behind her young savior.

Her decision was also decisive for Big-paw. He snarled slowly and paced menacingly back and forth in front of the transgressor looking for the best way to take him down. She-Paw continued to make the multitude of snarls, growls and yowls she did when she first spoke to the young suitor. Lupine-lion remembered her previous message of fear; now it was clear and strong. He now knew why she smelled as she did. It was her father who killed her cubs. Her message was "you must fight him." Even though he knew She-Paw was his daughter, Lupine-lion had to kill Big-paw.

Lupine-lion struck first. With the coil and speed of a high jumper, he leaped and aimed for Big-paw's neck, his claws popping out of their sheaths. Big-paw reared up to meet Lupine-lion head-to-head; Big-paw's weight held, and he pushed the young lion down and immediately went for his jugular.

Lupine-lion quickly slipped under him, and in a flash was on the big lion's back. Big-paw twisted his head around, snapping, and they locked jaws. Lupine-lion had the upper hold on Big-paw's nose, piercing and locking hard. Big-paw lifted and turned his head free, bleeding profusely. A brief second passed before they both leaped at the same time, claws ready to end the fight. Lupine-lion was faster and got in twice the rips for every one of his foes'.

The howls and screams from both animals filled the canyon like devils burning in hellfire. Lupine-lion's claws were sharper than the older male's and he was able to tear one of Big-paw's eyes almost completely out of its socket. Lupine-lion hooked his canines just below the old lion's ear and tore a huge gash only inches from the vein that meant sure death.

From that point on, it seemed to be the young lion's fight to lose. The older, heavier lion had the disadvantage of having travelled all night to meet his foe. The young lion did not let up, biting hard at Big-paw's face with his young sharp teeth. The worn canines of his enemy could barely penetrate his hide.

Lupine-lion charged again at Big-paw's neck, and this time caught his worn tracking collar with his teeth and twisted it off. Panting for breath, Big-paw backed away trying to rub his bloody torn eyes and focus on his now blurry enemy's next move. Perhaps it was then when he sensed Lupine-lion's superior skills and passion. Perhaps, he simply felt defeated in his body, but he backed up and started hobbling away. Big-paw, unlike his young competitor, was no longer willing to die for She-Paw.

Next, and perhaps more surprisingly, Lupine-lion did not go in for the kill. The victor sensed that he had mortally wounded the old master, and the young lion watched as the vanquished male trailed off into the bush. Lupine-lion turned to his partner, finding her a short distance away. She had witnessed the whole battle. Despite his wounds and exhaustion, Lupine-lion immediately mounted her and copulated several times in as many minutes, each time ending in a roar and a neck bite.

She-Paw purred through the pain. The two were different now. At rest and lying together, she licked his bloodied face and rubbed his scratched and swollen head with her head. For the next three days, the sex acts continued like clockwork, but in between there was conversation. He caressed her gently. She-Paw provided her new partner with a constant series of soft growls, kitten-like chirps, and lazy mews. There no longer seemed to be fear in her voice. She was pleased with her new master. She now would bear him the strongest kittens.

CHAPTER TWENTY-SEVEN

Monday morning Carole woke Reggie. He was still tired. Despondent.

By nine, Carole reminded Reggie that Joe was picking him up at ten for their meeting.

Reggie got up, gulped down a quart of milk, and ran into the bathroom. He still felt sick from his shitty vision quest, but he told his mom he was okay.

By ten Joe arrived to pick Reggie up. Despite not feeling well, Reggie wanted to go. Joe told him he'd drop him off at school by noon.

On the drive, Joe knew Reggie was more than a little sick. He looked gaunt, on edge, even fearful. Joe tried to engage Reggie about what they'd cover in the meeting; how the research supported the need for lions to move in and out of the Santa Monica's. Reggie only nodded.

When Joe broke the news about P1, he noticed Reggie's face change. He looked like he was in shock. Joe told him, "My team found the old dominant male's shredded, detached collar and evidence of a battle with another male—possibly P12. Tracking data showed them to be in the same general area, but they need to analyze the blood and DNA matter they found at the scene."

Reggie said nothing, just continued to stare at Joe.

Then Joe added, "They haven't found P1's body yet."

Reggie struggled to grasp this information in his head. Then, in his gut, he finally realized the connection to his vision quest. He projectile-vomited, covering the dashboard and windshield with a smelly yellow-white bile. Joe pulled the car to the shoulder.

"Jesus, Joe. I'm so sorry," Reggie sobbed in between the heaves.

"It's okay," Joe said as he helped Reggie to the side of the road for more retching.

Joe could still hear him struggling to say he was sorry while he cleaned the car. After Reggie settled a bit, Joe insisted on taking Reggie home, but Reggie believed there was nothing left in his system, so he insisted on going to the meeting. He told Joe he'd wash up when they got there.

Throughout the meeting, Reggie seemed only somewhat attentive, but at one point he told Joe he needed to go to the bathroom. Noticing he was absent for several minutes, Joe excused himself and went to check on Reggie. He found one stall occupied and heard what sounded like sobbing.

"Reggie, is that you? Are you okay?"

"Sorry, Joe, I'll be out in a minute. You need to get back to your meeting, I'll be right there."

When Reggie returned he didn't actively participate in the meeting, but when it ended, Joe, once again, wanted to take him home. Reggie wanted to go back to school and told him yes, he'd check in with the school nurse when he got there.

****

By eleven forty-five, Reggie checked in at the office, but not with the nurse. He still felt rank and rotten so he tried to wash up in the bathroom. Then he went into the lunch yard to find Stephanie. Stephanie saw Reggie come into the yard and ran over to him and gave him a hug. Then she jumped and stepped back. She saw that he looked sick, and smelled bad.

"Reggie, are you okay?"

Looking down, he barely noticed she had her hair in two braids, and said, "Sorry, but I must have caught some sort of flu bug."

"You look terrible! Why didn't you stay home?"

"I had that wildlife corridor planning meeting. I still went and everything, but I was too sick to participate. I really let Joe down."

Pulling Reggie along like an invalid, Stephanie said, "Let's go sit down at a corner table and you can tell me about it."

"Nothing to tell, really."

"What about your vision quest on Sunday? I called, you know."

Reggie put his hand to his throat and quickly faced away from Stephanie.

"Reggie?"

Reggie held back the churning feeling in his stomach and turned back to look at her.

"Oh my God, Reggie you look really bad. You should go to see the nurse. Like right now."

"It's okay. There's nothing left in my stomach. I've been barfing all morning."

Steph tugged at his arm. "What's really going on? You can tell me."

"I... I... had a horrible vision quest on Sunday that turned out to be more of a nightmare than anything. I was a wild animal and I was...

I... killed someone. I'm all messed up in my head and I had moments where I honestly didn't know if I was Reggie Youngblood—or a lion."

Stephanie put her arm around his shoulder. "I've had some bad nightmares, too, but when you look back, they're just stupid dreams. I'm sure it will fade soon enough."

Reggie appreciated her empathy, but he was not really comforted. "This is not just a dream, Stephanie."

Taken aback, she asked, "What do you mean?"

"My fucking vision quests are... are... they're coming true. I told you about the time I dreamed that P1 killed his cubs and... and... then I find out from Joe that he actually did it!"

Reggie started to choke up, but Stephanie nodded to him to continue. "Keep talking. Maybe you just need to get this off your chest."

"I wish I could empty my mind because on Sunday all I saw was me as a mountain lion and I had to kill a rival lion for his territory. And I did. I killed him. And in real life, Joe just told me that they think P1 is dead and P12 probably killed him."

"That's crazy!"

"Is it?" he asked, looking at her for understanding. "I've heard that how you feel in a dream is always the most real part of a dream. It's just too weird. I'm somehow connected to all of this. These are more than dreams I'm having. It's like I am being controlled by a supernatural force. I should never have done that vision quest."

The lunch bell rang and they both looked up and saw a kid, wearing sunglasses and a baseball cap, walking in their direction.

"Who's that?" Stephanie asked.

At first, Reggie couldn't believe his eyes. He thought that the school wasn't going to let him back in... but this kid looked a lot like Kevin. It *was* Kevin. He was bigger than Reggie remembered, and he had stubble growing on his chin.

Stephanie looked from Kevin to Reggie, and then from Reggie to back to Kevin.

As Kevin got closer, Reggie stood up. That's when Kevin started to run right at him. "I'm going to kill you, half-breed! You fucked up my life."

Reggie instinctively got into a fighting stance and pushed Stephanie behind him. "You fucked up your own life, asshole. What are you doing here?"

From across the yard, someone shouted, "STOP!" It was Mr. Suarosky running fast toward them.

Kevin reached for Reggie and bumped him hard with his chest. "Find yourself another lesbo girlfriend, little Reggie?"

Reggie's fists clenched so hard he thought his fingertips were going to burst right through his palms. He was just about to pull back and punch Kevin in the face when Mr. Suarosky jumped between them. The teacher grabbed Kevin by the triceps and pulled him in the other direction. "What the hell are you doing here, Kevin? Right into the Principal's office, now." Then, Mr. Suarosky pointed at Reggie and Stephanie. "You two get to your classes. Mr. Tremper will want to see you Reggie."

Stephanie slipped her hand into Reggie's and pulled him to leave the lunch yard. "Oh my God, Reggie! Who is that jerk and what was all that about?

"An asshole named Kevin," Reggie said as they walked into the building. "I got into a fight with him last year. A big one."

"Seriously? I didn't think you were the kind of guy who got into fights," she said, dropping his hand from hers. "Reggie, this is really scary."

Reggie reached for her hand and looked straight into her brown eyes. "It's okay. I promise. It'll be alright."

"Alright?" she asked. "After that nightmare or what the hell ever it was you told me about?"

"This has nothing to do with that. Look, I know this looks bad, but Kevin was expelled last year for starting the fight and bullying, not me. The only reason I fought him in the first place was to protect my best friend."

"But if he got expelled, then why is he back?"

"I'm just as surprised as you are. They told me last year that he could conditionally return to this school depending on counseling and parental intervention." Just as the period bell rang, he added, "Maybe something got screwed up. But you shouldn't have to worry about this crap."

"Crap?" she said. "I'm afraid. I'm worried that you're maybe someone who's always getting into trouble."

They stood in the middle of the hallway, both about to head in opposite directions, when Stephanie asked, "And what's that stuff about another lesbo girlfriend?"

"That's just some dumb shit," Reggie shrugged. "He's talking about Jennifer, who was really just a friend, not a girlfriend. She moved to Georgia. Bottom line is that Kevin is an asshole and he'll probably end up in juvenile hall."

"But this fighting and what Kevin said, it's...it's confusing and it scares me." She let go of his hand and began to walk down the hall, away from him. Without turning around, she said, "I don't like this whole thing, Reggie."

Reggie stood watching Stephanie disappear around the corner, and all he could think about was one thing: *I'm gonna kill Kevin.*

He headed off to his chemistry class. There, he nodded off within five minutes of Mr. Jasko's review of the periodic table of elements. Later, Reggie jumped awake when he felt something on his shoulder and saw Mr. Jasko tapping him with his pointer.

"Mr. Youngblood, we haven't gotten to the inert elements yet, but you need to come alive now. Mr. Tremper is here to see you."

The principal stood in the door and waved to him. Reggie climbed out of his chair and followed him to the office. Mr. Tremper ushered him into a chair and said, "I am sorry about what happened with Kevin, he was not allowed on our school grounds."

"I thought he was permanently expelled?"

"He was. Kevin and his parents did not comply with our requirements for re-admittance and Kevin showed up unannounced. Good thing Mr. Suarosky recognized him in the lunch yard before anything happened."

"Um, yeah," Reggie said.

"The Encino Police Department will be contacting you about whether or not you want to file an assault complaint and restraining order against Kevin." Reggie nodded and let the principal continue: "I'm sorry all this had to happen on our school grounds. I can assure you it will never happen again. Can your mom or your dad come and pick you up now?"

"Yeah. My dad's at home. I'll call him."

"Good. Tell your parents I will call them tonight, I have to head off now to a school board meeting. Take care, Reggie."

****

John arrived at the school at three, and when he picked up Reggie, he looked pale and was non-communicative.

John asked if he was feeling okay, and Reggie said he wasn't. That his stomach hurt and he wanted to go home. John didn't want to push it and let him be for the rest of the ride. John dropped him off and then immediately turned around to pick Carole up at the Coffee Bean.

Reggie was watching TV when the phone rang. He let the answering machine get it, and it was the principal, Mr. Tremper, wanting to talk to his parents. He immediately erased the message.

When his parents returned, his mom didn't have any luck talking with Reggie either, except for when he agreed to have mac and cheese for supper.

After he managed to keep his supper down, Reggie went to his room. He tried to call Steph, but there was no answer. He immediately tried her again, but it went straight to voicemail.

Sitting in his room with the lights off, Reggie grew more and more despondent—about Stephanie, his Dad, Kevin, the mountain lions. Everything. But most of all, what he thought about, was that he was becoming afraid of himself. Just a few weeks ago he thought things had turned a corner and his future was starting to take shape, but it seemed like all that was now falling apart.

He could understand why Stephanie was so put off by Kevin coming at him in the lunch yard and what he said. *She must think I am a friggin' psychotic. This whole thing, my whole life is like a fucked up curse. I don't know what's real anymore.*

It started with those damned mountain lions. Why, he thought, *did I ever feel this thing for them? Now they are haunting me.*

Why is this happening to me? When is this violence going to stop? How can I end it?

Tap! Tap! Reggie heard his mom's familiar knock on his door.

"Reggie, how are you doing?"

"Still feeling sick."

"Can I come in for a moment?"

"Okay."

She entered and turned on a lamp. "Is it your stomach?"

"Yeah, my head too."

She went over and put her hand to his forehead to feel for a temperature. Her touch brought Reggie momentarily back to reality and to the love his mother had for him.

"You don't feel hot, but you still look pale. Did you get real sick at school?"

"I just felt like I was going to throw up again when I called Dad to come and get me."

"Do you think you will want to stay home tomorrow?" she asked.

"I might, but I'll let you know."

"Is there anything you want to tell me? Anything you want to talk about?" When Reggie didn't reply, she continued: "You know, Reggie, if you keep emotions and hurt and anger pent up inside you, they can explode later and hurt you and others."

"Like with Dad?" he asked.

"Like with Dad."

"Things are just messed up now, that's all." He stood up and grabbed his laptop. "I'm just going to stay up a little longer because I've been getting lots of messages from the mountain lion websites that I've got to follow up on. Then I'm going to go to bed."

"Sounds like a good plan," she said as she patted his shoulder and left.

There on his monitor was a big headline from the *Cougar Observer: "NEW KING OF THE MOUNTAINS?"* It was there in black and white. Quotes from Joe verifying that although they cannot be sure P1 was dead—it was highly likely after finding his detached, but still beeping, collar. P12's tracking collar showed he was in the vicinity when P1's movements stopped, and P12's tracking collar still showed him roaming the mountain range.

The discussion boards showed there was little surprise in the wildlife community as P1 was quite old and it was typical for a young male such as P12 to want to take over his territory. Reggie was surprised to read a lot of comments saying they were happy at P1's 'dethroning.' Most mentioned the importance of new blood, and some indicated they were thrilled that the incest perpetrator was finally dealt with.

Although Reggie knew better than to attribute human social morals to wild animals, he too, was happy that P1 was gone. Most people didn't know he also killed—and maybe even ate—his own grandchildren. Starting to feel sick all over again, he went into the bathroom to find some aspirin or something to help.

His mom and dad were watching TV and both spoke at the same time, "You feeling okay, Reggie?"

"Feeling a little lousy again. There some antacid in the medicine cabinet?"

"There should be some on the top shelf," his mom said.

He took a couple, and then he noticed his dad's sleeping pills. He figured he might as well take a couple of those too, guessing he'd probably have another restless night. He took three for good measure.

On his way back to his room, his mom asked if he wanted anything else. Reggie answered, "No, I'm good, but I think I better stay home tomorrow."

"Makes sense," his Mom said. "I'll call the school in the morning before Dad takes me to work."

"Thanks, Ma."

"Have a good night."

Reggie felt a little better knowing he didn't have to go to school on Tuesday, so he went back to the mountain lion forums to put in his two cents. At first, he commented that a lack of genetic diversity and inbreeding might become a cause for more abnormal inter-species behavior. He then made his case for a wildlife corridor. His first postings were well thought-out and rational, but as he kept posting comments throughout the night, his thoughts became more erratic, and angered.

He wrote: "What makes humans... the supposedly higher order species... so willing to judge other species? We humans have been killing other humans over territory for most of our existence on earth. I guess sometimes, we humans, are like animals and have to eliminate the undesirables—those members of society who are evil."

By 10 o'clock, Reggie's head was spinning. He started hitting the wrong keys and writing nonsense: "use forced to protec uss --- men peopl...kill rsm shoot...deader." He shook his aching head and pushed send. Then he went to bed.

CHAPTER TWENTY-EIGHT

"I'll call the school. You get better now. I'll see you this afternoon." Carole's voice came through the crack in Reggie's door. He raised his head off his pillow for a second before rolling over and going back into a long, deep sleep.

"*CLINK ... CLINK... POP!*" Reggie woke up to a series of hollow, tinny sounds. He tried to go back to sleep, but then was startled awake by a louder *POP* sound. He sat up and looked at his clock: it was after ten.

What was that stupid noise? He wondered as he slowly put on his sweatpants. Half-asleep, he schlepped to the bathroom. But then he saw something out of the corner of his lidded eyes and stopped cold in his tracks. His dad was slumped down at the kitchen table, his head buried in his arms. Empty beer cans spread over the floor.

It took a moment before Reggie saw what was across the table from his father, and when he did, his heart jumped into his throat.

There, on the opposite chair, was a rifle with the butt tied with bungee cords, its barrel lying on the table aimed right at his dad. Towels were wrapped around the rifle from butt to muzzle.

"Dad!" Reggie gasped, running over to his father. No response. He smelled for gun powder in the air and looked for blood on his dad's clothes. Nothing. Reggie gently pulled his dad's head back. He moaned but did not open his eyes. He was still breathing. Reggie was relieved. He was just passed out.

My dad was going to fucking kill himself. Reggie wanted to shout and shake his dad and then slap him across the face for attempting such a thing. Reggie was paralyzed by the scene and instead just sat down and tried to think. *Should I call Mom? Should I call 911?*

Think.

No, I have to get these guns out of here. What if he still wants to kill himself when he wakes up?

Stepping behind the chair, Reggie carefully removed the towels from the rifle. That's when he saw his dad's hand, his finger resting on the trigger. *I have to get that off the trigger without waking him up.* Carefully, he pulled the finger away. Then he removed the bungee cords from the rifle and walked into his parents' bedroom where he spotted the open gun case in the closet. He placed the rifle, together with the other guns and the ammo into the case and lugged the heavy thing to the doorway.

He stopped and looked at his dad and the beer cans. *My world is fucked up. I have to end this. Somehow.*

Then it hit Reggie. He had to act. He had to get to school.

Dad's totally passed out, he thought, *I'll let him sleep it off. I'll call Mom when I get to school.*

Reggie slinked past his dad and quietly opened the apartment door and set the gun case down outside the hallway. He ran back into his room, put on his blue hoodie and grabbed his phone. John was still in the same position, so he plucked the car keys off the table and headed out the door. When he got to the Impreza, he unlocked the trunk and lifted the gun case into it. He took the same route the bus took to school, driving with deliberate speed, but careful not run any lights and get pulled over.

At stoplights, people's faces flashed through his mind. He thought about his dad slouched on the kitchen table, alive only because he got too drunk to actually pull the trigger. Stephanie's face came to him next. He saw her turn and walk down the hall. *If it weren't for that asshole, Kevin,* he thought, *she'd still want to talk to me. She'd still trust me. Jesus. I can't turn off my freaked-out brain anymore. I need to make it right. I need to end this.*

The light changed and his mind and eyes returned to the road, picturing every turn he needed to get to school.

HONNNNK!

SCREEEEECH!

Reggie slammed on his brakes just in time. A line of cars were in a standstill right in front of him, clogging the road as far as he could see. A sure sign of an accident. Hurried drivers turned their cars around. Reggie looked over and saw the long, deep concrete channel that he had passed many times in the bus. He used to laugh when someone told him it was the Los Angeles River. Other cars pulled to the shoulder and onto a side road that ran next to the channel.

A few blocks behind him he could see emergency lights flashing in his rearview mirror. He pulled to the curb and put the car in park.

Gazing down at the thin stream of water at the bottom of the concrete channel, he recalled his dad telling him how these channels spider-webbed the whole city. When the rains came, all the debris from the wasteland ran free to the ocean. He stared down at the two narrow rows of scrub and weed on either side of the water. He wondered how the scrub could suck green life from that small brown trickle. It made him think how little his dad must have now valued his life.

WHOOOSHH! A car whizzed by, bringing Reggie's thoughts back to his mission. He envisioned the lunch yard filling soon with kids. He could picture Stephanie sitting in her usual spot. He had to get to school. Looking around there were no cars or people.

He got out of the car, opened the trunk, and pulled out the gun case. With a flick of his fingers, he unlatched the case and grabbed the 30.06 Winchester rifle when another car shot by. Reggie stood frozen.

I need to end this. These fucked-up guns. It's crazy that Dad said he needs to have these guns to protect his family. Guns do not solve problems; they make things worse. It's sick. More guns mean more killing. It's fucked up. He'll kill me when he finds out, but I have to do this.

He made sure no one watched and threw the Winchester down into the channel. It gave a satisfying crash. He immediately began to toss the other guns.

"Stupid twenty-two!" He shouted as the small rifle skipped down the channel from end to end. "Stupid Ruger pistol!" It landed all the way to the other side before it slid under the brush and into the water to rust. Now the bullets. "Stupid fucking guns and bullets!"

Let them rust. Let this fucking violence finally end.

When he finished, Reggie gazed down at the bottom of the channel. The guns were totally covered by the brush. Minutes passed before he got back in the car. He pulled back into the line of cars just as it started to move again. Checking his phone for the first time, he saw there were four attempted calls from his mom. He didn't call her back; he was only a few blocks from school, from Stephanie.

He parked the car down the street from the school, ran and checked into the office. The secretary was surprised to see him and told Reggie his mom was looking for him and that she would call her back and let her know you're here. He ran into the lunch yard. He saw Stephanie sitting with her girlfriends. He approached her, fearing that the surprised, leery look on her face meant disaster.

"Hey, Steph," he said.

"Hey, Reggie! I thought you were sick? How did you get to school?"

"Drove."

"For real? You don't even have a license."

"Whatever. I need to talk to you."

"About what?"

"I wanted to explain..."

"Look, Reggie," she interrupted, "Can we wait to talk until I speak with Jennifer?"

"Jennifer?" Reggie asked. "Why Jennifer?"

"Yeah," she said as she looked across the table. "One of her girlfriends from last year told Jennifer about the latest incident with Kevin and Jennifer told her that I should know that you're not at fault. So I called her and left a message. I think I need to talk to her and see what she has to say."

Reggie just stood there, not knowing what to say or do next. This was definitely not a part of his plan.

"I'm glad you're feeling better, Reggie. Talk to you later." Stephanie said, and then went back to talking with her friends.

Reggie wandered away and found an empty table. He absentmindedly ate his crackers while wondering what Jennifer would tell Stephanie.

Reggie's phone rang. It was his mom.

"Reggie! Are you alright?" his mom yelled into the phone.

"I'm good, Ma. Sorry I didn't call you."

"How did you get to school?"

"I drove." he said quietly so no one would hear him.

"With dad?"

Reggie hesitated. "Nope, I took the Impreza."

"Without your dad? And where is your father? I can't reach him. Reggie, why did you think it would be okay to take the car to school by yourself?"

"To see this girl, Stephanie."

"Jesus, Reggie. To talk to a girl?"

"Yeah."

"Where was Dad when you left home?"

"Passed out at the kitchen table. There were beer cans all over."

"Oh my God, Reggie, why didn't you tell me?"

"I'm sorry."

"Reggie, we have to get to him, the doctors said drinking with the drugs could kill him. Hold the phone, Reggie." In a couple of minutes, his mom came back and said, "I can get a ride home from Joan, we'll come and pick you up?"

"No, mom, I'm going to drive back myself. I can handle it."

"Reggie, you could get picked up for driving without a license."

"Bye, Mom. I'll see you at home."

"Reggie..." *CLICK.*

Reggie told the lady in the office his mom was coming to pick him up and went to the front door where he pretended to wait. In a few minutes he took off down the street to where he parked the Impreza. He'd try to connect with Stephanie again tomorrow. On his drive home, Reggie kept thinking about her and how much he needed to win her back. *Why wouldn't she let me explain? She was so stand-offish. Does she really think I'm an aggressive guy? Always getting into trouble? That I was in love with a gay girl? I was,* he remembered.

What would Jennifer tell her? That I was always hallucinating? Maybe, just maybe, he thought, *Jennifer would tell her about Isaac. She is the only person who knew it was the fight and Isaac's fear of coming out that caused my suspension.*

But as soon as Reggie started driving home, the reality of what he would face filled his mind. What would his dad do to him when he found out he took the car and trashed his guns? *I need to tell Mom that he was going to kill himself! Better hurry, she'll get home before I do. Will he still be messed up when she gets there? Drive faster. Will she finally stand up to him? Watch the stoplights. Fuck. He may hurt her.*

****

"Thanks for the ride, Joan," Carole yelled back as she ran to the apartment, fumbling into her purse and dropping the keys on the sidewalk. Opening the door, she yelled, "John!"

No answer.

"John, are you here?" She stumbled over the beer cans toward the empty bedroom. She turned around and saw the bathroom door ajar. "John?"

There he was, on his knees wiping up the floor around the toilet.

"John, are you okay?"

He looked up at her, reeking of vomit, and snarled, "Well, I'm alive."

"What the hell were you doing drinking again? You know what the doctor said."

Still wiping the floor, he said, "Fuck the doctors! And fuck the therapists!"

Offering him a hand up, she said, "Leave that mess. What are you saying? What's wrong?"

Standing up and clearing his throat, he said, "Reggie took my guns and the car."

"The guns?" she asked. "He took your guns, why?"

He threw the towel into the wastebasket, took off his shirt, and went to the sink to wash his face.

"John?"

Looking into the mirror, he said, "He should have let me do it. I...I...didn't have enough guts to pull the trigger."

"What?" she shouted.

"I want it to end, Carole."

"Stop it, John! It's your PTSD! We have to get you to the hospital, now!"

He raised his hands in the air, "I don't know what's happening to me."

"John, you've got to let go of your past, or you'll always be cursed."

"Cursed?" John's eyes widened with the shock of her words. They looked at each other in silence for a moment before hearing Reggie shout on his way up the stairs.

"Mom! Dad!"

Carole put her hands on John's shoulders, shook him, and said, "John, you have to quit feeling sorry for yourself...re-living your life...Your failures, through Reggie. Because, Jesus, John, he just saved your life. Reggie loves you."

"Does he?"

"Yes!" she said as they heard Reggie unlocking the front door.

Reggie, fearing the worst, yelled, "Mom! Dad!" and ran into the bathroom and pushed his way between them. He looked at his mom and said, "Are you alright?"

"Yes, Reggie. I'm alright. We have to get Dad to the hospital."

Reggie looked at his Dad who had dropped down hard on the bathroom floor and buried his head in his hands.

Reggie put his hands on his dad's shoulders. He could see he was crying and looked so small and defeated. As he lifted him from the floor he said, "Come on, Dad."

"I'm sorry," his dad whispered as he looked up at Reggie.

Reggie took his hand. "That's okay, Dad. Let's go."

****

After John was re-admitted under supervised care, Reggie and his mom talked on the drive back.

"Mom?" he said. "I heard you stand up to him when I was coming up the stairs. That's good."

She took one hand off the wheel and held it to her chest and said, "I'm going to stand *by* him, too, Reggie. I know he's been hard on both of us, but at his core, he's a loving man."

"I wonder about that," Reggie said.

"He loves you, Reggie, just sometimes in the wrong ways. He's fighting *for* you."

"Seriously?"

"I know it's hard to understand, but in his wrong-headed way, he doesn't want you to end up in a dead-end job or become a jarhead marine like him. You know, Reggie, he gave up on his dream to follow his dad's dream. He settled, and he's regretted it all his life."

"Then why the fuck doesn't he get that I need *my* dream?"

"Reggie, I know it doesn't make sense, but he thinks that a love of nature is from the old Indian ways and wants you to break away and become rich like the white man."

"Jesus, Mom. That's so lame."

"I know, Reggie, but I hope you can come to forgive him someday."

Reggie took a deep breath and mumbled, "Yeah. Maybe."

As soon as they got into the house, Reggie's phone rang. It was Joe.

"How you doing?" Joe asked as Reggie headed into his room.

"Okay, I guess," Reggie answered.

"I was more than worried about you. At the office, I saw some of your website postings and I called your mom who said you were at school."

"Oh, right. I was having weird, I dunno, hallucinations." Reggie hesitated, "Joe? I'm worried about the wildlife corridor meeting?"

"How come? It's two weeks away."

"It's... it's...hard to explain, but I'm getting freaked out about mountain lions. It's like this connection I once felt I had with them has turned into... like... getting too weird. You know, I hoped my vision quests would find my power animal. Now the lion is becoming more like a *bad* spirit, some kind of demon."

"I'm not following exactly what you're saying. Can you tell me more?"

Reggie sighed and flopped down on his bed. "It sounds stupid, but it's like the lion is talking to me... Talking through me, from another world. It's a mixed up half-man, half animal thing."

Joe remained silent, so Reggie went on: "Remember, P1 killing the cubs? During my quest, I had a vision that I was trying to save the mom and cubs... I saw the cubs being killed *before* they were actually killed."

"Reggie, that's just a coincidence," Joe said.

"I thought so, too, but then..." Reggie paused. "I dreamt about P12 killing P1 the day before it actually happened! And in the dream, I was actually a part of it. *I* killed P1."

Joe was silent for a long while. Finally, he said, "God, Reggie, I honestly don't know what to say. Maybe you have to quit trying to connect with the mountain lion in the spiritual world. I mean, I don't doubt what you've gone through, but I worry about what's happening to you."

"I know; that's what scares me," Reggie said.

"Understand Reggie, but you're only seeing these things, you're not making them happen... You're not the demon... Maybe you have to quit trying to reach beyond reality. Get your feet back on the ground and help me protect the lions we have here today. In the *real* world."

After a long pause, Reggie said, "Maybe you're right. Sorry for bothering you about all this stuff. I'll let you know about the conference. Thanks, Joe."

Reggie and his mom shared three chicken pot pies for supper—Reggie only eating the insides—and just as they were cleaning the dishes, the phone rang again.

Reggie read the caller ID and said, "Hi Captain Arnold."

"Hi, Reggie. I wanted to talk to you about the business with Kevin."

"Yeah Mr. Tremper told me you were going to call. But I've already made up my mind, I don't want to press charges."

"Have you talked to your parents about this?"

Reggie hesitated then said, "Yes, and we're sure. Thanks for calling."

As soon as Reggie hung up the phone, his Mom asked, "What did you tell him?"

"I told him I don't want to press charges."

"Why did you tell him that? You were trying to protect your best friend and he used a weapon on you, we can't let that kind of behavior go unpunished."

"Yeah. You're right in a way, but I found out from one of his old buddies at school that the county took him away from his parents, because of his dad's abuse. He's in a youth shelter now. Maybe he will learn that violence doesn't solve things. I just want this to end and not add to the kid's misery."

"What about your Dad? Don't you think he would want to pursue charges?"

"Ma!" Reggie interrupted. "Maybe, but I don't want payback—it never ends."

"You're being too kind," she said. "And that reminds me, before you got home, your Dad told me how ashamed he felt for how he treated you. He told me that you had more courage than he ever did."

"That's nice to hear, Mom, but it would have been better if he actually told me that himself."

"I know, Reg, but I think there's hope now." After a pause, she asked, "Reggie? Did you get to settle things with that girl? Stephanie, I think you said."

"Not really, Mom, but I don't want to talk about it."

"You must care a lot about this girl."

Reggie was taken aback by his mother's blunt, but true, characterization of his actions and feelings. He worried that Stephanie thought he's stupid about girls and has a mean streak.

He looked out the window, not wanting to talk about Stephanie with his mom.

"Well, Reggie," she tried to confide, "what you do shows who you are as a person. I'm guessing the more she knows you, the more she will like you."

Reggie continued to not respond, knowing that this was just what mothers say to their kids.

"You know, Reggie, I'm also a woman, and I wasn't much older than you when I fell in love with your dad. And despite his problems and flaws, he is, at his core, a good man; that's what matters and that's why I choose to stick with him."

Reggie listened to his Mom's words, but there was no way he was going to come out with his own.

Then she said, "I'm betting she'll give you another chance. If you're open with her, and speak from the heart..."

Reggie knew the finger snap was coming.

"She'll come back to you, just like that!" SNAP.

"Okay, Mom. Whatever."

She got up, reached over to rub his head. Reggie ducked, she smiled and walked out of the room.

Reggie picked up his cell thinking he might try and call Stephanie. Staring at her profile for a full minute, he dropped the phone on the bed. *What am I going to say to her?* He asked himself.

She said she'd talk to me after she talked to Jennifer. What did I say to her that made her shut me out? Screw it; I'm going to call her, he decided. Maybe the news about Kevin being expelled would soften her up and they could talk.

"Hi, Reggie," she answered in a fairly bright tone. "How are you feeling?"

"Better. Thanks for asking."

"Well, that's good," she said.

"Hey. Can we talk?"

"I suppose."

Thinking that maybe she thought he really was at fault for starting the fight, he said, "I wanted to tell you that Kevin has been permanently expelled from the school and Mr. Tremper apologized to me."

"Okay."

"Did you talk to Jennifer?"

"I did."

Reggie waited then asked, "What did she tell you?"

"A lot."

"About the two of us?"

"Yeah."

"Did Jennifer explain everything?"

"Quite a bit."

"So, what did she tell you?"

"She told me what she thought of you."

"And?" Reggie said with a little irritation.

"You know, Reggie? I'm more interested in what you have to say."

"Say about what?"

"What you said to me about her and Kevin in the lunch yard."

"What do you mean?"

"That's what I mean; if you don't get it, you don't get it."

"I'm... I'm confused, Stephanie. I was hoping she'd tell you all you needed to know, did she say bad things about me?"

"Not at all."

"Then, we're okay?"

"Reggie, I care about you, but I want to hear what you have to say directly about the whole thing, not only Jennifer. Think about it, and we can have a real talk at lunch tomorrow, I'll see you then. I have to go. Bye."

What the hell was that? Reggie wondered. *Talk about the supernatural. I don't think I'll ever understand girls.*

****

That night, Reggie didn't sleep well; this time he wasn't dreaming about fighting lions, but about Stephanie. He kept waking up, picturing her and trying to piece together their last conversation.

Why was she focused on what he told her about Jennifer and Kevin? All he told her was that it was all crap and that she shouldn't be bothered. What was wrong with that? *If only I could picture her face,* he kept thinking as he tried to get back to sleep.

After first period, Reggie headed over to the east wing, knowing he might catch Stephanie in the hall on the way to her history class.

There she was. He caught her attention and ran over to her.

She stepped away from her girlfriends. "Hi, Reggie."

"Hey, I wanted to make sure you knew I was in school today and that I'll see you at lunch."

"Good," she said as she ran back to catch up with her girlfriends. "I'll save a corner table."

By third period, Reggie was nervous, going over and over what he would say to her, hoping he could straighten things out. In the lunch yard, there she was, as promised, smiling. He sat next to her and took a deep breath.

"I've been thinking what you said about what I said after that incident with Kevin." As he looked at her, he could see that same dejected look on her face that she had when he told her it was all

188

crap and she needn't worry. He could see the hurt in her eyes, the sad in her mouth.

"I know what I did wrong," he said as he reached across the table and held her hand, "I wasn't open with you."

Her eyes brightened up.

"I was trying to hide my past from you like it didn't matter, like you didn't need to be bothered with my problems...Right?"

She squeezed his hand. "Yes, Reggie, if we are going to be friends, we need to trust each other." Now, they held hands together across the table.

"I know now that I was being a jerk to dismiss you and not confide in you, and for that, I'm sorry. It was my stupid ego. I was trying to protect you."

She got up and sat next to him. "I know you were, Reggie, I just wanted to hear it from you."

The bell rang and she put her hand on his cheek and kissed him on the mouth.

It was a short, soft kiss, but Reggie felt the girl this time, not just the thrill of her lips. He felt her feelings for him mingling with his feelings for her.

CHAPTER TWENTY-NINE

At the next hiking club meeting, the president and vice president sat in their usual chairs next to each other. When the group got to discussing hiking plans for the coming weekend, Stephanie had an immediate suggestion; one that she thought would please Reggie.

She suggested the Viewridge Trail in Topanga. "It's a little off the beaten path," she explained, "but I know a secret path to get to a real cool cave. Inside the cave are these really beautiful Chumash rock paintings. My dad took me there once when I was in grade school and I remember the cool drawings of these half-animal, half-human figures.

"Amazing! Let's go!" one club member yelled.

Reggie smiled at Stephanie, but on the inside, he felt so done with ancient Indian beliefs—especially knowing that tribes considered caves to be portals to the supernatural world.

"What do you think, Reggie?" Mrs. Horton asked.

Reggie scratched his bushy head, looked over at Stephanie and said, "Sure. Sounds good."

At 1:30 on Saturday, about half-way to the trail, the bus began to sputter and chug until the driver pulled over to the shoulder. The engine popped and gasped its last breath. The driver made a phone call and relayed the information to Mrs. Horton. She turned to the kids and said, "Well, here's the deal, a new bus will be here in about an hour. So, we can either go back home..."

"No! Boo!" the kids moaned

"Or," she said, "We can continue on to the hike."

"Yeah! Hike!" the kids yelled.

"Okay, okay," Mrs. Horton said, "only thing is that we can't goof off a lot on the trail; it's two hours to the cave and two hours back and it'll be getting dark after that, okay?"

"Yes, Mrs. Horton," one boy mocked in a grade-school way. Everyone laughed.

"Funnnyyyy!" Mrs. Horton said. "Now, everyone call your parents and make sure they know we may be an hour or more late. Call them now please. I'm serious."

The new bus pulled in at the park, and by three, they were heading up the trail. As usual, Stephanie constantly snapped pictures along the way, but after a while, Reggie asked her if he could carry the camera.

"Seriously?" Stephanie asked. "You know I need to do lots of practice if I'm going to be a photojournalist."

"I know," Reggie said. "And I know you will be a great one, I just want to hold your hand for a while."

Stephanie handed him the camera, gave him a kiss on the cheek, and then they interlocked their fingers. They slowed to the rear of the line. The trail was quite wooded in places, and when the rest of the kids rounded a bend, Reggie stole a kiss, sometimes, two.

The group made good time with only one short rest break, and by five, they stood on top of a high ravine looking down on some large rock outcroppings with a slow creek running in front.

"That's it!" Stephanie pointed. "That's the Santa Maria Creek. You can't see the cave from here, but I remember it was a steep climb down."

Reggie looked down and felt a strange, not-so-good feeling. It was heavily wooded around the cave due to the moist environment. *It's a place Native peoples would choose to make sacred animal paintings,* Reggie thought, *and a place animals would come for water.*

"Come on, Reg." Stephanie grabbed his hand and started down, walking sideways over the dusty gravel-strewn path.

Behind them they heard a couple of kids slip and slide, followed by Mrs. Horton's warnings to take it slow. At the bottom, it was quite dark in the wooded shadows, but when they got there, Stephanie took the lead, climbing over several large boulders.

Catching his breath, Reggie asked, "How do you remember so much about this place?"

"Photographic memory, I guess."

"Now I get the picture," he chuckled.

"Good, and we have to keep this path to the cave secret so vandals and camera flashes don't destroy the paintings. "Here it is!" she shouted. With Reggie in hand, they bent down and squeezed through a narrow opening. She set her SLR camera on macro and a low light manual exposure, and immediately began shooting.

"Look at this one, Reggie, looks like a snake with antlers." *CLICK.* It seemed like the shutter clicked every ten seconds. "Whoa! Here's a man with big long claws for hands." *CLICK.*

****

Then she got real excited when she spotted a large ochre-colored circle with lines radiating outward. By this time, the whole club gathered around Stephanie. "My dad thought this one represented the sun," she said. "There was a full eclipse of the sun in the 1600s and maybe this recorded the event from their eyes... Can you imagine what they thought was happening to their world?"

As the kids gazed at some stick figures with rays and halos around their heads, Reggie wondered what meanings the drawings had. *Was there a message for us?* He wondered. Wrenching his head far back to see a drawing on the ceiling, he saw a figure in red looking kind of human, but with pointed ears and a tail. Thinking of his dreams, his head started to spin and his stomach turned.

He made his way toward the opening, his hand on his stomach. "Come on, Steph, finish shooting, will ya? This musty smell is kind of making me sick. If you want, I'll wait for you by the creek, okay?"

"Sure, Reg, won't be long." *CLICK.*

The fresh air seemed to help Reggie breathe easier for a while, but as he scanned the dense brush surrounding the area, he knew this could be a dangerous spot for smaller animals. With the cave behind him and the precipitous climb out, and with the thicket on either side, prey would have little chance to escape.

Reggie smelled a faint, but foul odor. It gave him the creeps. He shouted at the group, "Hey! It's getting late, guys! We better think about heading back!"

Mrs. Horton checked her watch. "Reggie's right! Let's wrap it up, okay?"

Then Reggie heard a buzzing sound. The buzzing of flies? He slowly followed the creek for a few yards. Then he saw it. A raised area in the sage brush, covered with leaves: two rear hoofs sticking out.

A mountain lion kill.

Without turning around, he shouted, "We have to leave right now!"

He heard and saw some kids were starting to come.

"What's wrong, Reggie?" Mrs. Horton asked.

"This is not a good place to be," Reggie said as he pointed to the pile. "That's a cougar kill right there and he may be coming back soon to feed."

"Got it, Reggie," Mrs. Horton said. She turned around and shouted, "Let's go kids!"

As they started their climb, Reggie didn't see Stephanie, so he ran over to the rocky path to the cave, shouting her name. She smiled as she climbed over the last boulder, camera dangling from her neck.

"I'm coming, I'm coming," she said. "What's the hurry all of a sudden?"

Reggie grabbed her hand. "Come on, there's a cougar kill nearby, it's dangerous to be here."

As they caught up with the rest of the group, Mrs. Horton was nudging some of the kids up the ravine, when she let out a scream: "STOP! Come back down!"

They scrambled down as everyone looked up to the top of the ravine. There stood a mountain lion looking down at them. The light surrounding the lion at the top of the ravine made the animal look huge and threatening. Everyone, including Reggie, felt vulnerable in the shade at the bottom.

"Oh my God!" one girl screamed.

Staring down at the group, the lion twisted his head and made a low snarl.

Reggie jumped out in front of the group and held up his hands.

"Just stay together." Knowing what he knew about the local cougars and its size, it was likely P12. But that didn't matter; the lion was probably surprised to see a group of humans, and probably not happy to see them hanging around his evening meal.

Reggie knew they had to leave the area before dark, and up was the only way out.

"I'll call 911," Mrs. Thornton said.

"No, don't," Reggie said. "They'll just bring a noisy crowd of nervous, shotgun-wielding police. Let me call Joe Sartor, he'll know how to handle this. He lives and works near here and knows the trails and the animals." But Reggie knew it would take more than an hour for even Joe to get there. And darkness was approaching soon. He called Joe, but only got his voice mail and left an urgent message telling him where they were on the trail and that a lion was on top of the ravine and to hurry.

The lion didn't move. Reggie could see his nostrils flaring and his whiskers twitching. Reggie tried to remember all that he had read about lion attacks and what Joe told him about the best ways to fend them off in an encounter.

Reggie was scared, but he felt he needed to prove himself. He needed to push past his fear. He knew that mountain lions are afraid of humans and that a large group of them advancing toward him would eventually scare him off. *Besides,* he thought, *it would be a lot scarier staying put after nightfall.*

He knew the lion did not consider humans prey and it was highly unlikely it would attack if it had an escape route, but he was a wild animal—a powerful animal. The group's advantage was being a group. Reggie turned to everyone and said, "Follow me. Nice and steady."

Mrs. Horton said, "No, Reggie, it's too dangerous."

"It's too dangerous to stay," he said. "The lion will not confront a herd of humans coming at him. He'll run."

"How can you be sure?" Mrs. Horton asked.

"I just know," Reggie answered. I know these animals. Let me go ahead, leave some space behind me, and follow one at a time. And, make lots of noise." Looking back, he saw Stephanie jump on to the trail behind him and that made him feel even stronger.

Reggie started slowly up the ravine. He held his arms high in the air and talked to the lion.

"Hey, lion, we're coming up! Don't worry; we're leaving your kill. You can come back when we're gone."

Reggie knew to look the lion right in the eyes, so the lion knew he wasn't going to run like a prey animal would.

The lion stared back.

Their eyes locked on each other, and each time Reggie spoke, the lion's ears would twitch as if he was straining to understand.

The climb was slow. After a few minutes, Reggie looked back and everyone was in line on the trail with Mrs. Horton at the end. Stephanie was only five yards behind him holding that ever-present camera. He gestured to her to pull back and he continued climbing.

"Reggie, he's not moving!" Mrs. Horton yelled. "You better stop!"

Reggie was within 20 yards or five seconds of the lion's charge and contact. Fear returned to Reggie's body, but his mind told him something else. *This lion was put here for me,* he thought, *I have to do this.*

"He'll move, keep coming!" Reggie yelled back, without looking back. Reggie stood up and waved his arms at the lion and shouted. "Hey lion, time to leave!"

The lion looked back up the trail, then at Reggie and the approaching people. It dropped its ears, flicked its tail, and Reggie could see that it pushed down on its muscular hindquarters, ready to leap.

The lion's eyes met Reggie's. There was no fear in them.

But Reggie saw something else in the lion's eyes. He saw himself flash by in a movie; a young boy with his mom and dad, Jennifer, Isaac, Kevin, Joe and Stephanie—they were all there. Then Reggie blinked.

When Reggie blinked, the lion blinked, and in an instant, it was gone like a ghost.

Reggie scrambled fast and pulled himself up to the top of the ravine to see where the lion went. About 100 yards up the trail, he saw the tip of the lion's tail veer off into the bush.

"He's gone!" Reggie shouted back to the group.

Cheers went up.

"Hurry!" Reggie yelled. "And make lots of noise! He's on the run!" Looking quickly back and forth to between where the lion departed and the ravine, he reached his hand out to Stephanie. He pulled her to him and they hugged until a sweaty-faced boy in a Nike t-shirt reached the top and said, "Hey! Move your butts."

The pair moved aside and let the laughing line of hikers reach the top. One at a time, they high-fived. *CLICK*, went Steph's camera. Shook Reggie's hand. *CLICK*. Hugged Reggie. *CLICK*. Reggie smiled. *CLICK*. He was both surprised and embarrassed when finally Mrs. Horton pulled herself up and said, "Reggie, you're our hero." *CLICK*. She gave him a big hug, holding onto him almost like his mother did. *CLICK*.

"Let's just keep moving," Reggie said, blushing. "Stay close together." Even though the kids couldn't stop talking, Reggie added, "And keep up the chatter."

When Reggie got to the spot where the lion entered the brush at the side of the trail and gestured for everyone to gather around, he said, "This is where he went in. For good measure, I want everyone to yell and scream at the top of their lungs on the count of three. Okay? One, two, three!" The roar of the chorus careened through the canyon and the lion's sensitive ears, no doubt, cued a fast retreat. After the echo, they all cheered.

"Great," Reggie told the group, "but we have to still be cautious and stay together on the hike back. There's a slim chance he might be stalking us." Then Reggie went over to Mrs. Horton and asked her to be the tail on the trail and to frequently check behind her in the rare event the lion was following.

Reggie's phone rang. It was Joe.

"Hey, Joe, we're okay. The lion left."

"Thank God. We're on our way. Stay cautious."

"See you soon, Joe."

Reggie turned to the group and said, "Joe's on his way. He's that lion expert and he's bringing his crew."

A cheer went up and Reggie gestured to keep moving. On the hike back, Reggie and Stephanie held hands the whole way, even though the trail was mostly narrow and they had to go single file. Since the group was close by, they didn't talk much. At one point, when they had to scramble over some rocks and there were a few feet between them and the group, Stephanie whispered behind Reggie's back.

"You know something, Reg?"

"What?"

"I like you a lot. Not just for what you did back there, but for who you are."

Reggie turned around, met her eyes and wanted to kiss her; then he caught the eyes of the approaching group, and said, "Thanks, Steph."

As the light of the day started to fade, the group marched on increasingly tired and quiet. In the lead, Reggie spotted a movement far among the tree shadows. He blinked his eyes and shook his head, thinking he was fading, too. It was only a passing blur as it disappeared below a hillock. *Was I seeing things?* He wondered. He knew the light could play tricks with your eyes when you're moving in the woods.

He decided to be cautious in case it really was the lion stalking them. He turned around, held up his hand, and said, "Hey group! We gotta keep up the chatter!" Then he checked his watch, "We've got an hour to go!"

Mrs. Horton yelled from the back, "Come on troops, let's hear some club spirit!"

For a laugh, one girl starting singing, *"Over the hill and through the woods, to grandmother's house we go..."*

Some kids joined in while others laughed. Just as the 'boos' drowned out the melody, Reggie froze and everyone else froze behind him.

There, beyond a rise, a bright light pierced the evening sky. It bounced back and forth as it got closer. Brighter.

"What's that?" a girl whimpered.

Reggie knew instantly what it was: the powerful LED flashlight on top of Joe's helmet.

"It's Joe!" Reggie yelled, just as the full figure of a man appeared over the hill, followed by his Agency team of scientists and some rangers.

Reggie pulled on the hand he never let go of, and he and Stephanie ran to meet them. Cheers went up as Reggie hugged Joe.

One by one, the kids gave Joe and the rescuers hugs—telling them how happy they were to see them.

"It's getting late, folks, we better head back." Joe announced.

Soon, Reggie asked the question that was knocking on the back of his mind ever since he saw the lion. "Joe?"

Joe turned around and saw the look on Reggie's face. "Yes, Reggie it was P12. The last blip on our tracking monitor had him right here."

"I knew it," Reggie said with a big smile.

Then Joe said, "I'm not sure if you got a visit from your power animal, or if it was the power of reality that guided you, I don't know. But from what your teacher told me you did back there, it took a hell of a lot of courage."

"And smarts," Stephanie said.

CHAPTER THIRTY

"How was the big hike?" Carole asked when Reggie got home that evening.

"Fine," Reggie said, but his wary smile told of a better-than-fine time.

"You look really beat."

"Um. Yeah. It was a long day and I'm wiped out." Reggie grabbed a coke and a bag of Doritos. "Think I'll go to bed."

"Sure. You can fill us in tomorrow," she said as Reggie headed to his room. "Remember, we're driving up to the mountains. It'll be good for your dad to get a break from the hospital."

Sunday morning started off quietly. Reggie and his mom picked his dad up at the hospital and went to Outback for lunch, his dad's favorite spot. Then they took the long drive on the Rim of the World Highway. Reggie noticed how the woods and the vistas seemed to bring peace to his dad, and Reggie felt it, too.

"Remember all those switchbacks on the Timberline Trail, Dad?" Reggie asked. "We doubled back on ourselves so many times, I thought we were lost."

His dad let out a laugh. "Yeah, I remember. You kept asking me to check the compass."

Reggie remembered all the good times they had. He started feeling a greater acceptance of his dad. Reggie felt good, he suddenly realized, about himself. As he gazed out the car window, he savored the success he had on the trail the day before, but didn't want to brag and thought he would share it with them later. He felt like he wanted to savor his victory over the lion, *or was it over himself?* He thought.

After their hike, they checked John back into the hospital. They walked him to the fifth floor common room. A crowd of vets played cards at a table and one guy in a wheelchair made small endless circles in the middle of the room. Other vets sat along the perimeter, staring at the ceiling, or what Reggie thought, staring at some distant moment in the past.

John thought he'd watch a bit of TV and went to sit down. When they waved goodbye, Reggie looked at his dad and the other men and felt a little depressed. He saw many had lost their limbs, and thought that many had also lost their minds and their lives.

As soon as Reggie and Carole got back to the apartment, the phone rang. It was John.

"Turn on KTLA-TV!" he shouted.

"What?" Carole said.

"Channel Five, right away. I'm hanging up to watch, bye."

"Dad says we have to watch TV," she said as she flicked it on. Reggie looked puzzled.

They heard the news anchor say, "And we'll be right back with more of that incredible video of the teen lion-tamer who saved his friends in the Santa Monica Mountains."

Ping! Reggie looked at his phone and saw a text from Stephanie telling him to turn on Channel Five news.

There was a car commercial after a Ross commercial, followed by a Stater Brothers commercial, then another car commercial filled the screen as Carole asked, "Do you know anything about this, Reggie?"

"I'm not sure, Mom."

The anchor finally came back on the screen: "Here's Vera Chu with an exclusive live interview with an Encino High student who recorded the daring rescue in Topanga Canyon from a possible mountain lion attack. Vera?"

A short woman standing on a mountainside appeared. "I'm standing here, live in Encino with Stephanie Demancik, an Encino High Junior who was on a hike in Topanga Canyon yesterday and caught on her camera the remarkable footage of a fellow student who stared down a mountain lion. Can you tell us, Stephanie, about this young man and what happened?"

"Reggie?" his Mom gasped. "Is this the same Stephanie that you—"

"Yeah..."

And there she was, Stephanie talking to the reporter with a huge smile on her face. She spoke, "Well, Reggie Youngblood, who's the president of our hiking club at school, climbed to the top of a ravine where a mountain lion was looking down on us and we were all freaking out because we thought it was going to attack us. And Reggie just went up and talked to it and it ran away."

"What do you mean, talked to it?" the reporter asked.

"Reggie has been studying mountain lions and their behavior and their relationship with humans, and so he used his understanding of the animal to coax him to leave us alone. It was incredible."

Carole turned to her son with her jaw on the floor. "Reggie, why didn't you tell me?"

"Mom, just watch!" Reggie said as he remembered that Stephanie's uncle worked at KTLA.

The reporter shook her head. "Reggie must be a very brave guy."

"He is, and he showed all of us how we can share the lion's habitat."

"Go, Stephanie!" Reggie yelled, pumping the air.

"How did you capture that exciting rescue on video?" the reporter asked.

"Reggie told the hikers to follow him up the ravine and make lots of noise... I was behind him about ten yards and I turned my SLR onto video."

"Well, thank you, Stephanie, for sharing your exciting video. Back to you in the studio, Mike."

The anchor popped back on the screen and said, "Here's another look at that incredible video taken by Stephanie Demancik in Topanga State Park."

Together, Reggie and his mom watched the footage of Reggie saving the day. "Reggie, I can hardly believe what I just saw," his mom said as she scooted over on the couch and gave him one of those choking hugs.

"Enough, Ma," he said.

The anchor came back on, "Watching these kids hugging their hero shows what brave young leaders we have. We'll be right back."

The phone rang and it was John: "Can you believe it? That's our son!"

"I know!" Carole shouted. "And here he is..."

"Reggie, you're a hero!" John yelled. "I ran around the TV room telling all the guys 'That's my son!' I knew you knew a lot about cougars, but geez, Reggie, where did you learn that?"

"I don't know, Dad, it was just in me somehow."

"Well, I'm real proud of you, Reggie."

"Thanks, Dad. How are you feeling?"

"Right now, super."

"Say Dad, can we talk later? I have to call Stephanie, if that's okay."

"Go for it, hero," John laughed. "Talk to you soon."

Reggie ran into his room to call Stephanie.

"So, did you see it?" Stephanie asked.

"I can't believe it, actually. I had no idea you were taking a video the whole time... Guess I can't get frustrated with your constant picture-taking anymore. Nice interview, by the way."

"My God, my hair was a mess and I stumbled over my words."

"You did great."

"Guess what?" she asked.

"You've got another surprise?"

"My uncle, you know the producer at KTLA, he told me that the CBS network has picked the story up for a feature piece to be broadcast on Monday. You'll be famous!"

"That's, um..." Reggie whispered as he heard his mom knock on the door.

"It's Joe on the phone, Reggie, want to talk with him?"

"Yeah... wait... hold on Steph... it's Joe, can I call..."

"Hey, take it. My parents want to go out to dinner—they want to meet you by the way—I'll see you on Monday, okay?"

"Definitely." *Click.*

The home phone rang. Carole picked up, said hello and handed Reggie the phone.

"Joe? Guess you saw the news," Reggie said.

"Not really, I'll catch it tonight, but the commissioner did and Mr. Callahan called me to confirm that you'll be at the wildlife corridor meeting on Thursday. He said he thinks your story will help the meeting and shore up public opinion. Congratulations, by the way."

"Thanks, and I'll be there for sure. I'll have my Mom call the school. Ten thirty, right?"

"Right, I'll see you then. Thanks, Reggie."

"Thank *you*, Joe."

Another call came in.

"Isaac?"

"Hi, Reggie. My parents told me you rescued your hiking club from a mountain lion yesterday and you're a big hero. Did you fight him off?"

"Nah, I did what I had to do and it worked."

"Mr. Modest!" Isaac laughed. "Who's the girl who took the pictures?"

"My new girlfriend, Stephanie. You never met her."

"My Mom says she's cute."

"Totally, dude. Long brown hair, brown eyes and a super personality."

Reggie got a signal on his phone, another call was coming in.

It was Jennifer. "Say Isaac, hold on a sec, I got another call coming in."

"Hey, Jennifer. How are you?"

"Hey there, superstar. You must be floating on air 'bout now."

"Yeah. Right. Jennifer, can I call you right back? I've got Isaac on the other line."

"How's he's doing? Haven't talked to him in a long time. Why don't you put him on and we can have a three way call?"

"Hold on, let me see."

"Isaac? Jennifer's on the other line. Wanna say hi?"

"Yeah. Put her on."

"Hi Jennifer. How's things with you?"

"Real good, Isaac. This art school is awesome and I've got a girlfriend now."

"Good for you," Isaac said. "Guess what guys? I've got a boyfriend too."

"Cool. You're a fast mover," Jennifer said.

"Good news, dude," Reggie said.

"Yeah! His name's Javier, and we fit right in at this liberal school. He's good-looking and super athletic. Even got me into martial arts. And, Javier's modest, just like you, Reggie."

"Hey! Give it up!"

"I miss you Reggie," Isaac said.

"Me too," Jennifer said, "It's just like old times."

For a moment all three paused, then Isaac said, "You know, Reggie. I need to thank you for always sticking up for me. You too Jennifer. And...and Reggie, I'm sorry for being selfish after the fight, I could have been a better friend then."

"Don't worry about it, Isaac. Both of you were, no, sorry, *are* great friends. You know what's funny guys? I always wondered why you two picked me as a friend."

"Simple, Reg," Jennifer said, "You're a hopelessly sensitive and sweet straight guy."

"Ha. Don't make me laugh. You two are the best friends a straight guy could have."

"Let's not get too mushy here," Jennifer said, "And on that note, I gotta run, Terrie's pulling my arm. Congratulations on rescuing that cute girl."

"Bye Jennifer," Reggie and Isaac said at the same time.

"Alright, I better split too," said Isaac, "Take care, buddy. And kiss a mountain lion for me."

"Ha! Take care of yourself too, bye."

CHAPTER THIRTY-ONE

Reggie's return to school on Monday was, as one can imagine, considerably more friendly. Reggie and Stephanie instantly became the hottest couple in school and the hiking club doubled its membership. When Reggie asked around about Kevin, one of his old buddies told him that Kevin was in foster care. *At least he's safe,* Reggie thought, but wondered if he'd ever get out of that choke-hold of violence.

There was only one thing now that was bothering Reggie—his dad. Reggie wanted him to come with his mom to the wildlife corridor conference on Thursday, knowing he needed a break from his hospital room. But his dad kept declining, saying that that meeting was all about Joe and Reggie's efforts. Reggie pleaded with him, but John kept begging off saying he was proud of him, but that he didn't play a part.

On the day of the conference, Joe picked up Reggie early so they could prepare their testimony. By the time they got into the conference room it was already packed with many others who were going to give testimony, politicians, the public and lots of press. As soon as Reggie and Joe sat down, the Commissioner of Fish and Game, Mr. Callahan, jumped down from the podium and came over to greet them.

"Good to see you, Reggie," Mr. Callahan said, smiling and pumping Reggie's hand like a circus clown. "You, too, Joe," giving him a quick nod. "I want to thank you, Reggie, for all you've done for us. I look forward to your testimony."

"Okay, sure," Reggie said before turning to Joe with a 'what was that all about?' look on his face.

"I think he's hoping the press coverage will lift the standing of his department in Sacramento," Joe whispered.

The conference kicked off with various conservationists who argued that humans needed to balance consumption and growth with the respect for nature and the health of our planet.

Broad thinking, Reggie thought.

Then came the spokesperson from an organization called The People for Responsible Growth, who argued that Southern California is in a housing shortage and the area needed to first invest in an improved infrastructure if the region wanted to be viable in the future.

Developers and contractors, Reggie figured.

Then the National Rifle Makers Association lawyers argued for repealing the California statute that gave mountain lions protection from hunting. They came out in favor of the corridor if it meant more lions and that they could hunt them in the Santa Monica Mountains.

The gun manufacturers sure suck a lot of hunters into their bullshit, Reggie thought.

The Mountain Lion Foundation spokespeople made an eloquent statement that humans needed to protect cougars because they, more than any other animal, represented the freedom and independence that the nation was founded on.

Huh! Reggie thought, *they represented a lot more than that to the Native Americans.*

When the conference moved into the second half to discuss funding and building the wildlife corridor in the Santa Monica Mountains, Joe was introduced to describe the result of his department's ten year study of the mountain lions. Both Reggie and Joe moved into the front row facing the microphones.

Joe presented detailed charts and maps showing how the cougar population was trapped by highways, and how increased development and the lack of genetic diversity from new lions could result in more in-breeding and ultimately, the demise of their own tiny population.

At the conclusion of Joe's testimony, the commissioner thanked him, and then addressed the crowd. "Ladies and Gentlemen, I want to now introduce a colleague of Mr. Sartor's—a special guest who also has firsthand knowledge of our mountain lions. I'm sure by now, everyone in this room knows of this young man's remarkable rescue of his high school hiking club. Mr. Reggie Youngblood! Please stand up, Reggie."

The whole room stood up and clapped a thunderous applause. The TV camera zoomed in and the camera flashes blinded Reggie. The more they clapped, the weaker Reggie's legs felt. The commissioner finally raised his hand and motioned for everyone to sit. Reggie was relieved, but still nervous.

"First, Mr. Youngblood," Mr. Callahan said, "on behalf of the citizens of our great state, I'd like to personally thank you for your courage and leadership. You've set a fine example for young people everywhere." After allowing a few more photos, Mr. Callahan asked the press to clear the area so Reggie could speak.

"Thanks again for coming, Mr. Youngblood, could I ask you what your feelings are about the proceedings today?"

Reggie fidgeted with the microphone, and then said, "I want to say that I really didn't rescue my friends from the lion. I mean, I knew he wasn't going to attack us."

Looking surprised, Mr. Callahan asked, "Interesting, how did you know that?"

"Well, humans are not his prey and the lion saw the power and the numbers of us and he backed off. And, I'm happy to say that Joe is still tracking P12, who's roaming free in our mountains."

The crowd began to whisper and Mr. Callahan regained control by asking, "Thanks, Reggie. Can I ask you if you think we ought to consider building a wildlife corridor?"

"Well," Reggie said after a pause. "Yes." Everyone wanted to hear more, but Reggie simply rested back on his chair.

Mr. Callahan waited a few moments more, and then asked, "Could you tell us why?"

Joe gave Reggie an encouraging nod.

"Well," Reggie started. "I guess it's due to my views of our two species and how they relate to each other. I think if you believe that the human animal species is *superior* to all other animals, then you'd consider mountain lions an inferior species. And I think that would be like...like being a racist."

You could hear a muffled gasp from the audience. Most shuffled uncomfortably in their seats and looked around the room.

"Okay," Mr. Callahan said nervously, "Can you elaborate?"

"I believe the cougar is a fellow species, an equal member of our global community of animals." Then Reggie grabbed the microphone and leaned in, "And they have as much a right to live and survive as we do."

Silence came over the crowd. The commissioner wanted to move back to the subject at hand and asked, "Do you think we can afford to build the corridor?"

"Yes," Reggie replied. "We've already re-shaped the cougar's natural habitat in Southern California with cities and freeways to suit our needs. I think now we can afford to re-shape a tiny bit back for an animal that was here thousands of years before we showed up."

Mr. Callahan jumped in, "It sounds like you're making a moral argument for the corridor?"

Reggie sat back in his chair, feeling like he had already been saying too much, but then looked at Joe, got a smile, and leaned forward again. "I guess I am. With our superior intelligence, technology, and resources, if we can't help preserve a much less powerful species, then maybe we won't be able to preserve ourselves."

The audience remained silent for a moment, expecting Mr. Callahan to speak, but then a single clap was heard way back in the standing-room-only corner of the room. Reggie looked back to see his dad had come and was the one who started the clapping. Soon, everyone followed, and Reggie was back to another standing ovation.

Above the din of the crowd, the commissioner spoke as loud as he could, saying, "Thank you, Mr. Youngblood, for your input."

The audience continued clapping and the press rushed in for photos and comments. Reggie gave them short, polite answers, and then he and Joe left to see Reggie's parents.

Joe said, "Thanks, Reggie, you did a great job."

Reggie shook his hand. "Thank you for mentoring me. Do you think the news coverage will help?"

"Absolutely!" Joe replied. They continued through the crowd and finally reached the corner where Reggie's parents were. Reggie's mom hugged him in her usual uber-exuberant way. This time, Reggie didn't tell her he was choking. While she held on, he could see Joe and his dad finish talking and his dad tapped his mom on the shoulder.

"May I have the next hug?" he asked, smiling.

"Glad you came, Dad," Reggie said.

"Me, too."

In the middle of the bear hug, his dad whispered in Reggie's ear, "Can we go out in the hallway and talk for a bit? Is that okay?"

"Sure, Dad."

John gestured to Carole, waved off a reporter, and they found a bench down the hallway.

"First, I want to say," his dad started, then halted.

"Are you mad at me about the guns?" Reggie jumped in.

"No. I want to thank you for saving me, giving me another chance... and..." His dad looked down trying to bring up the next words. "I... I didn't want to come here because... because I felt Joe was a better man than I was. You know, because I tried to teach you to hunt animals, not protect them."

Reggie could see how low his dad felt. Reggie didn't picture in his mind the shooting of the wounded deer. This time he remembered the way his dad would thank any animal he just killed and bless it by placing some grass in its mouth.

"It's not like that, Dad. It was *you* who showed me the beauty of animals. *You* taught me how to respect them in the old Indian way. Joe only gave me a direction."

His dad stared dumfounded at his son, then finally said, "It's bigger than that, Reggie."

"What do you mean?"

"I'm sorry for all the years I didn't listen to you." Rubbing his temples and taking a deep breath, he continued, "I'm sorry for trying to make you into somebody you aren't."

"I'm glad you see that now, Dad."

Taking another deep breath, his dad said, "Took me way too long." Then he pointed at the conference room and said, "But you got here all on your own. Your great grandmother Wanchuat would be so proud of you. Congratulations."

"Thanks, Dad. We better get back to Mom."

The crowds were still mulling around the hallway when the two of them reached his mom.

"You guys have a good talk?"

"Yeah. We're cool." Reggie said as he smiled at his dad.

"She's here, Reggie," his mom said, tilting her head toward the crowd.

"Stephanie?" Reggie almost screamed.

"Yup, I recognized her from the TV."

Reggie made his way through the crowd and when they spotted each other, ran and hugged. Reggie lifted her off the floor and twirled her around. Facing his Mom, Reggie held up his hand, smiled at her and snapped his fingers.

A word about the author...

Growing up in the boondocks of Northern Minnesota, Tom dreamed of becoming a game warden. He loved the woods and vowed he'd never sit behind a desk working in an office. He left home, moved to New York and started his career in a cubicle as an advertising copywriter.

After a lifetime in business and living in the Northeast, the journey of a wild animal caught his interest. A young male mountain lion travelled 1,700 miles from South Dakota to Connecticut in search of a mate. He was killed on a highway not far from Tom's home. Soon after the author moved to Santa Monica, California, another mountain lion was killed by police a few blocks from his new home, on Tom's birthday.

The author's love and respect for wild animals was rekindled. At least he could now write about them. So Tom wrote this story to inspire young (and older) people to not give up on their dreams.

To learn more, contact the author:
https://TomBerquist-Author.com

Facebook: /people/Tom-Berquist/100010214148721

STALKING LOS ANGELES by Tom Berquist
DISCUSSION GUIDE

ABOUT THE BOOK

Fifteen-year-old Reggie Youngblood has a lot to be angry about. His father is deployed for a second tour of Iraq, his mother works long hours at a low-wage job, and a bully torments Reggie and his few friends at school. While struggling to find where he fits, Reggie stumbles upon an unexpected passion for studying the wildlife in his new Los Angeles surroundings. By studying the elusive mountain lion and its habits, Reggie discovers more about himself, his family, and his relationships than he ever could have imagined. In this coming-of-age novel that explores what it means to be a man and what it means to be an animal, Reggie learns to define the balance between instinct and intent, as well as fear and love.

PREREADING ACTIVITY

Stalking Los Angeles is about the delicate and dynamic relationship between humanity and the natural world. In particular, the novel highlights Animism, the Native American belief of humanity's connection to nature through power animals. Either individually or in small groups, ask students to research the Native American belief of Animism. Based on their research, ask students to write a short response or give a brief presentation about which animal they feel would be their power animal, and why.

DISCUSSION TOPICS

- *Stalking Los Angeles* is a coming-of-age tale not only for Reggie Youngblood, but also for Lupine-boy. Compare and contrast both characters' progression from confused youth to dominant male over the course of the novel. Topics to consider include physical changes, sexual awakenings, and social changes, among others.

- One of the reasons that Reggie and Lupine-boy struggle in their lives is the presence of strong, dominating males in their lives. Just as Lupine-boy must mature into the strength to stand up to Big-paw, so must Reggie learn to control his impulsive anger to overpower the bullies in his life. Who is a bigger foe to Reggie's success, Kevin or his father? How does the novel present Reggie's emotional growth? What does it mean for Reggie to be the dominant male in his own life?

- During Joe Sartor's lecture to Reggie's biology class in Chapter 2, he discusses the process of tranquilizing a mountain lion for research. Reggie thinks to himself, "*Tormenters... You trap the poor animal so he can't move for hours as he tries to chew the wire off, they shoot him with something that makes him sleep in the middle of the danger, then poke and prod him before he wakes up in a daze*" (Page 13). How does the novel justify this treatment? Can the justification be expanded to larger animal issues like hunting or animal testing?

- In Chapter 5, police officers shoot and kill a male mountain lion that has wandered into Santa Monica: "The crowd took a collective breath, and a mixture of cheers and moans broke out. Then silence. Ralph watched the lion take its last breath and bleed out on the concrete. As the cops muttered amongst themselves, Ralph turned to the crowd and saw Joe running toward him with his gear" (Page 23). After reviewing the various reactions of witnesses, discuss what this scene suggests about fear in society. In what ways do these reactions demonstrate a society's varying views and priorities?

- When discussing mountain lions with the class, Reggie says, "Maybe God put both beauty and violence in all animals" (Page 38). In this scene, he is talking about mountain lions but thinking about his father. Do you agree with Reggie's statement about beauty and violence being found everywhere? What does this mean for characters like Big-paw, Kevin, and John?

- One of the largest environmental issues that the novel tackles is the co-habitation of humans and wild animals, particularly in regards to the urban sprawl that continues to claim natural habitats. What does the novel suggest about the possibility of co-habitation between humans and large, potentially dangerous animals like lions? What does Reggie's relationship with Lupine-boy suggest about the human responsibility to care for nature? What insight does this novel give you into the need for, and effects of building, wildlife corridors? (Page 138).

- In both Lupine-boy and Reggie's worlds, females play the dominant role in ensuring the survival of younger generations. The fathers in the novel – both human and animal – are uninvolved in their offspring's upbringing, and the novel opens with a scene of Lupine-boy's mother saving her children from a vicious attack. In light of this, how does the novel represent female characters? Consider She-Paw, Carole, Jennifer, and Stephanie. In what ways are these characters strong? In what ways are they weak? Overall, do these characters live up to the novel's expectation for female strength?

- When considering his relationship with Joe Sartor, Reggie thinks to himself on page 107, "when you were in nature and got quiet, you felt more open to others and to new ideas." Consider the different ways characters in the novel open themselves up to new ideas – vision quests, meditation, discussion, etc. Which of these methods seems to be most effective for truly opening the mind and changing opinions?

- Discuss how reading *Stalking LA* has affected or changed your views of wildlife conservation, particularly in your own community. Has the novel opened your eyes to ways that you, as an individual, can help preserve nature? What changes could you make in your daily life to help ensure that local flora and fauna be given the opportunity to thrive? How does this novel challenge your views of human rights versus animal rights? Which species has more or less right to live freely in a space? Why?

- *Stalking LA* incorporates a lot of mountain lion research into the story. Discuss how the author manages to balance fact and fiction. How does the incorporation of scientific fact affect your overall enjoyment of the novel? In what ways is this novel both educational and entertaining? Which scientific aspects most captivated your imagination, and why?

- When discussing life choices with John, Joe says, "Sometimes family survival needs take precedent and life throws you a bad deal" (Page 155). What does he mean by this? How do you see this sentiment reflected in the novel's major themes, in both the human and animals worlds?

- Discuss the novel's presentation of the use of anti-coagulant rat poisons (Page 109). How do these poisons travel through the food chain? What are the results, both intentional and unintentional, of their use? What policies should be put in place – if any – to control the spread of these super toxins? What other methods might be effective in controlling rodent populations?

- When an animal population is restricted to a confined area, the gene pool of a species dwindles. What effect does this have on a species' survival fitness? How did inbreeding affect the mountain lion population in the novel specifically? What can scientists do to help ensure that new genetic variants enter a territory and animal population?

Discussion Guide prepared by Amy Holwerda, a freelance academic writer who lives and writes in Chicago, IL
www.amyholwerda.com

Tom Berquist

Stalking Los Angeles